THE FALLOUT

THE FALLOUT

S. A. BODEEN

SQUARE
FISH

FEIWEL AND FRIENDS

NEW YORK

For Martine Vokt

SQUARE FISH

An Imprint of Macmillan
175 Fifth Avenue
New York, NY 10010
macteenbooks.com

Square Fish books may be purchased for business or promotional use.
For information on bulk purchases, please contact the Macmillan
Corporate and Premium Sales Department at (800) 221-7945 x5442
or by e-mail at specialmarkets@macmillan.com.

Library of Congress Cataloging-in-Publication Data Available
ISBN 978-1-250-05078-6 (paperback) / ISBN 978-1-4668-4842-9 (e-book)

Originally published in the United States by Feiwel and Friends
First Square Fish Edition: 2014
Square Fish logo designed by Filomena Tuosto

10 9 8 7 6 5 4 3 2 1

AR: 4.1 / LEXILE: HL580L

The truth is rarely pure and never simple.

—OSCAR WILDE

CHAPTER ONE

THE STALE AIR IN THE OVERHEATED BOARDROOM AT YK Industries made my red silk tie feel tight. Way too tight. With trembling fingers, I tried to loosen the noose slowly strangling me. Finally, I yanked hard enough to release the knot, and then just let the tie hang there as I sucked in a breath.

Sitting next to me on one side of the long oak table was my twin brother, Eddy. Like me, he wore a black blazer and white button-down shirt, but his tie was blue. He'd gotten his hair cut about the same length as mine, but gel made his stand straight up, so at least we didn't look as identical as we could have. Mom was on the other side of Eddy, along with our lawyer, John something or other. He was trying to explain to Mom why Phil was still running our family's billion-dollar software company.

Phil. The right-hand man of my father, Rex Yanakakis,

founder of YK, his own Yanakakis family legacy. Together, they kept our family in the Compound.

Roughly two thousand days. Two thousand days of my life spent underground. And why?

Because my father lied.

Lied to all of us. To my mom, to my sisters. To me.

He made us believe there was a nuclear attack and our only hope for survival was to enter the Compound, the lavish underground refuge he had built, so we could survive what no one else on the planet could. We were desperate; we willingly entered that silver door beyond which lay a sanctuary of my father's making. A place of the kind of luxury and excess that we were used to.

A place of safety.

Were we stupid? To enter so blindly?

The memory of that night had dimmed. My ninth birthday. I remember the fire, the screams. I remember my heart pounding so hard I thought I would die. I remember running until I thought my legs would give out. And the terror in the eyes of my mother and my two sisters, terror that mirrored my own.

Mostly I remember my relief as the silver door closed. The screaming was done. And the fire, the apocalypse: They were outside.

As was my brother, Eddy. My twin. My other half.

I was not whole without him. And my own selfishness had been the reason he was not with us. I had set him up, lied to him, so that he hid in the car with our grandma as she drove away. So, when the time came to enter the Compound, neither of them was there.

I was the reason Eddy was left on the outside. All those years underground, I believed he was dead. And I blamed myself for his death.

The rest of us were safe. Six years we stayed there, believing it was our only choice. The rest of the world was gone.

Or so we thought.

My father's lies were good. Better than good. His lies were brilliant. And his planning was nothing short of genius.

Planning he could only have done with Phil working for him on the outside. While we were stuck on the inside.

But my father didn't count on me figuring out it was all just a game. Figuring out my twin brother was still alive, alive and living in the world that was still there, still oh-so-totally frickin' there. And my father didn't count on me being strong enough to get us all out: my mother; my little sister, Reese; my older sister, Lexie; and . . . the ones born inside.

The Supplements: Four-year-old Lucas. Two-year-old Cara. And Quinn, nearly one year old.

They were the ones who lived behind the yellow door. They were the ones created for an unmentionable, unholy purpose.

The ones who never knew the other world. The ones who only knew the Compound.

My brothers and sisters gave me the strength to stand up

to my father, find the code that opened the door, and get us all out.

I didn't feel guilty for getting out, even if it had led to my father's death.

Because I had to believe he did it to himself. He never should have put us down there. He never should have made us stay for so long. He never should have made us believe the lie.

I hated him for the lie. He deserved to burn with the Compound.

Maybe it made me evil, but I was glad my father was gone.

But Phil?

Phil was right in front of me, strutting through the double doors of the boardroom in his thousand-dollar suit and alligator loafers, hoisting a leather briefcase emblazoned in gold with the initials P.A.W. He set it down in a chair across the large table from us and stared at me, a smug grin on his face.

I looked away and tried to tune in to what our lawyer was saying to my mom.

"Their only option was to assume you were all dead and follow the instructions in the will. I'm sorry to say it that way, but except for Eddy, it appeared you were all . . . gone. So Rex's will instructed that Phil would remain CEO until Eddy turned twenty-five."

"But I'm not dead, obviously. Neither is Eli. We're here," Mom said. She glared across the table at Phil. "And he needs to go."

The lawyer cleared his throat. "Obviously, the judge will have to revisit the will, and Rex's instructions, now, in the event of his death."

Eddy asked, "How does it change things? Is Phil still in charge?" He looked across the room at Phil, but my twin's gaze was soft, his forehead unlined. Apparently, he didn't harbor the animosity I did.

The lawyer rubbed his forehead. "Well . . ."

Mom frowned. "What?"

The lawyer said, "It doesn't change much."

I sat up straighter, causing the leather chair to creak. "How can that be? My mom is still here."

The lawyer shook his head. "Rex didn't name your mother to run the company. He named you boys once you turn twenty-five."

Mom asked, "So who *did* he name to run it until they turn twenty-five?"

The lawyer looked across the room and nodded at Phil. "Mr. Whitaker."

"After what he did?" Mom slammed her hand on the table. "No!"

The door opened and a tall bald man in a gray suit entered the room. He shook hands with our lawyer, then turned to Mom. "Mrs. Yanakakis, I'm Henry Dodge, Mr. Whitaker's lawyer."

He smiled at Eddy and me.

Eddy smiled back. I sure didn't.

Dodge took a seat beside his client and opened a folder. He handed us each a sheath of papers. "This is Rex's will,

5

which I'm sure your lawyer has shown you, Mrs. Yanaka-kis. It clearly states that—"

Mom jumped out of her seat and yelled at Phil, "After what you did, you should be in jail! Not running my husband's company."

Phil held up his hands in a gesture of submission. "It's what Rex wanted. I'm simply following his wishes."

Mom sat down and looked at our lawyer. "How do we fix this? How do we get rid of him? Can we contest the will?"

"There are only a few circumstances in which a will can be contested." Our lawyer lifted and lowered a shoulder. "We would have to prove Rex was mentally incapacitated when he made the will, or that he didn't sign the will, or that the will doesn't meet state requirements."

I drummed my fingers on the table. "Let me guess: None of those circumstances apply."

Phil said, "Really, kid?" He shook his head a little, his mouth turned up at the corners. "You think your dad didn't know how to dot his *i*'s and cross his *t*'s?"

Mom ignored Phil and turned to her lawyer. "What if we prove Mr. Whitaker was complicit in keeping us prisoner for six years?"

Her lawyer nodded. "That would certainly—"

Phil interrupted, "You've got no proof of anything."

I stood up and practically leaped across the table. "You were there with the helicopter!"

He smiled and tilted his head a bit. "I was there to rescue you."

"After six years?" I scoffed. "You were a little late."

Eddy pulled on my arm to get me to sit back down.

Mom pointed at Phil. "One way or another, I will get you out of here."

Phil leaned back and crossed his arms. "I'm not going anywhere."

Mom shoved away from the table and headed for Phil, who jumped to his feet. I followed Eddy, who quickly grabbed her arm and said, "Mom, we'll figure this out. Just calm down."

Phil turned to his lawyer. "I have to get back to work." He looked my way, a smirk on his face. "I have a company to run."

In an instant, I had my finger in his face. "This isn't over."

"Oh, really?" Phil shook his head. "I think—" Dodge pulled him away and they huddled together, heads down, their backs to me.

My heart was pounding, and I looked down, trying to stop myself from doing something I would regret later. Phil's briefcase was open on the chair right by my leg. A flash drive sat on top of a few folders. Without thinking, I reached in, closed my fingers around it, and slipped it in my pocket. Then I backed away and stood beside Mom and Eddy. "Let's get out of here." And I glared at Phil one more time before we left the room.

Out in the hallway, Mom turned to our lawyer and said, "I want him gone." Her jaw clenched and her eyes grew dark. "One way or another."

I'd never seen that look in her eyes before.

THE LIMO RIDE HOME WAS QUIET. QUIET AND UNEVENTFUL, thanks to our recent move to Mercer Island in the middle of Lake Washington. After spending a few weeks at Gram's in Hawaii, we had flown home to Seattle, arriving one night at a private airfield near YK, and then piling into two big SUVs. As we neared our mansion, the road swarmed with news vans and satellite dishes and reporters. Fortunately, the windows of the vehicles were tinted, but that didn't stop the cameras from flashing. It took forever to get through the gates and onto our driveway.

The second I'd opened the car door, our chocolate lab, Cocoa, jumped out and ran around to the back, probably wanting to see if her doghouse was still there. Inside, our housekeeper Els had been waiting for us. Ever since we'd gotten out of the Compound, she'd been getting the mansion ready for us, and our extra siblings. Reese went right to her old room, leaving Eddy and Lexie and I to help get the little ones ready for bed. I took Lucas to a former guest room that had been repainted in primary colors. A big red fire-engine bed rested on one wall. He squawked, then ran to it and climbed the ladder to the top. He waved. "Look how high I am!"

I grinned. "Can you sleep that high up?"

He nodded and flopped down on the mattress, disappearing from view.

I walked over to the curtained window and peeked out. Although the street itself wasn't in view, the glow from all the lights was, and cameras still flashed. How long were they going to stay there?

I let the curtain drop and went over to the bed, then climbed up the ladder. Lucas was already asleep.

I tucked him in, then backed down the ladder a step before dropping to the floor.

Downstairs, Mom, Gram, and Els were in the kitchen. Mom was holding a snoozing Finn. I said, "Lucas is asleep."

Els set an apple pie on the counter and held up a knife. "Hungry?"

I smiled. "Sure." I reached out to get the knife.

Els gently slapped my hand away. "I can still get things for you."

"Fine." I made a face at her and climbed up on a stool beside Mom. Els slid a piece of pie over to me. I picked up a fork. "Thanks. May I have some milk?"

Els nodded and went to get a glass, her white orthopedic shoes squeaking as she walked across the tiled marble floor.

Weird. Being served again after so many years of doing things for myself. I took a bite of pie. "Yum. Els, this is great."

She set a glass of milk in front of me and handed me a napkin. "Wipe your face."

Without a word, I obeyed.

Mom handed Finn to Gram, who said, "I'll take this babe up to bed."

I asked Mom, "What are we gonna do about all those news crews?"

She shrugged. "We'll deal with it tomorrow."

Those first two days, being home in our mansion was surreal. Paparazzi and news vans surrounded us. Our home wasn't visible from the street where they camped out, but helicopters could fly overhead. We didn't dare go outside, not even to take Cocoa for a walk. One day I stopped by an upstairs window that looked out over the pool and the basketball court, wishing I could go out there. Beyond the basketball court, something new had been built. I couldn't tell what it was, but I saw a lot of concrete.

Did it really matter? After being cooped up all those years, I was once again denied the coveted freedom of the outdoors.

After three days of virtual house arrest, the YK helicopter came one night and took us to the office. There, we switched to several white windowless vans, which secretly transported all of us to a new house on Mercer Island, bought under a name that would never be traced to us.

While not our mansion, the new house was still huge: seven bedrooms, six-and-a-half baths, on over an acre of lakeshore property, next door to a home that was even bigger, with even more security than ours. Which meant we had a pretty good chance of not sticking out, at least for a while.

My room had a massive bank of windows looking out onto Lake Washington. In front of them was a state-of-the-art treadmill, which I ran on every morning. Running outside would have been better, but we had tried that. Once. Our security force had all been hired for their bulk, not their stamina, and those guys couldn't keep up with me for more than a mile.

Cocoa followed me to my room, where I inserted the stolen flash drive—initials p.a.w. etched on its side—into my desktop computer. Of course, I also had a new YK tablet, which made my old laptop in the Compound seem laughable, but I found myself still using the desktop most of the time. The list of files on the flash drive popped up, and I hoped one of them had something that would shed light on Phil's connection to my dad and the Compound.

But as I opened the first several files, everything appeared to be legitimate business: schematics of products, meeting notes, schedules. After about an hour, I couldn't stop yawning. I rubbed my eyes, ejected the flash drive, and put it in my desk drawer.

Cocoa had been curled up at my feet, but when she felt me stir, she sat up and put her head in my lap. As I petted her, I realized I would have to figure another way to get Phil out of the company. And out of my life.

CHAPTER TWO

THE DAILY ROUTINES THAT HAD BEEN SO CONFINING, SO infuriating, while I was underground became something to cling to once we got out. Maybe it was because every morning I still woke up feeling angry and trapped. But then I looked around, saw the late-summer sunshine, smelled coffee and cinnamon, heard birds singing outside my open window. An extra dose of my new-and-improved reality came that morning when Lucas's foot kicked me in the gut, and I realized he'd snuck into my bed sometime in the night. And then Cocoa stuck her cold nose in my face.

Every morning I got to realize it all over again; the nightmare was done. We were out. Safe. Together as a family.

Lucas was still zonked, so I covered him up and took Cocoa outside, then filled her dish with food. In the kitchen, Els was busy making breakfast on one of the two stoves and

Gram was the only other one awake yet. She didn't ever speak in those early-morning moments, instead she simply set a hand on my shoulder and squeezed, then set a steaming cup of coffee and milk in front of me as I slid up on a bar stool at the counter.

She passed the box of natural sweetener to me, along with a spoon. As I stirred, I wondered if she knew how much I was still adjusting. For whatever reason, I appreciated it, this early-morning time with just the breeze ruffling the lace curtains at the window above the sink as I sipped my hot drink. The quiet moments that ended when the rest of my family woke up.

First Finnegan—Finn—the baby, wailing, until Mom pulled him out of his crib to snuggle with her. A few minutes after that my younger sister Terese—Reese—staggered in, long dark hair loose and mussed, wearing an old Seahawks jersey of Eddy's, so long that it skimmed the top of her skinny knees. She carried our cat, Clementine, and took her into the laundry room. Cat food rattled, then Reese came back out and stood still for a hug and kiss from Gram before climbing up to sit next to me. I put an arm around her shoulder and she leaned in to me. Reese smelled clean, like shampoo. Little wonder, since both she and our older sister, Lexie, spent a lot of time taking baths in the big garden tub in Mom's master suite.

I didn't get the appeal of baths, never did. But it was some sort of therapy for them, apparently. Part of me was worried, still, that Reese had been too young when we entered the Compound, that she'd been too affected. I was worried that one day she'd revert, start speaking with the English accent she'd spoken with for her years underground. But in the weeks since we'd been out, she had changed. As far as I could tell she actually seemed like a normal eleven-year-old.

I'd like to give credit to the family time, that simply being in a nice place with Gram and Eddy was enough to make us whole. But I have to place the blame, or credit, with television. Even though she was limited to two hours a day, those two hours consisted of all the tweener shows that told Reese exactly what she'd missed of American civilization in those six years of being *away.*

That's what we called it when we had to refer to our time in the Compound.

Away.

When we were *away* . . .

The word soft-pedaled the messed-up reality of the situation. We weren't trapped or confined or unwilling prisoners. We were simply . . . *away.*

We talked a lot about that period of our lives. How could we not? That had been the reality of the past six years of our life, and Eddy and Gram wanted to know. We couldn't pretend we weren't there. But, as we replied, we could leave out the worst of the Compound; the worst of what my father did. And we could use euphemisms that took some of the pain out of answering the questions.

"What did you eat when you were *away?*"

"What did you do for fun when you were *away?*"

We'd been at Gram's in Hawaii for a few days when Eddy asked me, "Did you think of me when you were *away*?"

How to answer that one? Because to answer only yes would not have done justice to the truth, that he was never out of my mind; that I thought of him constantly as I blamed myself for his death. For six years, I wore that guilt like an ugly shirt I couldn't take off.

Since being out, being back with my brother, at least once a day I found myself having to touch him to prove he was real.

Usually I settled for punching him on the arm or elbowing him or putting him in a headlock. Because reaching out and touching him and saying, *"Just had to check if you were real because I think you are just in my imagination and I'm terrified I'm going to wake up and realize I'm still in the Compound,"* . . . well, that might make me seem like a freak.

And I already felt that way enough of the time.

Next in the morning parade came my older sister, Lexie, in pajamas with pink lip prints all over them. Her eyes were red and puffy, and I assumed she'd been crying again. Her room was next to mine and I often heard her at night. Her dark hair was twisted in a messy bun at her neck. In her arms she carried Cara, whom she handed off to me. "I checked on Quinn, but he's still asleep. Which I would be if this little poop hadn't woken me up." She kissed the top of Cara's head, then accepted a cup of Kona from Gram and went and sat on the flowered couch in the sunroom by the fireplace and television.

My older sister seemed to be affected the most. Honestly, I could barely remember what she was like before the Compound. Spoiled like the rest of us. Did any of us even think about one another before that experience? But we'd actually become friends since we got out. She was quiet, though, maybe too quiet; I wasn't sure I'd ever seen her that subdued. And she was sad.

Lexie had been closer to Dad than any of us had. So it made sense that, despite all he had done, maybe she was still grieving for him.

So I made sure to be nice to her. She seemed too fragile to not treat kindly. I couldn't help thinking she had secrets. But we'd all spent the last six years in a confined space. Not many secrets you can keep in a situation like that. Maybe she thought none of us would understand how much she was missing Dad. And maybe she was right; maybe none of us would.

Mom came in, yawning, with dark circles under her eyes. She set the baby monitor on the counter. "Sweet thing went right back to sleep."

Gram asked, "Why didn't you?"

Mom shrugged. "I tried. But I smelled coffee."

I knew the Phil thing was stressing her out. That was why she couldn't sleep. Cara twisted around in my lap, kneeling so she could put her arms around my neck. Then she settled in, as if she was going to go back to sleep, her breath warm on my skin.

Mom kissed Gram on the cheek, then came over and did the same to me and Cara and Reese. She doctored her coffee with cream and sweetener and then went to sit with Lexie.

Eddy walked in, carrying his tablet computer. Barefoot, he wore a pair of faded gray sweatpants with holes in the knees and a nearly threadbare Nirvana T-shirt. Gram shook her head at him. "I'm gonna throw those out the next time I see them in the wash."

"No way." Eddy grinned and put Gram in a gentle headlock. "They just got broken in."

I glanced down at the clothes I wore: black running shorts and an orange T-shirt, both brand-new, not even close to being faded. Neither had any holes. Neither was broken in. Like the rest of the clothes in my closet.

Our first two weeks in Hawaii, Lexie and Mom and Reese had spent hours online, ordering clothes for all of us. Other than some dress clothes, Eddy didn't need anything.

So everything I owned was new. I had no favorites. I hadn't been on the outside long enough to break something in.

And suddenly I wanted something like the clothes Eddy wore. Something old. Something with holes in it. Something of my own that I'd had for longer than a month, something that wasn't so frickin' *new*.

Eddy poured himself a glass of juice. Our cat, Clementine, rubbed against his leg. Thanks to some new allergy shots, the cat no longer bothered him.

I looked sideways at my brother.

He was so . . . relaxed. So normal, with his worn-out, comfortable clothes. He totally fit in wherever he was.

Eddy's eyes narrowed as he looked at something on his tablet. He put a hand over his mouth as he paled.

I asked, "What's wrong?"

Eddy turned the screen my way to show me the front page of the *Seattle Times*. "It's Phil."

I sighed and looked away. "What's he done now?" I'd had enough of Phil the day before.

Eddy's eyes were wide. "He's disappeared."

My mouth dropped open. "What?"

"They suspect foul play." He sunk down onto a stool.

Reaching out with one hand while still holding Cara with the other, I grabbed his computer and quickly scanned the story.

Philip A. Whitaker . . . 38 . . . missing . . . blood-spattered apartment . . . The article was short, but it got my heart pounding. What if something had happened to Phil? What if he was gone forever? I started to smile, but then I looked up at Eddy. "Why are you so upset?"

Eddy shook his head and wouldn't look at me. "I know you don't get it, but Phil was good to me and Gram while you guys were . . . away. I didn't know what had happened. I only knew you were all gone and Gram and Phil were all I had." He looked at Gram.

She nodded. "He made sure we had everything we needed. But if I'd known . . ." She made a fist and smacked it into the palm of her other hand.

I set the tablet down, then put a hand on Eddy's arm. "I'm sorry." But, really, I wasn't. Not even close.

Eddy went into where Mom and Lexie were watching television, and flipped the channel to the news. I followed, carrying Cara. The story about Phil was big news. "How long do you think they'll wait?" I asked Mom.

"For what?"

I shrugged. "If he's gone . . . I mean, someone has to run YK."

She nodded. "Yeah. But I don't know. We'll have to see." A funny smile played at the corner of her lips. She didn't seem surprised at the news.

Did she have something to do with Phil's disappearance?

No way. I shoved away the thought as Els held a platter of fresh cinnamon rolls in front of me. Cara stirred and reached out for one.

"Want one, Cara?"

She nodded, so I carried her back into the kitchen and put her up on a stool, getting her some milk and a small piece of roll. I picked up one and took a bite, then, as Els was passing them around to everyone else, I quickly poured myself a glass of milk and went back up to my room.

I went online and found the article Eddy had showed me and printed it out. I glanced at the picture of Phil and called him the worst name I could think of. Then I added, "I hope you did get what you deserved. And that you're gone for good."

I opened my drawer and put the sheet of paper inside, along with the flash drive. I planned on never looking at either again.

CHAPTER THREE

As nearly two weeks went by with no sign of Phil, it became clear that the company had to make some decisions. Since the will named Eddy and me to take over when we were twenty-five, and Mom was obviously in charge of us, the board named her temporarily in control of YK. She was happy at that, to have Phil out of the way, but she had no desire to actually run the company.

The last week of August, she and Eddy and I were with the seven members of the YK board, in the same meeting room we'd seen Phil the last time. Mom said, "I believe it is apparent to everyone here that I don't have the faculties, or the time, to run this company." She nodded at us. "And my sons aren't ready. But I want them to be part of this company, part of this process. One day this place will belong to them. They need to start learning about it now."

The company lawyer pulled out a sheath of papers and

passed them out to all of us. I glanced down at a list of names; all were people Dad had groomed, thus all were people loyal to my father.

He cleared his throat. "These are the choices to run the company."

My heart started pounding.

Who was to say any of them were better than Phil?

Any, or all of them, could have known about the Compound, could have helped keep us down there.

Mom pointed to a name. "Mr. O'Connor. Can we appoint him?"

I grabbed Mom's arm and whispered, "How do we know that—"

"Shh. Eli. I know him." She spoke up for the board. "O'Connor is capable, right?"

The president, a woman in a black pantsuit with a severe blond bob, nodded. "He's on the list."

Mom nodded. "Can we agree to appoint him for six months? See how it goes?"

The board conferred with one another for a moment, but they all seemed to nod. The president spoke again. "Yes, six months."

"And my sons can start being involved?"

My hands turned to fists. I hated that my mother, wife of the founder of YK, had to beg like this, had to bow at their feet to get what she wanted: her sons, the legal heirs of YK, to have some small fingerhold into the company that they would inherit in less than ten years.

I stood up and walked into the hall, letting the door slam

behind me. The door opened and closed quietly. Eddy grabbed my arm and swung me around to face him. "What are you doing?"

I shook my head. "I hate this. All of it." I let out a deep breath. "Mainly I hate that these people are all still loyal to Dad, after everything he did."

Eddy didn't look like he agreed with me. Not at all.

"What?" I asked.

He said, "You don't get it."

"Get what?"

He ran his hands through his hair and then let them drop. "You go on and on about Dad, how bad he was." He lifted a hand. "But he built this place from scratch. He started so many charities that have helped so many people."

"Seriously?" I felt my face turn red. "You're *defending* him? That's ridiculous."

Eddy looked at the floor and didn't say anything for a second. Then he looked at me, his eyes narrowing. "I lost my father when I was nine. You didn't. You had him for six more years. So you don't get to tell me what I can or can't say about him."

"But he—"

"What? He what? Kept you guys down there? Yeah. I know. I hear about it all the time. I *live* it all the time. Every frickin' day. I got my family back, but . . ." He paused for a second. "What exactly did I get? A bunch of people trying to get over something that happened to them that I wasn't a part of. You tell me Dad went nuts, did all this. But that's not the father I remember." He shook his head. "You don't get it. I lost everything when I was nine. Everything! And now I have most of it back. But it's not the same." He stopped and looked down at the floor. "I have to adjust, too."

"Eddy, I—"

He held up a hand. "You need to let me do it in my own way. I lost my dad when he was still my hero. So that's what he's been the last six years whenever I've thought about him. My hero." He shook his head. "You're not going to change that kind of thinking so fast."

None of that had ever crossed my mind. That the last time Eddy saw our father, Dad still towered over him in more ways than one, still seemed someone to look up to. Eddy hadn't known the father of the past six years. The man I knew, who slowly went mad, and tried to take his family with him.

I would have thought Eddy would be on my side. That he would start thinking differently about our father based solely on what I told him about the past six years. It would take longer for him to see the truth, and I needed to give him the time.

I put my hand on my brother's shoulder. "I'm sorry. I should have thought of how it would make you feel." But the truth was, I couldn't.

"I know." He sighed. "We'd better go back in."

I opened the door and we took our seats again.

"Here they are." The president took out a YK tablet and tapped it with one long red fingernail. "I'll set up a date for them to come in and decide what they want to do." She looked up. "I'll have the director of charitable contributions clear her schedule for tomorrow morning. Will that do?"

Mom looked at me and Eddy. We both nodded, and she said, "Yes."

There were a few more things to discuss, but Eddy leaned over to me and whispered, "Do you even know what you want to do here?"

I started to speak, but then had to pause. Other than getting rid of Phil and making sure Mom was listened to, what *did* I want?

I hadn't thought that far ahead. I had no idea.

THAT NIGHT WE ALL SAT AROUND THE DINING-ROOM TABLE eating Mexican food. Except for Cara, seated next to me, banging her spoon on the table, none of us said anything. There was only the clinking of silver on china as we devoured Els's chicken-and-cheese enchiladas with green sauce.

I dumped another spoonful of guacamole on top of mine, then reached for the crystal bowl of sour cream.

Food was still a bit overwhelming for us all. In the Compound, we'd gotten so used to eating the dregs: lame nourishment that wouldn't have even made the cut for a typical food pyramid.

Stale, broken pasta.

Limp, nearly flavorless produce from the flagging hydroponics.

Canned and boxed goods well past their prime.

Meat had been but a memory, something I'd last eaten when I was thirteen; dairy products had disappeared long before that.

The tastes and textures we had missed for so long became something to focus on. Except for the little kids making noise, our meals tended to be silent as we all dug in, savoring the fresh flavors. Only when everyone was full did we start talking.

Eddy said, "School starts soon."

"I want to go to college," said Lexie.

Mom looked up at her. "I was thinking more along the lines of online school for you all. Just for this year, anyway. Until you are all used to being back."

Eddy looked at me, then back at Mom. "I thought we'd go back to our old school."

Mom shook her head. "There's already so much speculation. I'd rather we give it a chance to all blow over."

"Right!" Lexie rolled her eyes. "The richest guy in America keeps his entire family prisoner underground for *years,* and you expect it to blow over? God, Mom, we're never going to stop being freaks. Might as well let us out of the house to be freaks. I want to study something. Take actual dance lessons. Be a real person for once." She shook her head. "I turn eighteen in less than three months."

"I realize that." Mom sighed. "I just think it's too soon."

Lexie glared down at her plate. That was the most outspoken she'd been for weeks. And I had to admit,

I was actually glad to see her mad for once, after being sad for so long.

Gram said, "Eddy was with me in Hawaii most of the time, at the local school. No one around here has seen him since you left."

I blurted out, "No one knows what we look like now." I glanced at Lucas and Cara and Quinn. "And no one has ever seen them. We could use a fake name. Like you do." Mom had been using Gram's grandmother's maiden name for everything: buying the house and all our online ordering. No one had any way of knowing it, and it kept the Yanakakis name off all our mail as well.

Reese said, "Yeah! I don't want to be online. I want friends. Mercer Island has a middle school."

I wasn't sure I could see myself walking into Mercer Island High, pretending to care about making the honor roll and football games and asking someone to homecoming. After what I'd been through, how could I?

Mom narrowed her eyes. "And what will all of you do when your friends want to see where you live? Meet your family?" She shook her head. "I just can't allow anyone in here. I'm not ready."

Reese was quiet a moment, then said, "I could go to their houses until you're ready. And by that time, they'll be my friends and they won't care who I am."

"Good luck with that." I sighed. "People always care who you are." I shoved my food around my plate.

I'd spent enough of my life trapped. Even though our new place was great, I didn't need it to turn into another bunch of walls keeping me prisoner. "I can't be stuck here like we were stuck there." I met Mom's eyes. "I just can't. I want to get my GED and go to college, too."

Mom said, "Eli, you're fifteen years old."

"So? I've done nothing but study the past three years. I can get my GED and take the SATs while I'm working at YK." I didn't mention that there was no way, after what I'd been through, that I could immerse myself in the shallow, day-to-day dramas of the average teenager. I'd lost any chance there'd ever been to be that person.

Mom shook her head. "You're not working at YK."

"You said you wanted us involved!"

She sighed. "Not in an actual position." She held up her hand before I could protest. "Stop. All of you. I get it."

Eddy said, "We can protect each other."

Mom looked down at her plate. "You have to understand that this is hard as a parent. I worry about every one of you, each and every moment of the day. At least in the Compound . . . I always knew where you were. I always knew you were safe. And the thought of just letting you all go to school, out there, where I won't always know where you are . . ." She trailed off.

Lexie said, "Mom, you can't hide us forever. We have to grow up and have lives at some point." She added, "Otherwise, you're no different from Dad."

Mom's mouth fell open and she dropped her fork.

"Lexie!" Eddy snapped so sharply that Cara dropped her spoon and looked up at him with wide eyes. She was still skittish around Eddy most of the time, so I set a hand on her head to reassure her as I quietly added, "Yeah, Lex. Slight difference there."

Lexie glared at me. "Really? You know you're thinking it. We left one prison for another one with better food and more natural light."

"Stop it, you two." Mom put an elbow on the table and leaned her head into her hand. "I know. I understand what you're all saying. But can't we just hold off a little while?" She looked at Lexie. "Until your birthday? That gives you a couple months to just . . . adjust. In the meantime, you can do things online, study for your SATs—for this first semester—and then decide?"

Eddy looked pissed off, but he didn't say anything.

Reese said, "I want to go out and do stuff. We haven't been anywhere for so long."

I nodded. "I agree. If we do stay home for school, we need to be able to go out." I tilted my head toward Lucas and Cara. "They've never seen anything in Seattle."

Mom shook her head. "I really want you all to stay anonymous for as long as possible. Just . . . just until you all adjust."

She could have said *Just until you all stop being freaks*. That would have been more honest. Except for the fact it was never going to happen.

We would always be freaks.

I stuck my fork in an enchilada and it stayed there, pointing straight up. My appetite was gone.

Lexie said, "I have an idea." She looked around at all

of us. "Mom, what if we agreed to all go out together one day to someplace. Just for fun. Just to get out of here."

Reese asked, "Where?"

"Just a sec." Lexie pushed her chair back and stood up. "Hold on." She left the room and came back a moment later, several pens and a pad of paper in her hand. She held them up. "We all put down a place on here, then draw them out of a hat. Each week, or a couple times a week, we'll go somewhere different." She looked at Mom. "We'll take a car and a bodyguard and we'll stay together."

Reese said, "Yes! I agree with the idea."

I nodded. Eddy looked down at his plate, but I couldn't see the look on his face. Did he not want to go out?

Mom rolled her eyes and said, "Fine. But we're still sticking to the rest until your birthday, right?"

"Yeah," said Lexie. She started tearing off sheets of paper and passing them around.

Reese said, "Cara and Quinn are too little."

Lucas raised his hand. "I'll think of places for them." Then he put his hand back down and looked at me. "I don't know any places."

I beckoned to him. "I'll help you think of some." He came and stood beside my chair. I whispered, "Do you want to see animals?"

He nodded. "Yes!"

"What about an aquarium?"

He frowned. "There's one in my room."

I smiled. "No, buddy. I mean a huge one. Like with sharks and stuff."

His eyes got wide and he nodded. "And I want to see toys. Lots of toys."

"Okay." I tore the sheet of paper into four pieces, and wrote *Zoo, Aquarium,* and *Toy Store* on the first three. Then I thought for a moment and wrote *Mariners game* on the fourth. YK had a corporate suite at Safeco Field, which made that outing seem the easiest. And also the most obvious. I crumpled up that piece of paper and set it by my plate.

Lexie dumped the lettuce onto a plate and held out the empty salad bowl to Reese, who dropped in her paper. Eddy hadn't written anything on his. Reese glared at him, so he quickly scrawled something, crumpled the paper in his fist, and dropped it in. I handed the three sheets to Lucas. He dropped them in and Lexie stirred them all up with her hand. She walked over to Mom. "You want to do the honors? Tell us where we are going this week."

Mom shook her head as she looked around at us, but then she smiled. "Fine." She reached in.

Eddy started drumming on the table with his fists. Lucas joined in, then Reese, and soon we were all pounding, even Lexie. Mom held up the piece of paper. "This week's outing is . . ." Her forehead wrinkled and she looked around the table. Then she shrugged. "Costco!"

Reese squealed.

Eddy looked at me. "Seriously?"

Lexie said, "I'm staying home."

Lucas asked, "What's Costco?"

I sighed. "You'll find out."

CHAPTER FOUR

THE NEXT DAY, MY ALARM CLOCK WENT OFF AT SEVEN. I threw on some black shorts, laced up my running shoes, and stepped onto my treadmill. The view was mainly of Lake Washington, but also of the good-size woods, separated by the security fence at the edge of the property. I put in earbuds, turned on the music, and ran several miles.

I showered and then got dressed. Dressed up, actually, in khaki pants, a white button-down shirt, and a black blazer.

Eddy met me downstairs, dressed in new pants like mine and a black V-neck sweater with a white T-shirt underneath. We went out to the waiting black SUV, driven by our bodyguard, Lee.

Lee was Samoan, about six feet five and two hundred and seventy pounds. He'd played three seasons for the Seahawks. His grandpa's cousin's wife was some friend of Gram's, who had been the one to hire him. I suspected he got paid more being our bodyguard/driver than he had playing in the NFL.

Lee drove us to YK, where a blond man in a brown suit led us into an elevator and up three floors to a door with a plaque that read:

DIRECTOR OF CHARITABLE CONTRIBUTIONS
SHARON GREENE

Ms. Greene opened the door for us. She was tall, dressed in a slim gray skirt, white blouse, and low black pumps, her dark red hair pulled back in a tightly braided bun. With a wide smile she shook our hands and ushered us into her office. Eddy and I both took a seat on the jade-green leather couch in front of a low glass table.

Ms. Greene asked, "Something to drink?"

"Coffee, please," I said.

Eddy just nodded.

She went to her desk, pushed a button on her phone, and said, "Lila? Could you bring us a tray, please." She came over to us and sat in a matching leather chair. "So, what are you two interested in doing?"

Eddy looked at me and then back to Ms. Greene. "I think we just want to get involved." He seemed way more enthusiastic than usual.

She nodded. "One thing about a company that makes a ton of money? They also get to give a lot of money away." She clasped her hands together. "And, boy, do we give away the money."

There was a knock on the door. Ms. Greene called out, "Come in."

A petite, dark-haired woman in a gray dress, flowered scarf, and tall black boots entered, carrying a tray so full it nearly covered everything above her shoulders. She set it down on the table.

"Thank you, Lila," said Ms. Greene. "That will be all."

The tray had two small silver pots on it, three china cups, three plates and various silverware, as well as a basket of scones and muffins and assorted jams and jellies and creamers. She held out a hand. "Help yourselves." She tapped one of the pots. "This is hot chocolate. The other is coffee. I can also get tea if you like?" She looked from me to Eddy.

I shook my head. "This is great. Thank you." I reached out for the coffee pot and held it up. "Would you like some?"

"Oh, polite, aren't you?" She smiled. "No, thank you."

I poured myself a cup, and stirred in cream and sugar. Eddy poured himself some cocoa and took a raspberry scone. I chose a blueberry one, which was still warm, and put it on a plate. "So, what are you expecting of us?" I asked. "I guess I should say, what are we allowed to do?"

She reached over and plucked a thick pile of red folders off a nearby file cabinet. "These are our current contributions that are soon coming up for renewal. Do either of you have particular interests?"

Eddy shrugged and took a bite of his scone. That was more like the Eddy I'd seen lately. What was his problem?

I said, "I'm interested in medicine. Like research of some type?"

I ate half my scone as Ms. Greene flipped through a few folders, then extracted a small stack of files. She set them down on the couch next to my leg. "Look through these. They are the proposals that explain everything about the medical focus of the research. So they are a little fact heavy, but see if any strike your fancy." She raised her eyebrows at Eddy.

He said, "I'm more interested in technology."

She frowned. "Let's get one thing clear. You both are set to inherit this whole shebang. Your entire lives will probably be wrapped around"—she swirled her finger around in the air a couple of times—"this place." She leaned forward. "So if I were you? I'd find whatever it is I liked the best and get good at it. Learn to love it." She leaned back. "Or you will both be very unhappy people."

I looked at Eddy. He bit his lip and looked back at Ms. Greene. He shrugged a little. "I seriously have no interest in what charities we give to. I mean, I'm all for it, giving money away. But I don't think I want to spend my time on it."

I nodded. "And I do. At least, for now. To see what it's about."

Eddy said, "I'd much rather be involved in development."

"Oh, smart boys, aren't you?" Ms. Greene clapped her hands and stood up. "Eli, take a look at those files. Eddy, come with me. We'll get you going to where you want to be."

They left.

I picked up the files and started leafing through as I finished my scone. YK contributed to so many medical causes. Cancer, heart disease, you name it. Some of my crumbs fell on a file. As I brushed them off, I noticed the label. Progeria. I had no idea what that was, so I opened it and found a fact sheet on top.

Progeria (also known as "Hutchinson-Gilford Progeria Syndrome") is an extremely rare genetic condition in which aging progresses rapidly, starting at an early age. The word progeria comes from the Greek words pro, meaning "before," and géras, meaning "old age." The disorder occurs only in an estimated 1 per 8 million live births. Those born with progeria typically live to their mid-teens and early twenties. Though a genetic condition, it is rarely inherited. Scientists are particularly interested in progeria because it might reveal clues about the normal process of aging.

"Wow." I paged through to a set of pictures and gaped. They were of a young child with a bald head and no eyebrows. If it wasn't for the pink dress, I wouldn't have known she was a girl. She looked like a wizened little old man. "How sad . . ." I paged through more, reading about the Progeria Institute and everything they did trying to discover a cure for the disease. There were more pictures of young children, all who looked like small, wrinkled old people.

I finished the file and set it down just as Ms. Greene came back. "Find anything that looks interesting?"

I picked the file back up. "Progeria."

Her smile immediately drooped as she sunk to the couch beside me. "Oh, my gosh. Those poor children. It's the saddest thing."

I said, "I want to go there. To the research center."

She tilted her head a bit. "Let's get one thing clear. Just because you are interested in a cause doesn't mean you have to get personally involved. Your father rarely—"

I clenched my fists. "I am not my father."

She reached out and set a firm hand on my knee. "Of course not. It's just . . ."

I stiffened. "What?"

She took a deep breath. "Having the money? To fund these causes? Doesn't mean you should get involved. Personally, I mean."

"So, I should just learn to write the check?" I asked. "Not ever learn who the check is actually helping?"

"Or not helping," she said.

"What?" I didn't get it.

She tapped the progeria file with one long white-tipped fingernail. "This is one of those . . . lost causes. They won't find a cure. Maybe not even a decent treatment. Certainly not in my lifetime and probably not in yours either."

My eyes narrowed. "So we shouldn't fund it?"

Her words tumbled out, "Oh, that's not what I'm saying. But—"

"But what?" My face was getting hot. "We should just forget those children? Not help them?"

She let out a long breath. "YK is an industry that is all about progress. Development. Creating things today that weren't there yesterday." She looked sideways at the progeria file. "Some causes simply will not have that kind of progress."

I shook my head. "What happened to trying? Not giving up?"

"Oh, softhearted, aren't you?" She patted my hand. "But getting involved in causes like this"—she narrowed her eyes—"will only make you softer."

I yanked my hand away and stood up so fast that I knocked over my coffee. As I tried to grab it, the file fell open, and all the fluttering papers hit the floor.

Ms. Greene made no move to pick up the mess. She sat there, a smile playing at the corners of her mouth.

I shoved the papers into a pile and set them back on the table. "Let's get one thing clear. I want to see the Progeria Institute." Then I picked the coffee cup off the floor, and slammed it on top of the papers. "Tomorrow."

Her smile disappeared and I left.

CHAPTER FIVE

I THOUGHT MY LITTLE TANTRUM MIGHT BACKFIRE, BUT LATER that evening I got a call from Ms. Greene. Her tone was very formal. "Mr. Yanakakis, we've arranged for a car to pick you up at eight A.M. and take you to the Progeria Institute. The director has been informed you're part of a program for exceptional high school students with an interest in medicine."

I frowned. "And he's fine with that?"

She cleared her throat. "I implied that YK was rather vested in the program, and that further funding might be related to this visit going well, so . . . yes. He's fine with that. I told him your name was EJ."

My initials. *Elijah John*. Clever. "Do I have a last name?"

"Smith."

Not so clever. "What kind of stuff does he expect me to ask?"

She began talking faster, as if she had a million things

to do and wanted to get the call over with. "Take a note-book. Make a show of writing information in it. And just ask whatever it is that you want to know. This is your game. Play it as you wish. You're simply on a tour of the facility. Stick to my plan and I highly doubt anyone will suspect who you really are."

"Thank you." I felt a little bad about my attitude earlier in the day. "I appreciate you arranging this so quickly."

She let out a harsh little breath. "You were quite clear about your wishes when you were in my office."

There was no point in me making an enemy of her. "Still," I said, "I appreciate your quick work. So . . . thank you. Again."

"Of course." Her tone had softened, but only slightly. "Please let me know if I can do anything else for you."

In the morning after my run and shower, I went into my huge closet and looked at all the clothes hanging there. After so many years of wearing the same sweatpants and T-shirts, choosing clothes to wear every day was still something I hadn't gotten used to. Hanging around the house made for easy choices, but what would an excep-tional high school student wear?

I put on a black T-shirt, and then pulled a gray cashmere V-neck sweater over it. I'd seen Eddy wear a similar look one day, which is why I'd chosen the clothes during one of the online shopping sessions.

I ended up getting a bunch of clothes that were like some of his. Maybe it was because I liked them, but there was also another reason. Eddy just seemed to know what to wear, how to act, who to be. And even if I had ever known all that, I'd been out of the game for six years. So I kind of figured copying him would be a sure thing.

Then I grabbed some jeans and socks, slipped on a pair of low black Chuck Taylors. I stood in front of the mirror.

Exceptional high school student?

I shrugged. Maybe.

Teenage son of a billionaire?

I smiled. Obviously.

I had a quick breakfast of coffee and a banana. No one else was up besides Els.

As promised, a black sedan pulled in our gate at eight. There was a light drizzle so I jogged to the car, holding a leather journal and a pen in one hand. The driver was older, about fifty, with gray hair. He had just opened the back door on the passenger side when Lee showed up, putting himself between me and the car. Lee shut the door and turned to me. "I'll take you in the SUV."

I froze. "Why? This has all been arranged."

Lee shrugged a bit. "Orders from your mother."

The night before I'd told Mom about the whole thing. My shoulders slumped. No wonder she'd been so okay with it. She'd already been making plans to make sure she would be in control. "Fine."

I headed over to the SUV and got in the front. I brushed a bit of rain off my face, and fastened my seat belt. Lee must have figured I was pissed off, because he didn't try to start a conversation the entire ride.

I found it strange to be alone, none of my family with

45

me. Rain started hitting the car window as we headed over the Hadley Memorial Bridge, a long floating bridge that connected Mercer Island to Seattle. Westbound, it ran parallel to the eastbound Murrow Memorial Bridge. At that time of the morning, the lanes were full of commuter traffic. The Progeria Institute was almost to Olympia, and rush hour slowed us down the entire way. I wondered whether Ms. Greene had scheduled the early appointment on purpose.

Finally, we drove through the gate of a complex of red-brick buildings, all surrounded by high metal fences with ornamental, yet deadly looking, spikes on top.

Lee took me all the way to the first building, and stopped at the end of a short sidewalk that led to a large set of glass doors. "Thanks," I said, and reached for the door.

He held up his hand. "Hold on." Then he got out, walked around to my side, and opened the door for me.

I dropped to the ground. "You're not going in with me. I don't care what my mom told you, but you will totally blow my cover if anyone sees you hulking beside me." I swallowed. "No offense."

"None taken." He looked around at all the obvious security measures, then handed me a cell phone.

"What's this?" I asked.

"Your mother asked me to give it to you. Untraceable. I'm number two on speed dial."

I started to ask who was #1, then realized I didn't need to. I turned the phone over and looked at the screen. My first cell phone.

Eddy had one already, of course. What teenager didn't have a cell phone? He stayed in contact with his friends in Hawaii, I knew that. Sometimes it bugged me, and I'd thought about asking for a cell phone, but who was there for me to call?

Still, I felt a little thrill as I slipped it in the front pocket of my jeans.

"You've got an hour. Then I come looking for you." He got back in the SUV and didn't take his eyes off me.

I headed toward the front doors, which automatically swooshed opened before I got there, and I stepped inside. The floors and walls were white, and the place looked like a hospital. A short, stocky man with a graying, receding hairline came toward me. He wore a white lab jacket and black pants, and held out his hand. "I'm Dr. James Barkley." He had a slight accent, which I couldn't place.

I shook his hand. "Pleased to meet you. I'm—"

"EJ. Ms. Greene told me all about you. Perfect SAT scores at fifteen!"

What? Ms. Greene had certainly taken liberties with the truth in order to make me *sound* exceptional. I hadn't even taken the SATs, and was fairly sure I wouldn't get a perfect score when I did.

"Amazing." He smiled.

"I guess so." I hoped there wouldn't be any more surprises courtesy of Ms. Greene.

"I'm so glad to have you here on behalf of YK." He held out an arm. "This way, please."

We walked down a brightly lit hallway filled with closed

doors. It felt so familiar, so similar to the Compound that I shuddered slightly, and found myself relieved as I passed each door and found that none were painted yellow.

He stopped in front of one near the end of the hallway and opened it, then ushered me inside, where several people in white lab coats and plastic goggles stood over trays of test tubes. Some held eyedroppers and methodically added something to the test tubes. Others seemed to be recording data on laptops as the others worked.

Dr. Barkley spoke quietly. "This is one of our many labs. Research is where most of the funding goes."

"You're working on a cure then?" To complete the picture, I opened my journal and jotted something down.

He smiled. "That's the main goal. But just isolating data related to aging and the disease . . . that can be a victory, too." He lowered his voice even more. "Some years ago we had a fire that destroyed most of our research. We were so grateful to Mr. Yanakakis. He gave us enough funding to start over again. Although we'd lost so much, at least we were able to keep going."

My face had gotten hot as he talked about my father. Was I so sensitive that I couldn't stand to hear anyone speak about him?

No. I just couldn't stand to hear anyone talk about him, as if he were anything but what he had been: a madman. The thought of even admitting to anyone that I was his son . . .

I turned back toward the door. "Is that it? Just research?" My tone must have been a bit brusque, because

Dr. Barkley's smile wavered. "I can show you our therapy section."

I didn't know what that was, but I nodded. I wanted to get out of that lab that reminded me so much of my father. And my former life.

He led me down a hallway and outside. We dodged raindrops as we walked across a cobblestone road to another building. After a short hallway, he opened a set of double doors and we entered a glass-domed room, so high over my head I couldn't help but turn my focus upward. Plants were everywhere, and colorful butterflies flitted overhead. A large sparkling pool took up a major portion of the space, the rest of which was covered with grassy walkways and benches. "This is amazing."

Dr. Barkley glanced at his watch. "Our first children should be arriving in a little while."

"What is this place?" I asked.

Instead of answering, he motioned to a nearby cushioned bench. As soon as I sat down next to him, the phone in my pocket felt too bulky and uncomfortable, so I took it out and set it on the bench beside me.

He asked, "Do you know anything about progeria?"

I shrugged. "Just what I read in the prospectus."

"Well, these kids aren't going to recover. It's not like other childhood afflictions that they have the hope of leaving behind them as they grow up." He pulled out a YK tablet from the deep pocket of his lab coat and swiped a finger across it. "Do you mind?" he asked. "I find it much easier to make all this clear if I start from the beginning."

"Not at all," I said. "It's a really fascinating disease." I quickly backtracked. "I mean . . . not to make light of anything, I just—"

"I understand completely." Dr. Barkley set a hand on my arm. "Progeria is *fascinating*. And mysterious. Which is why I've dedicated my life to it." He held out his computer so I could see a photo of a newborn.

Dr. Barkley said, "Progeria is extremely rare, and only affects one in eight million newborns worldwide." He pointed at the photo. "As newborns, children with progeria appear normal. But . . ." He tapped the screen and the photo switched to one of an older baby. "Within a year, their growth rate slows. Soon they are much shorter and weigh less than others their age." Again he tapped, and the photo of a boy, maybe five or so, in a navy-blue sweat suit, appeared. He was bald, with a pinched nose and wrinkled skin that looked very aged. While his head looked very large, the face and jaw seemed very small, too small for the size of his head.

Dr. Barkley said, "These children are of normal intelligence, but their appearance is very distinct."

I asked, "Are there other symptoms? Besides the ones you can see, I mean."

He pointed at the picture. "They typically have symptoms that you would normally only see in much older people. Stiff joints, hip dislocations, cardiovascular disease."

"Heart disease?" I asked. "Like heart attacks?"

He nodded. "Some children with progeria undergo

coronary bypass surgery. But it's just for more time, really. On average, most die around age thirteen. Usually from a heart attack or stroke."

I looked away, at the glistening pool. I couldn't imagine knowing you would die at such a young age. "And there's nothing you can do?"

He motioned at the pool. "Hydrotherapy seems to help a little with the stiff joints, much like it helps senior citizens."

It seemed so sad to me, that they couldn't do more for the children. Or prevent it from happening in the first place. "Can't they test for the disease?"

Dr. Barkley nodded. "Yes. But first let me explain how the disease works." He swiped a finger across the computer screen, and a diagram popped up of the cross-section of a cell. "There's a cellular protein known as Lamin A, which is encoded by the LMNA gene. Lamin A helps maintain the structure of the nucleus, which of course contains all the genetic information. Progerin is a mutated version of Lamin A, and it's what causes progeria to occur." He stopped for a moment and shook his head, as if in disbelief. "Twenty-five thousand base pairs of DNA make up the LMNA gene, but nearly all cases of progeria happen because of the substitution of just one base pair."

I said, "So that's why it's so rare."

He nodded. "The strange thing is, parents and siblings of children with progeria are almost never affected by the disease. Which means that the genetic mutation must occur just prior to conception." He swiped across the screen until it was blank.

He held up a finger. "Now, this has all been around for quite some time. But what we discovered in our research about six years ago was this." He tapped and a diagram popped up of a tubular structure surrounded by what looked like small worms. "Here's a chromosome." He glanced down at the loafers on his feet, then over at my Converse. "Ah, good. Can I see your shoelaces?"

I nodded and crossed my legs, so that one of my shoes was right near my hand. Dr. Barkley reached out and pulled on my shoelace, untying it. He held the plastic tip at the end. "Do you know this has a name?"

I shrugged. "Um, plastic thing at the end of my shoelace?"

He smiled. "It's actually called an aglet." He dropped the shoelace and went back to the computer screen. He pointed at the tips of the chromosome. "Much like the ends of your shoelaces are bound by aglets, the ends of the chromosomes are bound by telomeres." He tapped again.

An animated video began, showing cell division. He said, "During cell division, those telomeres wear away. Eventually, they wear away so much that the cell stops dividing and dies. Our research has found that short or abnormal telomeres turn on the production of progerin, which, as we know, is related to cell damage caused by aging. Still with me?"

I nodded.

"As the telomeres shorten, the cell makes even more

progerin. But I wanted to know what was causing the production of the progerin."

"And did you figure it out?" I asked.

"In a way." He turned off his tablet and leaned back. He nodded. "As I was trying to answer this question, I stumbled upon something else. I had just figured out what I believed to be the gene that turns on aging." He didn't say anything else.

"That's amazing!" I said.

He looked down and sighed. "Yes, it could have been."

"What do you mean?"

"I was doing this on my own. Unfortunately, only I knew all my research. When my lab was destroyed in the fire . . . I had to start over." He smiled. "Which made YK such an absolute lifesaver. Mere weeks before the fire, I had applied for funding through YK. Starting over was bad enough, but starting over with all the funding we needed? Well, it lessened the sting a bit." He looked around, then raised a hand in the air. "All of this is what arose from the ashes of that fire. My research will get back to where it was. In the meantime, we do all the good we can."

Just then a door opened, and I heard the sound of a child giggling. A small bald boy came in through the glass door, wearing red surf shorts. He held the hand of a slim girl who looked about my age. Her dark hair was in a pixie cut, and she wore jeans and a long-sleeved Mariners tee. And she had the most beautiful brown eyes I'd ever seen. My heart sped up.

She saw Dr. Barkley, then smiled and waved.

Dr. Barkley took my arm. "Come. You can meet one of our patients."

The girl was watching me.

Trying to be as cool as possible, I stood up, took a large step, then immediately tripped on my untied shoelace and did a face-plant on the grass.

CHAPTER SIX

Dr. Barkley took one of my arms and helped me up.

"I'm fine, I'm fine." I brushed the grass off my knees, then got up on one knee and tied my shoe as my face burned. *Great.* Way to make an idiot of myself in front of the first teenage girl I'd met in . . . well, actually? The first teenage girl I'd ever met since I'd become a teenager myself.

The girl and the little boy walked over to me. She looked at me with an amused smile on her face.

I felt my face get even hotter.

Dr. Barkley introduced me. "This is EJ. And, EJ, this is Jamie and his sister, Verity."

Verity may have been close to laughing at me, but even so, it made her brown eyes sparkle. "Hi."

"Hi," I said.

Jamie looked up at me and said, "I'm five."

I smiled. "I have a brother about your age."

His face lit up and he looked around. "Is he here?"

Verity set a hand on his head. "Jamie, stop interrupting."

"It's fine," I said. But I didn't want to have to answer, and say that, no, my brother wasn't here, because he was perfectly healthy and didn't have to face the fact he'd be dead by age thirteen. I mustered a smile. "You going swimming?"

Jamie nodded and grabbed Dr. Barkley's hand. He smiled, and said, "Okay, I'm coming." They left Verity and I standing there.

She looked over at me. "Want to watch him swim?"

I nodded. "Of course." I reached over and picked up my phone off the bench.

As we walked, she asked, "So why are you here? Is your little brother a patient, too?"

I shook my head. "No . . . um . . . I'm part of this internship thing." I held up my journal. "This is sort of a research assignment."

"What kind of an internship?" She seemed interested, but I wished she would stop asking. My whole fake persona of exceptional-high-school-student was not all that solid.

"I'm just asking a bunch of questions as he gives me a tour, basically. And then I have to write out a report to get a grade from my teacher at school." *Nice, Eli. That sounded totally plausible.*

"What school?" she asked.

Seriously? Trying to put an end to the questions I couldn't answer, I asked, "Is this the Inquisition or what?"

She smiled. "Yes."

I wanted to stop answering her questions because I didn't want to be dishonest with her. This was my first conversation with a teenage girl ever. Well, a teenage girl that wasn't related to me. And I didn't want to mess it up by any more lying. Which was all I'd done from the moment I'd opened my mouth.

"Sorry," she said. "I'm naturally curious."

I smiled. "I thought we were going to watch him swim." I started to head closer to the pool, but she grabbed my elbow.

"Trust me; we'll stay much drier if we watch from a distance." She pointed to a bench near the pool, and we both headed for it and then sat down. I set my journal down on the ground and put my cell phone on top of it. The bench was small, and her jeans-clad leg was only an inch or so away from mine. I couldn't help but notice that she smelled nice.

Jamie had gotten in the pool with a woman in a black tank suit. He wore blue water wings, splashed a bit and laughed.

Verity said, "He loves coming here."

I tried to fend off more questions by asking some of my own. "It must be hard," I said. "The progeria."

She nodded. "He was always sort of . . . unhealthy. Even before we knew about the progeria."

I wanted to know how old she was, but didn't want to come out and ask. "How old were you when he was born?"

"Ten. My parents didn't really think they'd have another kid, but I'd always begged them for a little brother or sister." She stuck an elbow in my ribs and I jumped.

She said, "If you want to know how old I am, just ask."

I smiled. "How old are you?"

"Almost sixteen. How about you?"

"Same." Well, if almost sixteen meant fifteen years and barely a couple months. Close enough.

We watched Jamie dog-paddle over to the woman. Verity asked, "So you just have the one brother?"

I kind of laughed, and then realized I needed to lie again. "I have an older sister, too." Which was actually the truth, except that I happened to leave out a few siblings.

"Sometimes I wish I had more brothers or sisters." Verity pointed at Jamie. "I don't know what I'd do without him." She met my eyes and shrugged a little. "I mean, I know the day will come." She sighed. "Life expectancy is, like, thirteen."

"That's what Dr. Barkley told me. It must be hard, knowing he has a . . . shelf life." I winced. "I'm so sorry. That came out wrong."

"It's okay." She lifted and lowered a shoulder. "It's kind of true." She watched Jamie for a bit before going on. "It's hard on my parents. I just try to do everything I can with him. I take an independent study at school first hour of the day, so I can bring him here three days a week." She glanced at her watch.

She wasn't old enough to drive. "How do you get here?" I asked.

Her brown eyes turned my way again. "The bus. Our schools are right next to each other, so I run him there and then get back in time for class."

"Sounds like a pain," I said.

She nodded. "It'll be way better when I can drive."

Jamie called out, "Verity! Come watch me!"

She stood up and looked down at me. "I'm surprised he didn't yell before now. Coming?"

I nodded. "In a sec."

I watched Verity walk away.

For some reason, I wanted to call her back, tell her every-thing: my real name, the truth about my family. I swal-lowed. How stupid would that be? I'd known her for less than five minutes. And there was the fact that I would never run into her again.

Just before reaching the pool, Verity spun around on her heel and jogged back to me. "Before I go . . ." She knelt down and grabbed my phone; then before I could say anything, her thumbs were a blur. "There. I mean, in case you have any questions about this place. Or anything." She handed me the phone and headed over to the pool.

Dr. Barkley joined me again. He said, "I have to go to a meeting, but I'll have someone show you out. Please tell Ms. Greene . . ." He trailed off.

I stood up. "I'm sure you can expect to hear about the funding sometime soon." I realized my mistake. "I mean, of course I don't have much to do with it, but . . ." I picked up the journal. "She'll get a great report from me about it all."

He smiled. "There's no rush." He held out his hand.

I shook it. "Thank you very much for the tour." I wanted to tell him that, in my mind, it was done. He would get whatever funding he needed. I would see to it. But I'd have to let the people at YK deliver that news.

I smiled. "I hope you get the funding. And I hope you find a cure."

He nodded. "We'll do our best."

"I can find my way out," I said. And he left.

I picked up my phone and figured out how to get to my contact list.

1. Mom

2. Lee

3. Eddy

4. Verity Blum.

Verity Blum.

After fumbling with it a bit more, I got a message to pop up: **Erase this contact?**

Getting close to anyone was unwise, not while we were trying to lie low. And then I almost laughed. Close to anyone? When had I been close to anyone, ever, that wasn't related to me? I even had trouble with family most of the time.

Plus, who said she even wanted to get to know me?

I glanced back down at her name in my contacts.

That had to mean something, right?

She put her number in my contacts. Which meant she wanted some sort of . . . contact.

My gaze went over to Verity, who crouched near the

side of the pool as Jamie tried to splash her. Verity laughed. Her laugh alone made me want to know her better.

But it would never work. Could never.

I looked again at the message: **Erase this contact?**

There was only one realistic and rational answer.

My thumb hovered over the **Yes** button.

But then I pressed **No** instead.

CHAPTER SEVEN

I CAN REMEMBER GOING TO COSTCO ONLY ONCE AS A KID, way before we entered the Compound. Maybe because I had no reason to wonder where the groceries came from. Honestly, I never really saw food in packaged form. Even the Baby Bels were unwrapped and on a white china plate with a line of Triscuits by the time I got them, so it wasn't until we were in the Compound that I saw the red wax circles of cheese and yellow boxes of crackers. Well, for as long as the cheese and crackers lasted, which wasn't long.

Eddy swung open my door. "You ready?" He was dressed in jeans and blue polar fleece.

"Almost." I buttoned my jeans and pulled a long-sleeved red Under Armour shirt over my head. Even though it was August, the day was damp and chilly, much like the day before. I hoped we weren't done with sunny days just yet; I wasn't quite ready for the northwest gloom to descend before autumn had even begun.

As I tied my Converse, Eddy said, "The little kids must be excited—they're already sitting in the car."

"Lee should love that." I turned back to him. "What about Lexie and Reese?"

"Actually, they're in the car, too." He grinned.

I grabbed my black soft-shell jacket off the hook on the back of the door and followed him downstairs. Mom was there with Gram, Finn, and Quinn. She looked up at us. "Quinn has a cough and Finn is fussy."

I asked, "You going to stay home then?"

Mom nodded.

I'd just been out the day before. And she hadn't been out since . . . since we'd last gone to YK. Which had not exactly been an enjoyable outing. "Mom, why don't you go? I can stay and help with them."

She smiled. "Oh, that's sweet, but you go have fun."

"Are you sure?" I asked. "I don't mind." Truth was, I liked staying home. I found it much less stressful than going out in public.

"Positive." She stood and went over to the window seat, to her black bag. She reached in and pulled out her wallet. She handed me seven twenties. "One for each of you to buy something. And a twenty for Lee to have a snack." She frowned. "He always looks like he's hungry."

I put the money in my jacket pocket and zipped.

Eddy leaned down and kissed her on the cheek. "Thanks." I did the same and added, "Don't worry."

As we walked out the door, she called after us, "And please be safe."

I climbed into the back of the SUV with Reese and Lexie, who'd already strapped Lucas and Cara into the third row, where they were busy with green juice boxes. Lexie, apparently having decided a trip to Costco was worth her while after all, rolled her eyes. "About time." She was playing with the cell phone Mom had given her after dinner the night before.

Reese had pitched a fit she didn't get one, and from the way she was glaring at Lexie's, she was obviously still not over it.

Eddy started to get into the backseat beside Reese, but Lucas kicked the seat. "No! I want Eli to sit there."

Eddy got back out. "Maybe I should just stay home."

"No, you have to go." I set a hand on his shoulder. "He's just cranky."

"Whatever." Eddy got into the passenger seat in front.

I glanced at Lee. He did look hungry.

As we stopped by the front gate and waited for it to open, the two security guards came out of the white concrete booth. Both were in their twenties: Joe had a dark beard, while Sam shaved his head and had ice-blue eyes. Both grinned and waved as we pulled out of the front gate.

When we hit the street, my heart started to pound.

Was I this excited about Costco? Or was it just that I was getting to go out, out into the real world where everyone else lived normal lives?

The trips to YK and then the progeria lab the day before hadn't been normal teenager outings. Maybe my heart was pounding at the possibility that I could actually be normal again. Costco could do that, maybe. Hand normalcy back to me.

The windows of the SUV were tinted, so I took advantage and stared all I wanted at people walking and jogging and driving beside us, knowing that they couldn't see me. I wondered, if you mentioned the name *Rex Yanakakis* to them, what would they think?

Would it be like mentioning *Steve Jobs*? Someone who was gone, who they'd only seen on television and the Internet, yet was a visionary who had influenced components of their everyday life? Is that what they thought of my dad?

Or was it not that positive? Did his name call to mind a paranoid genius billionaire who stuffed his family away underground for years?

I wiped away the condensation on the window.

And what of me? What if someone said *Eli Yanakakis* to them?

What if I had said that to Verity Blum?

I'm not EJ, I'm Eli.

What would she have thought?

Filthy-rich heir to a technology fortune? Will never have to work for anything in his life? The freak who spent years underground.

I looked over at my sisters and my little brother. If people thought that about me, they must think the same about the rest of my family. And I couldn't handle that.

Eddy glanced down at his cell phone and the GPS feature he'd called up. He pointed to the left. "I think we can get there faster that way."

He was so relaxed, finding directions on his cell phone, showing Lee the way, while most of the time I still looked around at the outside world through the eyes of someone seeing it for the first time.

My brother seemed to be a part of this world; he seemed to be normal.

I felt a twinge of envy.

Who was I kidding? Eddy *was* a part of the world. Eddy *was* normal. Something I could never be. My dad made sure of that.

"Is that it?" Lucas kicked the back of my seat. "Are we there?"

"Lucas, stop that." I looked out past Lexie and Reese at the red-and-blue sign, my heart still pounding.

Maybe I really was simply excited about going to Costco.

Lee parked. We got the little kids out of their car seats. Rain was starting to come down, so Lexie carried Cara and I took Lucas and we all ran to the entrance, Eddy and Lee right on our tails. Lexie put Cara in a cart; I did the same with Lucas, and we went inside. Lee showed his Costco card to the attendant.

Apparently he was already a member.

The first section we encountered was a bank of televisions and computers. The latest animated Disney movie was playing, and Lexie pushed Cara closer so she could see the princess. She said, "You guys go on. I'll stay with her for a bit."

Lee frowned.

Did he want us to stay together? Was he that worried about the whole thing?

I said, "We're fine in here. I'll take Lucas and see what else we can see." Then I remembered. "Wait." I reached in my pocket and pulled out the money. "Everyone gets a twenty to buy something." I gave Lexie twenties for both her and Cara, doled one each to Reese and Eddy, and held one out to Lee. "In case you need a snack."

"Won't." He rubbed his belly and smiled. "They have samples." He pointed at the money. "But I have the membership card so we have to pay together."

I zipped the three twenties back into my jacket pocket. "Who wants to come with me and Lucas?"

Eddy and Lee stayed with Lexie and Cara, agreeing to meet me and Lucas and Reese up front when we were done. I pushed the cart past the televisions and into the clothing section. Reese immediately went to a stack of pink hoodies and started holding them up to herself.

I still had not gotten used to seeing all of us out of our stupid Compound uniforms, all those years of the girls in their matching velour tracksuits, me in my sweatpants and T-shirts. Ditching those had been liberating.

I told Reese, "That's a nice color."

Reese scrunched up her nose and put it back. "Maybe. I want to look some more." As we passed a display of velour tracksuits, she glared, looking for a second as if she were about to spit on them, then moved on to a stack of jeans with sequins on the pockets.

The books and movies were adjacent to the displays of clothing, so I said, "Reese, I'm gonna take Lucas over there. Stay where I can see you."

Reese didn't look up. "Oh-*kay*, Eli. I'm not stupid."

"Reese?" She was making me feel parental. "Can you please look where I'm pointing?"

She huffed, and then looked up at me through narrowed eyelids.

I pointed over at the books. She said, "Fine," and went back to the jeans.

I rolled my eyes and pushed the cart toward the books.

Lucas said, "She's salty today."

I laughed. "She's what?"

He repeated, "Salty."

"Where'd you hear that?"

He said, "Els."

"Figures. You're right. Reese *is* salty today. Good word." I held up my fist and he bumped it with his own. I stopped in front of a huge display of kids' books. "Anything look good?"

He reached for a colorful book about trains, but couldn't stretch far enough. I grabbed the book and handed it to him. There were novels at the other end of the row, so I said, "Hold on," and pushed him farther down. There was a thick, new Stephen King I hadn't read yet, and I picked it up to read the back cover. I read about two sentences and turned the book over to see the price. The suggested retail price was hidden by the Costco sticker that read $16.98. I had a brand-new e-reader at home, but I couldn't get used to reading a book that way. Maybe things would change, but for the moment, I preferred the feel of a real book in my hands. And this one happened to be right within my budget for the day. I set it in the cart.

Lucas was still paging through the train book, so I just stood there, gazing at all the people and merchandise. A table was set up behind me with little white paper cups. A short woman with a clear plastic cap covering her dark hair noticed me looking and held one up. "Sample today! Dark-chocolate-covered pomegranate seeds in a three-pound bag."

I touched Lucas's arm and said, "Be right back." I crossed the aisle and took the paper cup from her. It had several small chocolate candies in it. I said, "Thank you," and went back to the cart. "Want one?" I held the cup out to Lucas. He peered inside and plucked one out, then put it in his mouth. His eyes lit up as he chewed. "Yum."

I popped a couple in my mouth. The fruity burst mixed with the richness of the dark chocolate. "Wow."

Lucas nodded. "I like them a lot."

I went back over to the dark-chocolate pomegranate display and grabbed a bag. Maybe I'd have to use Lee's twenty for it. I put them in the cart. Lucas was still reading, so I looked for other samples and pushed the cart toward them.

Farther toward the back of the store, a woman had samples of Gouda and Havarti served on crackers. I couldn't get the cart very close, so I left Lucas a few feet away, grabbed a few of the samples, said, "Thank you," and returned. Lucas devoured the cheese and crackers, as did I. Dairy products had been nearly nonexistent in the Compound, and since our liberation, I think all of us had eaten enough cheese to choke an ample Holstein. I pushed the cart over to a garbage can and tossed away our napkins. Then I remembered Reese and quickly wheeled Lucas back toward the clothes.

Reese had moved over to the book section, so I parked the car next to the display. Lucas was content looking at his book, so I leaned on the cart, waiting for Reese. I let my eyes wander a bit, and then Lucas grabbed for a book on the display stack and knocked the entire pile onto the floor.

"Seriously, dude?" I squatted to pick them up, and as I popped back up, I caught a glimpse of a man in dark clothing and a black knit cap staring at me from about ten yards away. He quickly slipped around the edge of an aisle and disappeared.

I told Reese, "Stay right here. We'll be back."

Lucas said, "I want to look at the books!"

"Just sit there a second." I pushed Lucas and the cart toward where I'd seen the man. But when I got to the end of the aisle, no one was there. And then I saw him again, turning another corner.

Lucas said, "I want to go back!"

"We will, just hold on." I walked faster, shoving the cart in front of me, but as I got to the end of the aisle, an

71

employee with a huge, orange flat cart full of cases of cans of Diet Coke and plastic bottles of SunnyD cut me off, blocking the aisle in the process.

"Excuse me," I said. "I need to get by."

"Just a minute. This is heavy."

I grabbed the handle of her cart and yanked, pulling it past mine. Then I pushed past. But when we reached the next aisle, there was no one there. I kept on pushing up that aisle where the man should have been. When I got to the end, something crunched under my shoe.

I moved my foot.

There was a small pile of white powder. Like I'd crushed a small white tablet of some kind. Like a . . . Tums.

Those last few months in the Compound, my father was never without a pack of Tums.

Dad?

My hands started to tremble. It wasn't possible. He was gone.

"Eli?" Lucas grabbed hold of my sleeve. "Your face is all white. Are you gonna puke?"

Just then a woman in a plastic cap at a display next to us called out, "Samples! Calcium supplements. They're good for kids as well as adults. Sixteen-ounce bottle."

I took one of the paper cups she held out.

Inside were two round white tablets. I looked down beside my foot. Exactly like the one that lay there on the floor, ground to a powder when I'd stepped on it.

I breathed out. *Paranoid much?*

Lucas was still looking at me with a concerned expression on his face.

I smiled. "No, I'm not gonna puke." What a dweeb. I'd imagined some guy staring at me. And then I'd freaked out over some stupid calcium supplements.

I almost laughed. If I was ever going to be normal, I would really have to figure out how to stop being so paranoid.

I waited until the sample woman wasn't looking and tossed the little paper cup, and the tablets, into the trash.

CHAPTER EIGHT

WE MET EVERYONE ELSE UP FRONT. AFTER WE CHECKED out, we went to the snack bar where Lee bought a bunch of pizza slices and frozen yogurt berry sundaes. We all sat at a red picnic table in the food area to eat. Lucas and Cara couldn't decide what they liked better, so they would take a few bites of pizza, then go for a spoonful of sundae. Even Lexie, who always watched what she ate, had both.

Other than Els baking morning pastries a couple mornings a week, our meals at home tended to be healthy, no processed foods, mainly fresh, and Els and the other cook got no argument from any of us. We'd had enough boxed and canned food to last the rest of our lives.

At least I had.

But still. Pizza and ice cream once in a while was fine with me.

Back home on Mercer Island, Mom hugged all of us,

looking totally relieved that we'd survived Costco un-scathed. After everything we'd been through, letting her kids go to Costco was probably more nerve-wracking for Mom than we'd ever know.

I helped talk Lucas into a nap and then went to watch some television in the den. I liked that our new house didn't have humungous rooms like our mansion did. I loved all the windows and natural light, and the small rooms were just . . . homier. The den had a huge flat-screen TV mounted over the gas fireplace, both of which were on. Leather recliners sat on either side of a large leather couch, and Lexie sat in one, watching some talk show where peo-ple were screaming at one another. She quickly wiped her eyes and shifted so she faced away from me.

I plopped down in the other recliner. "This stuff will rot your brain."

Lexie tried to sound upbeat. "These people are crazy. See that woman? She's married to that guy, but she thinks the other guy is the father of her baby. They're going to find out the results of the paternity test right now."

I wanted to ask her how she was, why she was so sad. Instead, I just asked, "How can you watch this crap all the time?"

She shrugged. "Sometimes they have people find their long-lost relatives." She pointed at the screen. "This one girl went looking for her real parents after her adoptive ones died, and it turned out her biological mother was actually the gymnastics coach that she already was living with! Is that crazy or what?" She looked like she wanted to say something else, but Eddy walked in and started digging through the DVDs. "You guys want to watch a movie?"

Lexie murmured, "When my show's done."

I opened up the ottoman nearest me and pulled out a white blanket.

Eddy kept looking through the DVDs as Lexie and I sat there, not saying anything. Finally the credits started rolling. Lexie glared at Eddy and then looked at me. "Eli? Can we talk?"

"Um, yeah?" Weren't we already talking?

Her eyes flicked over to Eddy, then back at me. "Alone?"

Eddy stopped what he was doing and looked at her. "I'll go get us something to drink. You two have your little talk." He left.

Lexie said, "Is he mad?" She didn't sound like she cared if he was or not. She and Eddy had not exactly bonded in the past few weeks, and I was beginning to feel like I was their intermediary. So it made things worse when she made a point of leaving Eddy out of our conversations.

I shook my head. "Why can't you talk in front of him?"

Lexie glanced around a bit and then leaned closer to me. Her voice was a whisper. "What would you think if I wanted to find my real parents?"

I froze. "What?" Lexie was adopted, but it wasn't something I thought of very often. She was just my sister. It was easy to forget the rest.

She nodded. "My biological parents." She pointed at the television. "So many people have been reunited. It's really cool."

I shook my head. "Listen, just because people on these stupid shows do that doesn't mean you should. Those things are probably fake and set up anyway."

Lexie watched the show for a little bit. "Yeah. I guess." She didn't exactly look convinced, but I hoped that she meant it, and the subject was done. She tilted her head a bit and the corner of her mouth turned up. "It was a good day, wasn't it?"

"Costco." I snorted. "Who'd have thought?"

Her face lit up when she smiled. "I was very happy to get my industrial-size box of Tic Tacs."

Eddy came back holding sodas and plates, along with the pound of mango salsa and huge brown bag of tortilla chips he'd chosen at Costco. He handed me a plate, poured some salsa onto it, and then ripped open the bag of chips.

Lexie turned off the television. "I'm going up to my room."

As soon as she left, Eddy asked, "What was the big secret?"

I put a handful of chips on my plate, then dipped one into the salsa and stuffed it in my mouth. "Not a big secret," I said, my mouth full.

"Says the person who's in on the secret." Eddy sounded miffed.

"Really, it was nothing."

Eddy flipped on the television and started zipping through the channels, glaring.

"What?" I asked.

He didn't answer.

"Dude, it was nothing. She just feels more comfortable talking to me alone I guess."

Eddy turned to me, his eyes narrowed and dark. "That's Lexie. Don't you remember? She hated us. And we didn't exactly like her. And now, it's like . . ."

"What?"

He shrugged. "You two are BFFs. I'm the third wheel."

I frowned. "That's not it."

He said, "Yeah? Then explain it to me."

How was I supposed to explain that, until the last few days in the Compound, I'd isolated myself from everyone?

That Lexie and I had barely talked, been closer to enemies than siblings? That, for all those years, I had basically been alone?

How was I supposed to explain that Lexie and I had to finally put aside our differences in order to get our family out of the Compound?

Was it betraying Eddy to admit that I liked my sister? That maybe I even needed her?

Eddy waited for an answer.

"It's not that at all. Lexie's having a hard time."

"Yeah, I noticed. She doesn't do anything *but* cry."

"She was really close to Dad and she's taking it really hard." I tried to sound casual. "It's not a big deal. I'm trying to be nice, I guess."

Eddy held my gaze for a moment, then popped a chip in his mouth. "Okay," he said, his mouth full. "Just want to know where I stand."

I nodded. "You know it's you and me."

"Cool." Eddy turned to a movie and started watching.

I stared at the television.

Had I meant what I said? Some days I felt way closer to Lexie than to my twin, simply because of everything we'd been through. And sometimes . . . Eddy seemed like a stranger. Reese was beginning to warm up to him, but she still came to me for everything. Lucas would tolerate Eddy, but preferred me, and Cara . . . Cara was pretty much scared of him most of the time.

As for Eddy and Lexie, I had expected them to get along better than we all used to. We were older, more grown-up, and so much had happened since then. Maybe I just wished they would get along. Because as long as those two were at odds, I would be stuck in the middle. At least we were all together, and it wasn't as if I'd ever have to make a choice.

CHAPTER NINE

After my morning run a couple of days later, I showered, dressed in jeans and a sweatshirt, and headed down to the kitchen. As I passed Reese's room, I heard her talking. In an English accent.

For the last few years in the Compound, my little sister had spoken in an English accent, something I never understood or got used to. Finally, as things began to fall apart down there, she had stopped.

But, now to hear that again . . .

My heartbeat sped up. I rapped on the door. "Reese?"

The sound stopped.

Silence.

I rapped harder. "Reese? Can I come in?"

I heard a hushed thump, and then the door opened and she stuck her head out the opening. "What?"

What was I going to say? *Hey, I couldn't help hearing*

you were talking with an English accent, which totally freaks me out . . . "I just . . ."

She raised her eyebrows. "Do you want to come in?"

I nodded and stepped inside. The walls of her room were white, but all the material on her bed and other furniture was bright and full of flowers. The television on top of the dresser was on, but the sound was off. "What's up?" I asked.

She shrugged. "Just watching the telly—I mean television."

I let that slip go. "With the sound off?"

She quickly glanced over at the television and back at me. "I didn't . . ."

"What?" I asked.

She went over and turned up the sound. Reese had been watching the BBC News. I listened to the female newscaster's voice: "Authorities are perplexed by the recent disappearance of ninety-two-year-old Dr. Dmitri Isbayeva, a Nobel-winning geneticist, from the elderly living facility in London that had been his home for the past ten years. This is the fourth such disappearance of elderly scientists in the past six months."

I said, "That was the voice I heard."

Reese frowned. "You thought it was me?"

I bit my lip and nodded.

Reese flopped down on her bed. "You think I'm a freak and I'm going to start doing that again."

"No, no." I went over and sat down beside her, setting a hand on her back. "I was just—"

Reese interrupted me, "Worried that I was a freak. I know. The other night, what Lexie said at the table about us being freaks. It's true."

I cleared my throat. "No. It's not true. We went through something no one else has, but we are a family and we're here for one another. We'll get through this."

She sat up. "I just like British things. Hearing about England. Does that make me weird?"

I laughed. "No, not at all." I pulled her to me and gave her a hug. "I promise, we'll go visit England one of these days."

Her eyes widened. "You think Mom will let us?"

I nodded. "Eventually, we'll all get back to normal."

I hoped I was right. I was already worried about Lexie, so I was glad I didn't have to worry about Reese, too.

Downstairs, I found Eddy and Lucas sitting across from each other in the kitchen. Lucas climbed down off his stool and jumped up and down, clapping his hands. "You're ready!" He ran into me and threw his arms around my waist.

I looked at Eddy and raised my eyebrows. "What am I ready for?"

Eddy made a face. "Another family outing. The aquarium. Up for it?"

I shrugged. "Sure, why not."

"I'll get everybody." Lucas ran out of the room.

Breakfast items were set out on the kitchen counter, and I spooned some Greek yogurt into a bowl, then added granola and sliced strawberries. I snatched a small cinnamon roll as well and went back to Eddy. He was just finishing a bowl of cereal and wiped his mouth on the sleeve of his gray hoodie. "So, you never said how the thing at the lab went the other day."

"It was cool," I said. "I mean, not cool. But it's a good cause."

"Did you meet any kids with the disease?" He took a drink of orange juice.

I plucked a couple of raisins out of the granola and set them beside my bowl. "Yeah. A little boy."

He set his glass down and tilted his head slightly. "That's it? A little boy?"

"Yeah. And the scientists and all." I stirred the berries and granola into the yogurt and shoved a big spoonful into my mouth, giving myself time to decide if I should tell him about Verity. I decided not to and shoveled in another spoonful.

Eddy said, "Not everyone's going with us."

With a full mouth, I asked, "How come?"

"Mom and Lex and Reese are online shopping. Again. They'll keep Finn and Quinn, so we'll just have Cara and Luke."

I swallowed. "Does that ever seem weird to you?"

He pushed his bowl and glass away, then propped both elbows on the table, clasped his hands, and rested his chin on them. "What?"

I held up a palm. "All these kids. I mean . . . like you said the other day. You were left with memories of me and Lexie and Reese. And then, all of a sudden, not only do you have us back, but you have all these other kids to adjust to. Little ones."

Eddy shrugged. "I didn't like being an only child for those years. I was lonely. So this? All these kids?" He nodded. "It's cool."

But something in his words didn't convince me. I said, "Cara and Lucas are getting used to you," I said. "You've got to realize that they never saw anyone else in all that time."

"They seem to like Gram and Els okay," he said.

I raised my eyebrows.

He grinned. "Well, they seem to like Gram okay."

"Give it time," I said.

I didn't have time to think about it because Lucas came running in, dragging a giggling Cara by the hand. Her dark hair was in pigtails and she wore a purple fleece jacket. Her jeans were tucked into tiny pink Uggs, and she immediately tried to launch herself into Eddy's lap.

Eddy shot a look at me and I held out my hands. "See?"

He picked her up, then stood up and started throwing her into the air, making her laugh even more.

Lucas tugged on my arm. "Can we go now?"

"Hey, okay. Lemme finish eating." I pushed away from the table enough so he could sneak up into my lap, where he sat until I was done.

Lee was waiting outside in the SUV, and Eddy and I strapped Cara and Lucas into their car seats. Then Eddy sat in front by Lee and I sat behind him. Both little kids fell asleep on the drive over, and we had to wake them up when we got there. Lucas was fine, but Cara started crying, so I carried her into the aquarium while Lee bought tickets. There were rental strollers, so we got one of those for Cara. I pushed her as Eddy held Lucas's hand and walked toward a mammoth aquarium with a viewing window at least twenty feet high and probably twice that wide. The sign near it read, WINDOW ON WASHINGTON WATERS. I scanned the information and said, "Hey, Lucas. There's more than eight hundred fish in here."

Lucas pushed past me and went right up to the window, where he placed his hands flat against it and looked up at the bottoms of some huge salmon.

Eddy was reading the brochure and stopped. He glanced at his watch. "Hey, the dive show is about to start. There won't be another one while we're here."

"Let's do it," I said. I pushed the stroller closer until I was standing behind Lucas, and Eddy and Lee stood on either side of me.

The water inside the tank surged now and then, which made the blades of kelp sway slightly. Huge rock formations took up a lot of space, and tons of fish swam in and out as we watched. Anemones poked out of holes in the rock, and sea stars and sea urchins were stuck to the sides. Eddy bent down beside Lucas. "See the sea stars?"

Lucas's mouth was wide-open and he nodded. "Look at all the fish."

As we watched, a diver entered the water and swam

until he was on the other side of the window from all of us who were watching. A good-size crowd began to gather, mainly a lot of moms with preschool-age kids. The one man in the room caught my eye. He had a thick, reddish beard and wore camouflage pants and a black jacket. He held the hand of a little girl in dark braids who was sniffling. Her eyes were red, as if she'd been crying. She told him, "I want to stay!"

In the last few minutes before the program started, the crowd began to pack in tight around us.

My heart raced and my breaths became shorter. I felt like I wasn't getting any air. My hands began to tingle, and I pulled my collar away from my throat. I wanted to scream.

Lee grabbed my arm. "You okay?"

"I don't know. I—" Was I having a panic attack? All these people . . . Costco had been crowded, but the warehouse had been brightly lit, the ceiling high overhead, plenty of space. But here, in the aquarium, it was darker, and the ceiling was low, and I felt packed in with everyone.

"Take a deep breath," he said.

"I'm trying." I squatted down, so I was eye level with everyone's purses and strollers. Cara reached out to me. I took her hand and held it, squeezing probably harder than I should have, but having her soft little hand in my hand helped. After a moment I could breathe again, and my heartbeat had slowed back down. I stood up. Lee asked if I was okay and I nodded.

The diver started talking through his headpiece, telling us about some of the fish and other creatures inside the tank. Lucas was riveted by all the commotion inside the tank, and as I calmed down more, I found that I was, too. How long had it been since I'd seen something like the aquarium?

Since the Compound, I'd spent a lot of hours on the beach in Hawaii, but hadn't done any snorkeling. Even though the aquarium fish weren't as colorful as tropical ones were, they were amazing to watch. I found myself mesmerized and didn't really think anything of it when the diver offered to answer questions and Lucas raised his hand.

Lucas was little and cute, so of course the guy would call on him first, before I could pull his hand back down. And of course the guy would ask, "Where you from, buddy?"

Lucas said, "I used to live in the ground, but now we live in a new house." He turned to me. "Eli, where is our new house?"

So stunned I couldn't think, I managed to catch my breath in time to bark out a laugh and look around at the crowd, who were shooting odd looks at Lucas. "He likes to make things up," I said.

Eddy joined my fake laugh and added, "He's got the wildest imagination."

I nodded, and soon some of the crowd began to smile and looked at their own kids. I breathed a sigh of relief and figured we'd better play it safe and move on. "Lucas, what should we see next?"

He looked confused, as if he really wanted to pursue his annoyance at us, but he also didn't want to blow his chance to see everything. His face finally relaxed and he asked, "Is there a food place? I'm hungry."

I grinned. "Yeah."

I saw Eddy hold out his hand to Lucas, so I pushed Cara in the stroller, following the signs that said CAFÉ. I stood in line behind Lee, who turned around to ask us all what we wanted. Lee said he'd stay in line, so Eddy and I took Lucas and Cara to sit down at a table.

Lucas asked, "Where's the bathroom?"

I stood up. "Come on."

The bathroom wasn't far—down a short hallway—and no one was inside. Probably because it was a weekday and the aquarium was mainly full of moms, who would take all their kids with them into the women's room.

Lucas went into a stall and shut the door. I heard it lock.

"You okay in there?" I asked.

"Yes."

My cell phone rang. Eddy. "Yeah?"

"Cara is sick. She took a drink of her apple juice and threw it back up. Along with her breakfast. Oh God . . ."

"Seriously?" I sighed. "Well, clean her up and I'll be out in a minute."

"Dude, can you come now? This is gross."

"And it's gonna be less gross for me?" I sighed. "Lucas, you almost done?"

His voice echoed in the stall. "No!"

I sighed. "Eddy, you've got to come in here and wait for Lucas." Then I shoved the phone in my pocket and grabbed a bunch of paper towels, wetting some. "Lucas, stay there. Eddy's coming in, okay?"

"Yes."

I jogged back out to the table, which was a mess. Cara had thrown up not only the apple juice, but also the French toast she'd had at home for breakfast. Lee was holding his hand over his mouth and facing away from her. He shook his head at me. "Sorry. Sympathetic puker."

I wanted to groan. "That's fine. I'll clean this up and then we'd better get her home."

I heard an electronic beeping come from the direction of the hallway. It wasn't loud enough to be a fire alarm, just loud enough to be annoying, so I ignored it and started in with the paper towels.

Eddy was still standing there.

I frowned. "Go get Lucas."

"Sorry." He turned and left. I wiped off Cara with the towels as best as I could and stuck her back in the stroller. Our food had come by then, and Lee had it in bags so we could take it with us. Although eating was the last thing on my mind.

At the edge of my vision, I saw Eddy come back. "Ready to go?"

"He wasn't there."

I turned to face him and noticed he was alone. "What?"

Eddy's eyes were wide and he nearly spat out the words, "He wasn't in there. Lucas is gone."

CHAPTER TEN

LUCAS COULDN'T BE GONE. EDDY WAS WRONG. I LOWERED my voice and spoke slowly. "He's in one of the stalls."

Eddy grabbed my arm. "No, he's not. He wasn't in there. I checked everywhere."

Lee was already pulling on my arm. "There's only one exit. I'll go there, you check at the front desk."

Eddy took the handle of the stroller, and I said, "I'm checking the bathroom. He has to be there." I ran there, nearly smashing into a kid coming out. "Crap." Inside, I slammed open each of the stall doors. No Lucas. I whirled around, trying to get a grip. "Lucas!"

I ran back out and headed toward the front entrance of the aquarium. Eddy was at the front desk. He'd gotten rid of the stroller and was holding Cara. "Did they find him?"

Eddy shook his head.

Outside, rain was pouring down, and Lee stood at the

door, looking outside. I joined him. "Lucas has to be in here. He wouldn't go out there. Not when it's pouring."

Eddy came out. "No one there has seen a lost kid."

I covered my face with my hands. "It's my fault. I should have waited for him."

Eddy touched my shoulder. "No, I should have just cleaned it all up myself."

Lee didn't say anything, but from the look on his face, it was clear he considered himself at fault. Then he pointed outside, shoved the door open, and stormed through it.

We crowded under the overhang as a soaking wet Lucas came toward us, holding the hand of a boy who looked about my age. He wore a black knit cap pulled down over his ears, a dark green hoodie with frayed cuffs, and faded jeans with holes in the knees. His sneakers were black and beaten up, but his skateboard was nice. Like he only had so much money and the skateboard was way more important than clothes. Rain dripped down his face as he walked my little brother over to us and then dropped his hand.

I scooped up Lucas. "What were you thinking?"

He wiped some rain off his face. "I got lost and went out the door."

The boy pointed to his left. "I found him around the side by an emergency door. He must have gone outside and gotten locked out."

The beeping I'd heard while I was cleaning Cara up must have been the alarm on the door.

"Thank you so much," I told the boy. "We were freaking out."

Lee said, "Stay here. I'll go get the car."

Eddy told the boy, "Yeah, thanks a lot." He glanced at the board under his arm. "That a Plan B?"

The boy nodded, and some rain fell off the end of his nose. "Planned to meet some friends." He looked skyward. "Day turned to crap, though."

"Lucky for us," said Eddy.

Just then, Lee pulled up. Eddy said, "You need a ride or something?"

The boy shook his head, shedding more water. "The bus stop is close."

I breathed a sigh of relief. There had been too many strangers lately. I already had the phone number of one. I didn't want to meet any more, especially not one in our car.

Lee came around and opened up the back door. "Let's get them in."

The running and rain and getting lost seemed to have taken the piss and vinegar out of Lucas, who meekly climbed into his car seat. Cara, who obviously wasn't feeling any better, zonked out completely as soon as I strapped her in. I took my spot in the backseat. Eddy and the boy were still standing outside the car, rain soaking them even more as they talked.

Finally Eddy backed toward the car and held up his hand and the boy turned around and walked away.

Eddy was grinning as he got in the front. Lee sped

out of the parking lot, probably way faster than he should have. But I think we were all happy to put the aquarium behind us.

I wondered how we were going to tell Mom about what happened, because I knew it would be the first thing out of Lucas's mouth.

As we neared home, we had to wait to enter the gate because a FedEx truck pulled away. Joe was holding a box, and just as Lee turned into the circle drive, I caught sight of Reese running out the front door toward the guardhouse.

By the time we got the kids out of the car, she had returned, carrying the package into the house. Reese had gotten so helpful around the house. A few days before I'd seen her with the vacuum. I appreciated how much she had been helping. Maybe it made me feel less guilty whenever I went out and left Mom with all the little kids. I knew she had Gram and Els to help, but I liked knowing Reese was there, too, taking on some responsibility.

Lucas ran ahead of us into the kitchen where Mom was sitting, feeding Quinn lunch.

Lucas proclaimed, "I got lost!"

Mom smiled at him, and then up at me and Eddy. She winked. "I'm sure you did."

"No, I really did! I went out the door with the red light on it and it beeped and then I was outside in the rain and this boy found me."

Mom's smile disappeared and her eyes narrowed. She asked me, "What happened?"

I breathed deeply. "He came out of the bathroom and went out the emergency door."

"Where were you?"

"I was in the bathroom with Lucas." I pointed at Cara. "But then she was with Eddy and threw up, so he called me."

Mom frowned. "And you just left him?"

"For two seconds!" I said. "He was in the stall and I sent Eddy right back for him."

Eddy shook his head. "He had already left."

Mom shook her head. "This is done. This is all *done*. No more outings, no more—"

"Mom!" I interrupted her. "He's fine. We got him."

She crossed her arms and glared at us.

Eddy said, "Yeah, a guy found him and brought him to the front, and we were there."

"A guy? What guy?" asked Mom.

Eddy shrugged. "His name's Tony."

I flashed a glance his way. How did he know that?

Eddy continued. "He's cool. I got his number so we could send a thank-you."

When did he do that? And *why* would he do that?

Mom sighed. She looked at Cara, who was a mess. "I'd better get her a bath." She picked her up and started to head upstairs. Then she turned back around. "This discussion is not over."

It was safe to say the outing to the aquarium was a complete bust.

I made a turkey and Havarti sandwich with avocado and took it up to my room. I set the plate on my desk and slid the mouse back and forth. My desktop computer popped on and I hit Google. Our close call at the aquarium, the one before we lost Lucas, made me think.

What if Lucas had rambled on about us? Maybe called out our last name?

Would people have put two and two together?

Once again, it made me wonder what people were thinking about us. If they were thinking about us.

I typed in *Yanakakis*. Of course, thousands of entries popped up, most about YK and Dad, all related to the business. I scanned through, looking to see if anything was related to the family, and to more recent events. There were news reports from when we escaped of course, but not much lately.

Social media had changed so much since we'd been away. When I changed the entry to *"Eli Yanakakis,"* a post popped up. "Maybe saw Yanakakis twins at Niagara Falls! #YKsighting."

YK sighting? Was it a club or something?

I clicked on that and saw a bunch of posts. A bunch of posts that all seemed to be about encounters with me and my family.

"Saw them in Times Square!"

"Caught a peek at Disneyworld. Twins and a bunch of kids."

"My uncle in Vail said they've been there for a month."

I had to smile. They were all so full of it. No one was even close.

I shook my head, thinking I was dumb to be so stressed about it. Then I realized I had the order switched, and made the older ones go to the bottom. One popped up, by someone named @dpreppin, with an icon of a nuclear cloud.

"Tailed them at Seattle Costco."

I froze. The guy in black. *Was that him?* If so, I wasn't wrong to be paranoid. He *had* been watching us. I clicked on his user name, and a link on his profile took me to a website labeled:

Prepping for Doomsday: Be One of the Survivors

"What the . . ." I clicked and the screen scrolled down, revealing what seemed to be a site about people preparing for the end of the world. There were links to sites about ammunition and gun training and food preservation. I clicked on the Preparation tab. An entire litany about how much food you should stockpile in order to survive popped up.

I realized my hands were trembling.

Were these people disciples of my father or what? Were they watching us? Why? Because we had done what they wanted to do? Survived the end of the world? Granted, our doomsday was faked, but still. We had survived. I supposed someone who wanted to do the same saw us as role models.

I swallowed.

And they probably wouldn't stop until they found out what we knew. What we had been through and what we had done to survive.

I'd seen some of the stories about our years belowground: plenty of speculation, rumor, and conjecture. But some contained shreds of truth, which scared me, because the whole truth was something that I had to be sure they would never find out.

I went back to the original networking site and made up a fake account name. @1Turducken. A homage to the main course at one of Dad's nightmare Christmas parties when I was a kid.

And I posted:

"Whole family in Miami! Mansion on beach. #yksighting."

Immediately, responses popped up.

"Knew I saw them in Sarasota last week!"

"Camping 60 miles away, will check it out."

"That was them at Busch Gardens."

I blew out a sigh of relief. Those people would believe anything. Thank heavens.

But then @dpreppin replied:

"Untrue. In Seattle. Chickens return to roost."

I shoved away from the desk so hard the chair twirled me around, so I was facing outside.

He knew. @dpreppin definitely knew it had been me at Costco.

I stood up and went to the window, looking at our

front gate and the security guard there. What if he'd followed us? What if he knew where we lived?

I went back to my computer. Another reply had posted. The icon was a photo of a little girl, and the name was preppin.

"Definitely at aquarium today."

I glanced back at the icon. The little girl. I'd seen her before. She'd been crying, while the dad in camouflage had tried to get her to stop.

The guy in camo had to be @prep_man

We'd been seen twice. People were looking for us. And now they knew what we looked like.

CHAPTER ELEVEN

I SCOURED THE INTERNET, TRYING TO FIND OUT MORE about the guy with the doomsday preparation website. It was all vague, except there was a list of meetings in the Seattle area. Which made me wonder. Did the guy with the website just happen to live in the Seattle area? Or had he purposely moved here because of my father? Because of what the world knew about us . . . and the Compound?

A knock on my door made me jump. "Yeah?"

"Can I come in?"

Lexie.

"Yeah, come on in."

She opened the door and peeked around it, then stepped in and pulled it shut behind her. Her dark hair was down and she wore black yoga pants and a white T-shirt that bore a primping Marilyn Monroe. She walked over to my bed and sat down. She looked down at her hands and didn't say anything.

"What's going on?"

She had kind of half a smile on her face. "I know you thought it was dumb the other day, but I can't stop thinking about it and . . . I decided that I really want to find my biological parents."

Hadn't we been over all that? I sighed. "Why is this all coming up now? Before the other day you never even brought this up before."

Lexie rolled her eyes. "Well, let's see. Hmmm. The past six years I thought the entire rest of the world had been destroyed."

"Valid point." I scratched my head, wondering what I could say to talk her out of it. "Seriously though. Why now? We're just starting over, figuring out how to live in this world again."

"Exactly. I'm almost eighteen, I'm going to be an adult and I don't know the first thing about . . ." She trailed off. "I just want to know where I come from."

I didn't get it. "Why?"

"Because I do! I thought you would help me." She stood up. "God, just forget it. Obviously it was too much to ask."

I grabbed her arm as she started to walk past me. "Stop. Just stop."

She turned and stood there, tears welling in her eyes.

"Lex, I'm sorry. Sit down. Of course I'll help."

She leaned against the back of my chair. "I hate not knowing. I don't want to . . ." She sighed. "It's not like I want a relationship with them or anything, but I want to know." She waited for me to say something. When I didn't, she said, "Is that so bad?"

I shook my head. "But I have no idea what Mom will think."

"We don't have to tell her."

My mouth dropped. Was she planning to keep it a secret from everyone but me? "You'd actually do this without telling her?"

Lexie stood up and paced to my windows and back. "You're right." She leaned forward and put her hand on my arm. "Will you ask her with me? Please?"

Her eyes were tear filled and her expression was so sad.

"Tomorrow," I said. "First thing. We'll go to Mom and tell her you want to find your birth parents."

"Thanks. I'm glad I have someone to trust." My sister lightly kicked my shin, then dodged my reach as I grabbed for her. She laughed as she skipped out of the room.

Eddy walked in just as she walked out. "What was that all about?"

I shook my head. "Nothing. Hey, look at this, will you?"

I showed him the discussions I'd found about our whereabouts.

Eddy frowned. "It was inevitable, wasn't it? We can't hide forever."

True, but still . . . "Aren't you worried about it? People knowing where we are?"

He shook his head. "They don't know where we live. Maybe someone saw us at Costco. Maybe someone saw us at the aquarium."

I pointed at the icon of the little girl. "I definitely saw her at the aquarium."

Eddy said, "But they don't know for sure. One person jumps on the wagon, and they all jump on."

"Should we tell Mom?"

"No way. She's got enough to worry about. I really don't think it's anything to stress about." He squeezed my shoulder. "Holy crap, you're like one big knot."

I put a hand on each temple and rubbed. "I'm just stressed." I pointed at the screen. "Between this, and Lucas going missing and Lexie—" I stopped. How could I have let that out?

"Lexie what?"

"Nothing."

Eddy sat down on the desk and met my gaze. "What is she up to?"

I said, "Well . . . she's decided she wants to find her biological parents."

His eyes narrowed. "That's the stupidest thing I've ever heard."

I kept my tone light, tried to make it seem like no big deal. "People do it all the time. It's not like she wants to move in with them or anything. She just wants to know where she comes from."

Eddy raised his arms out to the sides. "Here! She comes from here. She has everything she wants. Why would she go looking for anything else?" He stood up. "She can't do this. All it's going to do is hurt Mom. I'm not letting Lexie do this. " He stormed out.

"Are you kidding me? Eddy! " I ran after him, wishing I had kept my mouth shut.

I reached Eddy just as he was knocking on Lexie's door.

"Eddy! Seriously." I grabbed his arm to keep him from knocking again. "She hasn't done anything."

He yanked his arm back. "She's about to break Mom's heart. There's been enough of that."

Lexie opened the door. "What?" Her gaze went from my face and then to Eddy's. She glared at me. "You told him?" She shoved me. "Leave me alone." She started to shut her door, but Eddy managed to get in the way.

He said, "You can't do this. Mom can't take this."

Lexie backed into her room. Like mine, it had a bank of windows, but instead of Lake Washington, hers looked out on the pool and veranda, and one opened onto a balcony. The room was all colored in oranges and yellows, with bold stripes on her matching bedding and draperies. She went over to her window seat and sat down, looking out the window, blinking fast. Clementine was curled up, sleeping, and Lexie dragged her into her lap.

I pushed by Eddy with a low "Way to go," and went and sat next to Lexie. "I'm sorry, he just asked and I told him."

She didn't look at me, and didn't answer either. She reached up and wiped her eyes. "I should have known not to trust you."

I breathed in deep. I was so stupid. "I'm sorry. You can trust me." I held out my hands, palms up. "I only told Eddy."

She narrowed her eyes at me. "Yeah." She flung out a hand toward him. "That turned out *so* well."

Eddy sat down on the end of Lexie's bed. "Don't you think Mom already has enough to worry about?"

"This isn't about Mom! It's about me." Lexie set a hand on her chest. "I want to know who my real parents are."

Eddy shook his head. "Your real parents are the same ones I have."

"Yeah, you're right." Lexie dropped her hand and leaned her head against the window. "We have the same father who made sure to leave his entire company to you and Eli. That the *same one* you're talking about?"

Eddy's mouth opened slightly, and then snapped shut. Apparently he didn't have an answer for that.

I sat down on the window seat. "He just did that because we're the boys."

She glared at me.

I bit my lip. "I mean, probably that's why."

Eddy added, "It was more to do with you being a girl than adopted."

"Oh, wow," said Lexie, scorn in her tone. "Now I feel *so* much better."

"That's not what I meant. It's a lot of pressure, to know we have to run the company. And Dad probably didn't want you to have to deal with that."

I shot him a look, trying to shut him up. If the plan was to talk Lexie out of searching for her biological parents, he was being his own worst enemy.

Lexie rolled her eyes. "Maybe I want to know for medical reasons."

Eddy stood up. "Did something happen when you were . . . *away?*"

I shook my head and saw Lexie was doing the same. She said, "There's just a lot I'd like to know. What if there's some medical history I should know about? What if I want to have kids someday and might pass something bad to them?"

"I understand that." Eddy sat back down. "I do. But you don't have to do it now."

She lifted and lowered one shoulder. "Fine, I'll wait."

What? Lexie would never give in so fast. Especially not to Eddy, given their current state of animosity toward each other.

"Really?" Eddy asked.

Lexie nodded. "Really. I'll wait until things calm down."

"Cool." Eddy smiled. "I just don't think Mom could deal right now." He stood up and looked at me. "Want to play some basketball?"

I shook my head.

"Lex?"

"No thanks."

After he left, I leaned over and set a hand on Lexie's arm. "You okay with waiting?"

"I'm *not* waiting." Her lip curled. "I'm just tired of him

thinking he can tell me what to do." She sighed. "I really don't care that much about you guys getting the company. It's not my thing." She looked at me. "Don't tell Eddy that though."

I leaned back. "You're still going to go through with it?"

She nodded. "I want to know. Now. I don't want to wait." She looked down for a moment as she stroked the cat.

"What? What's wrong?"

"I think . . ." She hesitated, then went on. "When we were down there? The last six months or so? I think something was wrong."

I let out a sharp laugh. "Uh, yeah. That's an understatement if I've ever heard one."

"No." She stopped petting Clementine and leaned forward, lowering her voice to a whisper. "With me. I was just so . . . depressed all the time. Or mad. Or something."

"Lex, we were all depressed. Or mad." I smiled. "*Or something.*"

Clementine meowed and stood up, then jumped to the floor and went out the door. Lexie bent her knees and hugged them. "What if it was more than that?"

I shook my head. "It wasn't. It was the situation."

"Then why can't I seem to stop crying? What if it is something? Eli, I need to know. I *have* to know. Will you help me?" Her eyes were shiny with tears.

I looked out the window. The afternoon sky was dark. A lot like the mood in the room. "Eddy wouldn't agree."

"I don't give a crap what he thinks."

I glanced at her. "I do care. And he wouldn't like me being involved when he's so against it."

Lexie said, "Eddy doesn't have to know everything you do."

Didn't he? I'd missed him for so long. I was so glad to have him back. How could I help Lexie, knowing I'd cause a rift between me and my brother if he found out? I was positive he would never keep anything from me.

Lexie grabbed my arm. "Please."

I whispered, "No."

She rolled her eyes and sat up straight against the wall.

I quickly said, "I mean . . . no." I shook my head. "Eddy doesn't have to know everything." I hoped I was making the right choice.

Lexie breathed out, a look of relief on her face. "Thank you." She smiled. "Thank you." She went over to her desk and opened the center drawer, then pulled out a manila folder. She came back to me and held it out. "Here."

I took it from her. "What's this?"

"All I know."

I opened it and pulled out a birth certificate. I quickly scanned it, noting Lexie's birth date and our parents' names. I frowned. "Why are they listed as parents? Wouldn't your biological parents be on there?"

"Believe me, I've been online, reading everything about this." She took a deep breath. "In a closed adoption, the records get sealed by the state of Washington. The judge, or whoever, issues an amended birth certificate with the adopting parents' names on it." She pointed. "That's my official birth certificate. At least, the one Mom and Dad used to get me passports and into school and everything."

I turned it over. The back was empty. "But how does someone even find their birth parents if the records are sealed?"

Lexie said, "I can get them opened with a court order."

"How do you do that?"

"I don't." She sighed. "Until I'm twenty-one, I need Mom's consent. But . . ."

"What?" I leaned back against the window, which was chilly on my back. "Are you still going to ask her?"

"I think there may be another way. I can get non-identifying information right now from the Department of Social and Health Services." She looked down at the paper.

"What does that mean?" I asked.

Her eyes met mine. "First name, occupation, heritage, education."

"That could be pretty vague. I mean, suppose your birth father is a white guy named John or Tom or Jim who is . . . a mechanic or a salesman or a plumber? You know how many men in the country fit any of those descriptions?"

"I know. It's a long shot. But Eddy *was* right about one thing. I don't want to make Mom upset." She looked around. "But what else do I have to do?"

I nodded. "So we could actually investigate without involving Mom. What information do you need for that?"

"Time and place of birth."

I pointed at her birth certificate. "Which you have, right?"

She nodded. "Just the county."

"So you know you were born in King County, and—"

"No. I wasn't."

"You weren't born in Seattle?"

She shook her head. The paper in her hand rattled. "Pierce County."

I thought for a second. "That's next to King. Really close."

"But it could be so many towns. What if I need to know the exact town?" She set the paper down on the bed. "I have to ask Mom."

I said, "I think we can do this without Mom. Without getting the court order."

Lexie held out her hands, palms up. "How?"

"Quinn's birthday is coming up and we can get Mom talking about when all of us were born." I paused. "I mean, I doubt she's going to really want to go on and on about a birth in the Compound. So we get her thinking about when Eddy and I were born. Or Reese. And then you. Maybe we can find things out."

Lexie said, "What if she doesn't know? I spent the first year of my life at the orphanage."

"Crap, I forgot that." I met her gaze. "Do you remember anything about that?"

She rolled her eyes. "I was one. I barely remember anything before kindergarten." She sighed. "Maybe Mom doesn't even know."

If Mom couldn't provide any information, I wasn't sure what else to do. But listening to Lexie worried me. Maybe the time in the Compound affected her more than I ever thought. Maybe she was clinically depressed at some point, but that was probably due to the circumstances. We all had to be at least borderline depressed.

But the thought of it being inherited had never crossed my mind. There were definitely valid reasons to actually find out more about her birth parents. In all honestly, I would probably feel the same way.

Which was something Eddy didn't get; he would never understand what we had gone through, how it affected us.

And for about the third time that week, I found myself feeling envious of my brother. Eddy *had* been acting superior to Lexie. Maybe even to me. Like we were visitors in his world and he needed to tell us what to do. So down deep, maybe I felt a little happy that I actually had a secret with our sister that I needed to keep from him.

CHAPTER TWELVE

BACK IN MY ROOM, I BEGAN TO PICK UP SOME OF MY clothes off the floor. I grabbed a pair of jeans and my phone fell out of the pocket. I picked it up. I'd forgotten to lock the screen, and my contacts were lit up. I couldn't help but notice Verity's name. Without thinking, I pushed the call icon and held the phone up to my ear.

Three rings, a click, and then a "Hello?"

I almost couldn't speak. She had to say hello again before I said, "Hey. Verity. This is E—" I almost said *Eli*. "EJ. We met at—"

"EJ."

I wasn't sure how, but I could tell she was smiling, which made me smile as well. "What are you doing?"

"Homework. Chemistry. Know anything about that?"

"A bit." I heard paper rustling and then a book slammed.

"That's enough of that. What are you doing?"

I sank down onto the side of my bed. "Not much."

"How's your paper coming?"

"Huh?"

"The paper? The one you had to write about your visit?"

Stupid. "Oh. I'm . . . still working on it." Trying to sound more certain of myself, I added, "I'm not a big fan of papers."

"Who is?"

I laughed. Apparently, being dishonest *and* talking to a girl my age made me sweat. I wiped off my forehead with the back of my sleeve.

"So." Verity breathed out. "Did you want something?"

"No, I just . . . called. I guess." I scrunched my eyes together and smacked my forehead with my hand. *Could I sound any dumber?*

"Want to do something this weekend?"

Did she just ask me out? "This weekend?"

She laughed a little. "Yeah. A movie or something?"

I swallowed. "I'll have to see. I mean, my mom is always planning stuff for us all. So . . . can I check and get back to you?" I knew Mom would never let me out of the house. But explaining the entire story was definitely not an option.

She sighed. "You don't have to make up excuses. If you don't want to, just say so."

I blurted out, "No, I do, I totally do, but I—"

"Okay." I could tell she was smiling again. "Just checking. I can't on Saturday. My family has this thing."

I took the easy way out and lied. "And I'm busy Sunday."

"Oh." The disappointment was obvious.

I felt bad. "But maybe I can get out of it."

"Okay." She was smiling again. "Text me when you find out."

I smiled. "I will. Text you."

"Cool. I'll be waiting to hear from you."

"Okay," I said.

"Okay." She hung up.

I sat there for a moment, smiling at the phone before I set it down.

What was I thinking? I couldn't go out on a date like a normal person. Especially not with people out there watching for us.

Watching for *us*.

Maybe no one would be watching for just me and a girl.

I sighed. *Not gonna happen.* Even if I had any idea what to do on a date, Mom was going to put an end to the outings after the aquarium fiasco. And if I told her what I saw online, she absolutely would.

I knew I should say something. Say that there were people looking for us, watching.

I stewed over it until dinner, and then went downstairs. I really didn't want to bring it up in front of everyone, so I decided to tell Eddy about everything later, see what he thought. I slid into the spot between Lex and Eddy and grabbed a piece of garlic bread.

"Grace!" admonished Terese, who bowed her head.

I dropped the bread on my plate. We all bowed our heads.

We'd barely gotten to amen when Mom said, "So, I have an announcement."

We all waited for her to speak.

She said, "I know what happened with Lucas was an accident and will never happen again, am I right?" She looked pointedly at me and Eddy.

We nodded.

Mom smiled a little. "So, I've arranged an outing for all of us. Saturday. The Mariners game."

"Yes!" said Eddy.

Reese and Lexie looked at each other, and my older sister said, "Seriously? Baseball?"

Mom shrugged. "It'll be fun."

Eddy asked, "Do we have the YK suite?"

Mom shook her head. "No, it's being used, but I rented a smaller one that'll work better for us. It'll be private, with just our family, and we can go in the VIP entrance, not have to deal with the general public."

Her words sounded so elitist, but I understood her meaning. If all went as planned, barely anyone would see us the entire game. A private, secure outing.

"Can I invite Tony?" asked Eddy.

I frowned.

Eddy saw my look and glared back at me. "What? It can be a thank-you for finding Lucas."

Mom started to shake her head, but Eddy said, "Please?"

"Let me think about it." The words were barely out of Mom's mouth when Lexie said, "I can't believe Quinn's birthday is almost here."

I shot her a glance, like, *Seriously, you couldn't wait five more minutes?* I started dishing some of Gram's lasagna onto a plate for Lucas.

Mom smiled. "Time goes so fast. Seems like yesterday he was born."

Lexie ignored me and turned to Mom. "You probably don't remember anything about when I was born."

Terese burst out, "But you were adopted. Mom wasn't there."

Mom frowned at Terese. "That doesn't mean I don't remember it." She looked at Lexie. "I know we didn't bring you home until you were one, but I was there when you were born."

Next to me, Lexie sounded like she had stopped breathing. "You were?"

Mom nodded at Lexie. "Well, maybe I wasn't there when you came into this world, but I was there the next day." She smiled. "Your father got a call from the orphanage. The flu had swept through the staff, and they were shorthanded when the call came to go pick up a newborn. Rex asked if I wanted to go . . ." She breathed deep and I saw her eyes mist over. "I'll never forget it. I don't know why, I just wanted to go. I dressed so fast I left the house in my bedroom slippers." She picked up a napkin and dabbed at the corner of her eye. "It was raining and your dad was driving much too fast. But he was as anxious as I was to get there."

Lexie shoved her elbow into my side.

"Where?" I asked. "Same hospital Eddy and I were born?"

Mom shook her head. "Gig Harbor." She went on, talking about when they got there and the nurse handed Lexie over to them. How she had fallen in love with her the instant she saw her. She went on about the next year, and how happy she was when the adoption went through months later, and Lexie was part of the family for good.

But I'd stopped listening and Lexie seemed frozen.

She took my hand and squeezed so hard it hurt.

We didn't need to know anymore. We'd gotten what we needed.

Gig Harbor.

CHAPTER THIRTEEN

As soon as dinner was over, Lexie grabbed my arm and whispered, "Your room."

I helped carry dishes into the kitchen, made sure everyone was busy, and then headed up to my room. Lexie was already there, pacing. Her eyes lit up. "Finally!"

On my computer, I pulled up the website for birth records. We found the correct paperwork to fill out online. But as I started to fill in her name, I stopped. "Crap."

"What?" she asked.

This was one time I couldn't use a fake last name. "I have to use your real name."

"So do it," she said.

I hesitated. "But if someone . . ."

Lexie grabbed my wrist. "Eli. I need to do this."

"Okay." I printed it out when we'd finished. Lexie held the papers in her hand and looked them over. "You're sure it's right?"

I nodded. "It's everything we know. We'll mail it out tomorrow and then we wait."

Lexie's eyes met mine. "What if—"

"What?"

"What if . . . they're weird or something?" Her eyes filled with tears. "Or worse, what if they're awesome? And they just didn't want me?"

"Stop." I reminded her, "You're not going to get any life stories. Not yet. You'll get nonidentifying information. Maybe it won't be enough to tell you anything." Honestly, I was certain we were in the middle of a wild goose chase that would end with my sister being very disappointed.

"Right." She nodded. "You're right," she said, and stood up. "Thanks, Eli." She closed the door after her.

My room was too quiet, so I turned on some music.

Since getting back to Seattle, I'd gone through a stack of iTunes gift cards that Gram had gotten for me when she'd purchased all the other cards for Lexie and Reese and all the online shopping. Maybe it made me seem spoiled, to have all this at my disposal, but I figured after all those years of being underground, a couple hundred new songs weren't going to morally bankrupt me. I had some punk band from Wisconsin blaring as the door opened.

Eddy came in, kicked the door shut behind him, and threw himself on my bed. "Hey."

I nodded at him.

He lay there on his stomach, chin propped upon his crossed arms. "What's going on with you?"

"Whadya mean?"

He rolled his eyes. "Come on. It started the other day when you went to that progeria place. And you were seriously quiet at dinner."

I didn't want to tell him what was going on with Lexie, that we were going through with the search for her biological parents. I also didn't want to tell him that I was still worried about the doomsday people who may or may not know where we lived. But I knew him. He wouldn't leave without something.

"The other day, at the lab"—I leaned forward, rested my elbows on my knees, and lowered my voice—"I met a girl."

Eddy's eyes widened. "Like a *girl* girl?

I laughed. "Living, breathing, yes."

"Sweet!" Eddy propped himself up on his elbows. "What's her name?"

"Verity. Her little brother has progeria."

Eddy lowered back down. "So did you call her?"

"How do you know I even have her number?"

Eddy laughed and rolled over onto his back. He grabbed one of my pillows and started tossing it up and catching it. "You totally called her."

"What if I did?" It pissed me off he was no longer looking at me, so I walked over to the bed and grabbed the pillow as he tossed it.

"What?" He looked up at me. "It's no big deal you called her."

I dropped the pillow on his face and sat down, leaning back against the headboard. "It's not?"

He shook his head.

"But what about . . ."

He raised his eyebrows. "What?"

I shrugged. "We're kind of trying to stay hidden, aren't we? I can't exactly start . . . I don't know . . ."

"*Dating*," said Eddy. "It's called dating."

"Really?" I grabbed a pillow and threw it at him. "When was the last date you went on?"

He rolled over to face me. "Just a group thing in Hawaii. With kids from families that Gram knew." He sighed. "There was one girl I talked to, but I couldn't tell her who I really was. None of my Hawaii friends know who I really am." His gaze met mine. "That's our biggest obstacle, you know. Does a girl ever like us for us—"

"Or because of who we are. And what we have." I'd never realized Eddy felt that same way. He just always seemed so sure of himself. I said, "But when we were younger and went to school like everyone else, we had friends." It all seemed so long ago. "Didn't we?"

He blew out a breath and fell onto his back. "Yeah, I guess. But we always had cool parties and stuff." He smiled. "You'd have to be stupid *not* to be friends with you and me."

"Well, *you* anyway. They put up with me to hang out

with you." I remembered that part of it pretty well. Eddy was popular. I was his bratty, tagalong twin.

Eddy said, "It's all different now. We're not just famous for being rich anymore."

"We're freaks," I said.

"No," said Eddy. "We're not."

"Right," I said. "*We're* not." I tapped my chest. "*I* am. Lexie is. Terese is." I shook my head. "I don't know what the little kids are."

Eddy reached over and grabbed my foot. "You are not freaks. You were put in a totally crappy situation. It wasn't your fault." He paused. "You might have experienced stuff no one else in the world has, but it doesn't make you a freak."

"Then why don't I feel that way?" I asked. "Even just talking to Verity that day . . ."

"What?" Eddy asked.

I shrugged. "It's, like . . . we had a conversation. A normal conversation. We just talked. And it seemed so normal. *I* even seemed normal. But . . ."

"But what?"

"There was so much still there, beneath the surface. So much still on my shoulders. How can I ever tell anyone who I really am? What I've been through?"

Eddy started to say something, but I stopped him.

"No, listen. What if I had said, 'Hey, I'm Eli Yanakakis'? There would have been this momentary pause on her face as the wheels started turning. And she would have thought, *Oh, Eli Yanakakis, son of Rex, who started*

YK, who—oh my God—he's been underground for six years." I sighed. "I can see it now."

Eddy said, "But you didn't say that."

I shook my head.

"So you don't know."

I rolled my eyes. "Oh, believe me, I know."

"It's too much pressure to keep everything a secret. We can't do it that much longer. Even Mom knows that." Eddy sat up. "One day you'll have to trust someone enough to tell them."

I nodded. "Yeah. I guess. But what if they want nothing to do with me after I tell them?"

Eddy smiled. "You'll always have me." He jumped off the bed. "Els made an apple pie earlier. Coming?"

"Yeah," I said. Pie sounded good. Anything to get my mind off a girl who, if I had any brains, I would never try to see again.

CHAPTER FOURTEEN

THE NEXT DAY I WOKE UP AND EVERYTHING WAS CLEAR. I wasn't ready to have to deal with telling someone, anyone, who I really was. I wasn't ready for a negative reaction from them.

Verity was nice. I could see myself hanging out with her. Maybe liking her. Maybe liking her a lot. But having her look at me strangely when I told her the truth? That my name wasn't even EJ?

That would hurt.

So I texted her to say I couldn't do anything that weekend.

She replied, asking about the next one.

I didn't answer.

Saturday morning we all got ready for the Mariners game. I pulled on a pair of jeans and then a throwback Mariners shirt. When we'd first arrived in Hawaii, Eddy had one like it. I thought it was cool, so when Mom started ordering clothes, I asked for one.

Downstairs in the kitchen, Mom was in her bathrobe, her hair up in a loose, messy knot on top of her head. She looked exhausted as she held Finn, who was fussing like crazy.

"What's up with him?" I asked.

Mom shook her head. "I don't know. But Lucas started throwing up in the middle of the night, and I think he's got whatever Cara had. Gram's with him. I think I'd better stay home with the three little ones."

"Why don't we just do the game a different time?" I asked. After the day at the aquarium, I was fine with delaying our next outing.

"Do what a different time?" asked Eddy, who bounded into the kitchen, wearing jeans and the same shirt I had on. Well, the same except that his was softer, more worn, and mine probably still smelled like the plastic bag it had been shipped in. He stopped and stared at my shirt, then said, "I'll go change." He headed back up the stairs.

My face turned red.

I got that it would be stupid for us to wear the same shirt, but the look on his face . . . it hadn't been a harmless reaction of *Oops, better change so we don't look like the identical twins we are*. It came across like it was more an annoyance, like I was someone he had to put up with.

Mom looked at me. "You okay?"

I nodded. "Yeah, sure."

She put Finn up on her shoulder. "You're fine with Tony going?"

I frowned. "Who?"

Mom said, "Tony, Eddy's friend that helped find Lucas the other day."

Eddy's *friend*? "He's going with us?"

Mom bit her lip. "You didn't know."

I asked, "When did that happen?"

"Eddy just kept asking and I figured it was okay."

My mouth dropped open. "How is it okay? Tell me how it's okay! You don't want anyone to know who we are or where we are, but then you'll let a stranger go to a baseball game with us?" I realized I was yelling.

Mom held up her palm toward me. "Sweetheart, calm down. I know I have to accept the fact that you all want to go out into the world, and it will happen sooner or later and—"

"Mom?" Reese walked into the kitchen in a flowered nightgown, her hair down and fluffed out around her face. She held her stomach with both hands. "I don't feel good." Then she threw a hand over her mouth and ran into the small bathroom off the kitchen.

We heard her throw up.

"Uh-oh. Another one down." Mom handed Finn, who had finally calmed down and was whimpering quietly, to me. "I'd better go check on her."

Just then, Eddy came back into the room, wearing a Cubs shirt. Almost the opposite of mine.

I said, "So your new *friend* is coming, huh?"

Eddy's face turned a bit red and he headed to the fridge and opened it. "I thought it would be a nice thank-you for helping with Lucas." He pulled out a gallon of milk and poured a glass.

"So you're going to tell this stranger who we are?"

He shook his head. "No, not really."

I rolled my eyes. "How is that going to stay a secret?"

Mom came back in and took Finn. "Reese is sick, too. Looks like it'll just be you two and Lexie."

I crossed my arms. "And *Tony*. Don't forget Tony."

Mom said, "If this is a problem, we'll just cancel. Forget the whole thing." She sounded miffed.

Eddy said, "No! I don't want to. God!" He shoved the milk back in the fridge and slammed the door. "It used to just be me and Gram and it was so much frickin' easier. Now everything has to be decided by a hundred people and I never get to do what *I* want!"

Mom's mouth fell open and I had to sit down on a stool. So that was how he really felt? That his life was easier when we were all . . .

"I'm so sorry we're not all *dead*!" I snapped.

"Eli . . ." He looked at Mom. "I'm sorry." Eddy paled and shook his head. "That's not what I meant. I didn't—"

"It's pretty clear you *did* mean it," I said. "Or you wouldn't have said it!"

"Eli!" Mom narrowed her eyes at both of us. "Just go. Both of you. I have sick kids to take care of and it'll be easier without you two around."

Lexie walked in the room, wearing jeans and a Mariners shirt, her dark hair in a loose bun on top of her head. She looked excited, but her face fell as she saw us. "What's wrong?"

Mom said, "Nothing's wrong. You look pretty, sweetheart."

"Where's Reese?" asked Lexie.

Mom said, "She's sick." Then she looked at me and Eddy. "Now go and take your sister to the ball game."

Eddy turned and headed outside. Lexie started to ask me something, but I just brushed past her and went outside. In the SUV, Lexie and I sat in the backseat and Eddy rode shotgun with Lee. Eddy pulled a piece of paper out of his pocket and punched an address into the GPS. "This will get us to where we need to pick up Tony."

I leaned forward. "You seriously are still bringing him?"

"Who?" asked Lexie.

Eddy said, "He texted me, said he'd be there."

I slumped in the seat. "We don't even know him."

"Who?" repeated Lexie.

Eddy turned around and looked at me. "We've been texting. Tony's cool."

Lexie grabbed my ear and twisted.

"Ow!"

She asked, "Who is Tony?"

"Let go!" I said, trying to get loose from her grip.

Eddy said, "This guy who helped us find Lucas when he ran off at the aquarium."

Lexie let go of me and I rubbed my ear.

131

Her eyes narrowed. "Does Mom know he's coming?"

Eddy said, "Yeah."

Lexie looked at Eddy and back to me. "And she's fine with some stranger knowing who we are?"

Eddy said, "It's easy now, with just the three of us." He pointed at Lee. "He's our uncle." He pointed at me. "You're EJ, since that worked so well for you before."

Lexie asked, "And who am I?"

Eddy shrugged. "You can be . . . Alex."

"Oh, just *awesome*." Lexie glared at Eddy. "I can't believe Mom is okay with you inviting some stranger to go with us! How would you have explained all the kids? And Mom? Everyone knows what Mom looks like."

Eddy said, "That's why this is way easier."

"Yeah," I said. "Because we know you like things to be easy. I'm sorry Lexie and I are here to mess up your day."

He shot a glance at me. "I said I was sorry. Just let it go."

Lexie raised her eyebrows at me, but I ignored her and looked out the window.

"Uh-uh." Lexie shook her head so hard a few strands of hair escaped from her bun. "That kid is not coming with us."

Eddy turned around. "Oh, come on. I told him we'd pick him up."

Lee took the next exit and we pulled into a sketchy strip mall that had seen its better days. The sun was shining over the blacktop, and a lone figure stood at the end of the parking lot near a bus stop.

Eddy pointed. "There he is."

"I'm the oldest here, which makes me in charge," Lexie said. "Mom must have been sleep deprived or *insane* to agree to this and I say no way. You just pull up there and Eddy, you tell him . . ."

She trailed off as we got close enough to see Tony. Instead of the ragged hoodie and jeans from the other day, he wore a Mariners shirt and clean jeans and running shoes. Nice ones. His hair, which had been covered by a cap that rainy day, was dark and curly. He saw us and waved, then smiled, revealing even white teeth and dimples.

I heard a click.

Lexie had unbuckled her seat belt and slid over into the middle seat. "Eddy, tell him he can sit by me."

My mouth dropped open. "Wait! What happened to him being a stranger?"

Lexie pulled on her bun until her hair fell down, loose around her shoulders. She ran a hand through it. "He doesn't exactly look *dangerous.*"

Resisting the urge to bang my head against the window, I watched as Tony opened the door. He smiled and greeted all of us, then got in the car.

I scowled the rest of the way, watching Eddy and Lexie gush over Tony. Eddy fist-bumped him and said, "Glad you could make it."

Tony said, "Me too." He turned to Lexie and held out a hand. "I'm Tony. Nice to meet you."

Lexie shook it and giggled a little.

Was she blushing?

Seriously?

Eddy said, "That's Alex. And EJ." He patted Lee on the arm. "This here's our uncle."

I rolled my eyes and glared out the window at the traffic. Great. Part of me had been hoping Tony would be so obviously not a good fit with us that Eddy would agree with me and never invite him anywhere again. But in less than five minutes, that strange teenager had my sister swooning.

Tony said something that made both Eddy and Lexie laugh, and I stopped listening.

When we got to the stadium, Lee pulled into a VIP parking area and we all walked in together through the sky bridge and up to the small, private suite that was ours for the day.

A buffet was laid out on a side table, and silver dishes of ice held a variety of sodas, juices, and bottled water. "Wow," said both Tony and I at the same time. We looked at each other, and then I looked away.

Sure, I'd grown up with similar layouts, never giving a thought to where my next meal was coming from, but it had been awhile. Having so many options of food and drink at my fingertips was something I had not yet learned to take for granted. I grabbed some napkins and dug in, taking a hot dog and dumping sweet relish all over it.

A couple tables were set up by the windows and I sat down at one. Our vantage point was high up, but right over home plate. Eddy, Lexie, and Tony were filling their plates, and Lexie came and sat with me.

Tony and Eddy sat down in leather chairs right beside us. Tony leaned back in a leather chair, looking totally relaxed as he and Lexie talked. How in the world was he fitting in so well with my family? Obviously from the wrong side of the tracks, so to speak, he should have been feeling uncomfortable, or at the very least, he should have been one of those people who rebels against the excess of the suite.

But he was just enjoying every moment.

I wasn't. But maybe I wasn't being fair to him. Maybe I was being elitist by thinking he should bow over backward with gratitude.

I finished eating. There was still time before the first inning started. "I'm gonna go find a bathroom."

Lee stood up to go with me, but I shook my head before Tony could notice my "uncle" wanting to accompany me to the bathroom. Lee didn't look happy, but he sat back down and pointed. "There's one down the hall."

I smiled at him and whispered, "I'll be fine."

Out in the hallway, there were a lot of people gathering at the door of a suite. There was an exclamation, and a little girl in a wheelchair was pushed inside, and several people followed her. A bartender had just walked out of the room with a tray of dirty glasses and headed my way. I moved out of his way and kept going past that suite to the bathroom. On my way back, I passed the open door and someone called out something.

I kept walking.

"EJ?"

The sound of her voice made me stop more than the name did, since I certainly didn't answer to it. I turned around.

Verity Blum was standing right in front of me.

CHAPTER FIFTEEN

WEARING A PINK MARINERS JERSEY, DENIM CAPRIS, AND white flip-flops, Verity just stood there, hands on her hips, looking at me with her eyebrows raised.

"Why are you here?" The words spilled out before I realized how rude they sounded.

She cocked her head toward the party going on in the suite. "We came here with my brother. A wish-filling charity thing." Her eyes narrowed. "Why are you here? Another research paper?"

"No. I'm just here at the game with my family." I started to motion toward the small suite, and then realized what that might lead to. So I gestured back toward the bathroom, and the steps that led to the general seating. "My mom surprised us. I'm way over in the nosebleeds but I wandered and ended up here." Way too many details. Truth is always simpler. I shrugged. "I better go before someone catches me up here."

"Wait," she said. "You could come in with me. They have tons of food."

I glanced inside the door. "I probably shouldn't. I better get back." I smiled at her. "Thanks though. I'm glad I ran into you."

She frowned. "Are you really? Because I thought, when you didn't text me back, that—"

"No, I was just . . . busy. Trying to write that stupid paper." I shrugged.

"So you'll text me?"

I nodded. "Definitely."

"Okay." She set her hand on my arm for a moment, then went back into the suite.

I breathed out, relieved, and went to head back to my suite.

As I turned the corner, I ran smack into a man in a black T-shirt and black jeans. "Oh, excuse me, I—" As I looked more closely at him, my eyes narrowed. Was he the man from Costco? The man from the doomsday preparation site? I started to doubt myself, but as he looked up at me, his eyes widened, and he started to back off.

I reached for him, but he dodged me and jolted forward, and I had to turn around to chase after him. "Wait!" I called. I ran after him, glad the hallway was fairly empty so no one seemed to notice.

What was he doing there? Following me again? Following us? But how did he know where we'd be?

I had nearly caught up to him when a door to one of

the luxury suites opened and a bunch of kids Reese's age poured out, cutting me off from him. I tried to swim my way through, but there were too many.

I saw the man farther down the corridor. He had stopped right at the stairway and was looking back at me. There was a smile on his face, like he was glad he got away. But then he reached in his pocket and pulled out a small white card.

A business card?

He held up the card, making sure I saw. Then he pulled out a pen, jotted something on the back of the card, and placed it on the railing of the stairs. He looked back at me.

I nodded.

He disappeared down the stairs.

As soon as I could get through the crowd, I headed over there and grabbed the card. I glanced at the back. A phone number. I flipped the card over. The front was a picture of a very nice kitchen with granite countertops. He obviously wasn't trying to hide from me, leaving the card proved that. But if he wanted to talk, why did he run?

After the game, we dropped Tony off at the strip mall. Eddy got out for a minute and walked him over to the bus stop. I watched them laughing, and then Eddy waved and walked back to the car.

I couldn't believe Eddy would trust him that much.

As soon as we pulled out of the parking lot, I asked, "Does he know who we are?"

Eddy said, "No. Duh. He just thinks we're some rich people. That's all."

Lexie said, "I think he's cool. You should tell him who we are, Eddy."

"Why?" I asked.

Lexie shrugged. "He wouldn't tell anyone, I bet."

I rolled my eyes. "Yeah, why ruin a good thing?'

I just stared out the window the rest of the drive. Back at the house, I went up to my room and pulled the business card out of my back pocket. The phone number on the back had a Seattle area code. I wasn't all that sure I was ready to call him up. What could he want from me?

I flipped the card over and looked at the photo of the kitchen. The top line read, TRINITY CONDOS. Under that were the words: *A Luxury Survival Development.*

"What?" My heart started to race as I went to my computer and typed in the website for Trinity Condos.

The first thing to pop up was a picture of a steel door and the words: **Click here if you want to survive.** "You've got to be frickin' kidding me." Still, I clicked and went into the site and read the headline.

Trinity Condos! Secure, high-quality living during a long-term survival situation. Our luxury condos are built to withstand a nuclear explosion.

Below that were several tabs. I clicked on the one labeled *Amenities.*

Each three-bedroom, two-bath condo contains a

five-year supply of freeze-dried survival food per person, for a maximum of six people. The food has a shelf life of 25 years and is stored in oxygen-free containers.

Dad should have thought of that.

The description of amenities continued, describing how the twenty available condos were all part of a larger space, which had, among other things, a community library, theater, gym, and . . . a hydroponics lab. *To provide fresh produce for the duration of your underground stay.*

I shuddered. God, it sounded like the Compound. I clicked on the tab labeled *History.*

The Trinity Condo units are inside a former US nuclear missile base in rural Kansas, six stories underground with elevator access.

I skimmed the rest, then went back to the home page and clicked on *Prices.*

Prices start at $2.5 million.

"Holy crap." Was the guy who left the card the developer of the condos? Did they really exist or was it a scam to get people's money? If they did exist . . . it meant people were on their way to being just as nuts as Dad had been. Except that, to my father, survival had turned into a game. A game that needed to be switched up now and then, a game to control.

But I doubted anyone spending that much money looked at survival as a game.

Before I could rethink it, I grabbed my phone and dialed the number on the card. There was one ring, then a click.

"Hello?"

I said, "You probably know who this is."

He breathed out. "Mr. Yanakakis."

"Why'd you run?" I asked.

"What?"

"If you want to talk to me, which you obviously do since you've been following us, why'd you run?" I waited.

He didn't answer for a moment, but then said, "You seemed a bit . . . volatile."

Volatile? "Seriously? Why wouldn't I be! You've been following me and my family and—"

"Please! Just give me a chance to explain." He sounded desperate.

Honestly, I kind of wanted to know what he had to say. "Fine," I said. "Explain."

"My name is Tom Barron. I'm a developer."

"Yeah." I glanced at the computer screen. "I looked up your site."

"Really?" He sounded excited. "What did you think?"

What did I think? I frowned. "I think you're nuts."

He was quiet. Then he said, "You of all people should understand the seriousness of the situation."

I had to laugh. "Are you kidding me? I spent six years under the frickin' ground because my father was insane! I think anybody who would willingly shell out millions of dollars to do the same thing is just as nuts as he was."

"Your father wasn't crazy," said Tom Barron. "Ever heard of Nightwatch?"

I let the name roll around in my head a bit. "No."

"Do you have a computer there?"

"Yeah."

He said, "Look it up."

I typed it in and waited. Several sites popped up, some with pictures. "It's a jet," I said.

"Not just any jet," he said. "It's the Doomsday Jet. There are some very solid stories to substantiate that it was flying around on 9/11."

I was sure that, if pressed, he would turn out to have "solid stories" to substantiate both Bigfoot and the Loch Ness Monster. Still, I wanted to know where he was going. "I don't understand," I said.

He said, "It can withstand a nuclear explosion, never has to land to refuel, and is a flying command post from which the president can command nuclear retaliation."

I sighed. "I'm sure all countries have something like that."

"On twenty-four-hour permanent high alert? They can scramble Nightwatch with five minutes' notice. Right now, there are crews sleeping nearby, ready to get it in the air at a moment's notice. It's an airborne ark."

"So?" I said.

Tom Barron raised his voice a little. "So it means nuclear attack is just as much a threat as it always was. Our government must believe that, otherwise they wouldn't have that aircraft on permanent high alert."

A chill ran through me.

He said, "Your father wasn't crazy. I'm not crazy. These are fearful times. Do you know there are people who spend every spare minute preparing a BOL?"

"What's that?"

"Oh, sorry. Bug Out Location. Somewhere to go when everything collapses."

I sighed. "Nothing is going to collapse. People are trying to cash in."

"Really?" He paused for a second before continuing. "Look online. Check out some typical seed companies. Even they offer survivalist seeds. Doomsday is coming, and people need to be—"

"God, just stop." I shook my head. All those people trying to survive. Underground. I'd been there. Been there long enough to realize survival wasn't all it was cracked up to be. Given the choice a second time? I'd stay outside. Die along with all the people who couldn't afford a BOL. I'd heard enough. "What do you want from me?"

"I was hoping . . ." He trailed off. "I was hoping you, or possibly your whole family, could act as a consultant on the Trinity Condo project. You've experienced survival-living underground, you know what works and what doesn't, and you—"

"No."

"But you would be so valuable—"

"No!" I snarled. "I won't do it. And stop following my family or I'll call the police and take out a restraining order." My tone hid the relief I felt at finding out the person following us was just an opportunist, trying to cash in. If need be, our lawyers would chew him up and spit him out. Still, I'd rather send him on his way myself, so no one else in my family would even have to know.

But he kept talking. "I never planned to follow you. But when I got that tip, I just couldn't resist trying to—"

I froze in my chair. "What tip?"

"Through the YK sightings website. I got a tip that you all were going to that Costco. Of course, I thought it was a joke, people send me tips all the time, but they always turn out to be fake—"

"Wait!" My throat tightened up. "Someone told you specifically what Costco we were going to?"

"Yes."

I swallowed and tried to keep my voice level, not betray my panic. "Who was the tip from?"

"I don't know. I mean, the first one was just an online message, but the second time he called and—"

Second time?

No one knew those plans but my family. I gave up trying to pretend calm, and demanded, "Who called? Who was he?"

"I don't know. His voice was . . . garbled, sort of? Like he was using one of those voice scramblers to disguise his voice? Heck, maybe it wasn't even a man . . ."

Oh, my God. Someone, other than Trinity Condo Idiot, was watching us, knew where we were, knew where we went.

He said, "I hope you'll think about—"

"No," I said. "No frickin' chance. You're lucky I don't

call the police." I hung up. My hands were trembling and my breaths were shallow.

Who was watching us? What did they want?

And how was I going to find out who they were, and stop them, before something happened?

I had no idea.

CHAPTER SIXTEEN

I SAT THERE, TRYING TO TALK MYSELF THROUGH IT ALL. Tom Barron wasn't a problem. But whoever tipped him off definitely *was*. Could it be someone in our security force? I went through the faces in my mind. Joe and Sam who minded the front gatehouse during the day; both joked with us whenever we went around them. Neither seemed capable of stabbing us in the back like that. William, the older guy who took over every night: very buff, with a tinge of gray in his hair. He had an adult child with special needs and was always thanking Mom for the job. No way would he risk his paycheck like that. I could be wrong, but my gut felt strongly about those three.

Then I thought about Lee.

I shook my head. "No way." Gram had vetted him herself. There was a family connection, a level of honor, and I was sure he wouldn't cross that. Other than those guards, and a few other loyal people at YK, no one knew where we were living. No one at YK would risk their well-paying job in order to tip off a guy selling survival condos.

And then I stopped trying to think of people who would give us away. Why *would* someone tip Barron off? A commission of some sort? He didn't mention anything.

And if the tipster was looking for us, well . . . obviously he'd already found us and seemed to know our every step.

He was watching us.

I went over to my window and looked out, first at the lake, then at the woods. The woods were just outside the fences, but if someone wanted to watch us, that would be a good spot.

Still, that didn't answer *why*?

Did someone want to mess with us?

No. Mess with *me*.

I had been the only one to suspect being followed, and I was the one who had just found out for certain that we were. Was that planned?

I went back to my computer and sat down, then swiveled slowly around in my chair. Should I tell Eddy? Mom? Or no one?

In order to know where we were, someone would have to have connections to YK. "That doesn't exactly narrow it down." I stopped twirling and drummed my fingers on the desk. "Who would want to piss us—me—off like this? Who at YK would want . . ."

Phil.

He knew about our new place; he was capable of finding out the license plates of our vehicles. He could have hired someone to follow us wherever we went.

I thought back to the places I'd been in the past few weeks, other than YK.

The Progeria Institute.

People at YK had been aware of that trip, had even arranged for a car. I didn't know the driver of the company car, and even though Lee ended up driving me that day, Phil could have paid the driver to keep tabs on me.

I shook my head. Too easy. So many people knew I was going there.

Costco. No one knew but Lee and us.

The aquarium. Same thing.

Someone had to be tracking our vehicles. I glanced at my phone.

Or us.

I grabbed the phone and went to Eddy's room. I held up my hand to knock when I heard him talking to someone. His voice was muffled through the door, but I could still hear what he was saying. "I know! That was hilarious." He was quiet for a moment. Listening to whoever was on the phone? He laughed. "Totally! We have to do that."

I stood there, hand frozen in the air. Maybe he was talking to a friend from Hawaii. I glanced down at my own phone, which held less than five contacts. His probably had dozens.

I dropped my hand and went downstairs.

Mom was in the kitchen, waiting for the teakettle to boil. She smiled at me. "How was the ball game?"

"Fine." I held up my phone. "Where'd we get these?"

Mom tilted her head. "Gram bought them."

"Where?" I asked.

"Why?"

"I just want to know."

Mom frowned, as if she were trying to remember. "I think she got them at Costco in Hawaii. They're not traceable, if that's what you're worried about. She made sure of that. They're just so we could communicate when we're not together."

I asked, "Why didn't you give them to us then? Why'd you wait until now?"

She smiled. "I was hoping you'd never leave the house."

I smiled back, relieved. Had the source of the phones been YK, Phil could have easily been involved in the phones, somehow added trackers to them. But he was obviously out of the picture. And maybe I was just being paranoid again. Barron could have made up the tipster for any reason. Maybe just to freak me out. Maybe just to make himself seem more serious than laughable, which is exactly what he was.

The kettle whistled.

"Making enough for me?" I asked.

She nodded. "Of course." She got another mug off the rack. "Lady Grey?"

I nodded and sat down at the counter. She poured water into each mug, then set one in front of me. She bobbed her tea bag up and down in her mug. "So what's on your mind?"

I shook my head. "Nothing." Part of me wanted to tell her about Lexie's quest to find her real parents. Instead, I asked, "Do you think that Eddy is embarrassed by me?"

Mom's eyes widened. "Why would you think that?"

I didn't answer right away, because I didn't know how to put into words the way I felt. Feeling bad about clothes was so stupid, but that was the only concrete evidence I had; he didn't want to be seen in the same clothes as me, which actually happened to make complete sense. We hadn't dressed alike since we were kids, a fact that took the air out of my argument. But he seemed so much happier around Tony. Like he couldn't relax around me. Couldn't have fun. I shrugged. "Sometimes . . . I feel like we kind of cramp his style."

Mom stiffened. "Is this because of what he said this morning?"

"Maybe."

Mom set a hand on mine. "We've been through so much that we expect him to understand. But we have to understand what he's been through. He had to adjust to us being gone. And now, he has to do the opposite."

"Wouldn't that be easier?" I asked. "To know we're here instead of gone for good? To just be normal again?"

"Who's to say what's normal?" Mom drizzled honey

into her tea, stirred, and took a sip. "He used to have three siblings, now he has four more. That would be hard enough to get used to. Give him some time, Eli."

She was probably right. Maybe Eddy's normal was him and Gram, on their own, and we had messed it all up. We'd even blown Eddy's whole belief of Dad as a hero. And Phil as a good guy.

I pulled my mug toward me and swirled my tea bag around by the string. Without thinking, I asked, "Do you think Phil is dead?"

Mom froze, then whispered, "What?"

"Phil," I repeated. "Do you think he's dead?"

"I don't know." She took another sip of tea, then set her mug back down and licked her lips. "Is it wrong of me to say that I hope he is?"

"No." I swallowed. "But . . . I think he's alive."

She looked at me, her forehead wrinkling. "Why do you say that?"

"Just a feeling I have."

She set a hand on my face for a moment. "He's gone. Whether he's still out there or . . . not . . ." She took a quick breath. "He's gone as far as we're concerned. He's out of our lives. For good."

I only hoped she was right.

CHAPTER SEVENTEEN

I ENDED UP WITH WHATEVER STOMACH VIRUS THE OTHER kids had, and with all of us recovering, we didn't go anywhere that week. Besides feeling sick, I was kind of relieved. Going out was stressful.

I had to be the only teenager in the world who preferred staying home to going out, and I wondered if that would ever change.

Mom and Lexie were busy planning Quinn's birthday party, an event that caused a bit of tension in the house, ever since Eddy had asked Mom, "Can I invite Tony to Quinn's party?"

"I don't think that's a good idea," she said.

"Why?" He frowned. "We can trust him."

Mom shook her head. "I'm just not ready to invite a stranger. The ball game was one thing."

Eddy said, "He doesn't know who we are."

Mom swiped her hand through the air. "He'll figure it out as soon as he meets all of us."

"Fine." Eddy rolled his eyes.

On Friday, Mom sent Els and Lee out to get supplies for the party. They came home with a penguin cake, and shopping bags from Whole Foods. I helped unpack drinks and whole-wheat buns. There were a bunch of chips and snacks as well.

Els said, "There are balloons in the car you could bring in."

I went out to the SUV and found almost a dozen silver Mylar balloons, all with various designs, all proclaiming HAPPY BIRTHDAY! I grabbed a handful of balloon strings, holding on tight so I wouldn't lose any to the breezy day. Inside, the kitchen was chaos. Gram was at the oven, checking on her Kalua pork for sandwiches, while Els arranged buns on a glass serving tray. Lucas was running around the tiled floor, Cara running after trying to catch him, both of them screeching so loud that Cocoa was curled up in a corner, looking like she'd rather be anywhere else.

Eddy set the cake on the counter, where Els immediately pulled off the cover and frowned at the penguin, obviously not happy with the workmanship. "Hmmph." She stuck a candle, a large blue 1, in the center of the cake and went back to stacking buns.

I walked up behind Gram and told her, "That pork smells wonderful."

She shook her head. "Roasting in the oven for a few hours is not the same as roasting in a pit for three days."

I hugged her. "It'll be delicious."

She patted my arm. "Go help your sisters. They're setting the table."

"Okay." The dining room table was spread with a bright blue tablecloth covered with penguins. "I'm sensing a theme."

Lexie was bent over a pile of silverware. "What was your first clue?"

I split up the bunch of balloons, tying some on to a few of the dining-room chairs, then I went back into the kitchen. Lucas and Cara had disappeared, and Gram was pulling apart her pork with two forks, which she set down on a towel when she saw me. "Can you fill a pitcher with ice water and take it in?" She wiped her hands on her apron.

I found a pitcher and filled it, then carried it into the dining room.

Everyone else was inside the dining room, clustered around one end of the table, except for Cara. She was stopping at each chair with a balloon, untying each and watching it float up to the fifteen-foot ceiling. Five already bounced around up there. "Hey!" I said. "Does no one see what she's doing?"

No one looked up from whatever they were doing. I set the pitcher on the table and picked Cara up. "If you let all the balloons go, you won't have any to play with."

She scowled and wriggled her way out of my arms, back to the ground where she ran over to Mom.

"What are you guys doing?" I asked.

"Quinn is opening a present," said Reese.

"Aren't you gonna wait for all of us?" I asked.

Eddy said, "It's from me. Just a little kid's skateboard."

Just then Gram walked in with a platter of pulled Kalua pork on whole grain buns. Els followed her with coleslaw and a fruit salad, which she set on the table. She said, "We're ready."

Dinner was nice, with no arguments or tension, and everyone just enjoying the food. When we had finished, Eddy and I went into the kitchen and lit the candle on the cake. Then we carried it into the dining room. Lexie turned off some of the lights, so it was dim, the light of the small candle glowing.

I looked around at all of us. The little kids all had smiles and wide eyes. Actually, Reese and Lexie did, too. I couldn't help but think of the lackluster birthdays we'd all had in the Compound. Everything to do with a celebration had been a task of making do with what we had.

I glanced over at Mom, who had tears in her eyes as Quinn squealed at the cake.

She had always tried so hard to make things special for us the past few years. I wondered if she was relieved to be out of that situation, and back in the world we'd all been used to. A world where anything we wanted was at our fingertips. A world where a birthday celebration meant a fancy cake and candles and presents.

Reese helped Quinn blow out the candle, then Gram got dessert plates while Els started cutting the cake.

Eddy, on the other hand, didn't seem particularly thrilled. He was smiling and laughing at the little kids, but it was different. Maybe because he'd never done without, had to make do like the rest of us had. The little ones would forget. Soon, they'd never know anything but this world, a world where they could have anything.

But Reese and Lexie would never forget what those years had been like. And neither would I.

Els set a plate of cake in front of me. The layers were made of red velvet, and the filling was white. I took a bite. Cream cheese. I shut my eyes and nearly moaned. "Wow." Then I took another bite, and another.

I smiled as I watched the members of my family eat their cake. Except for Quinn, who wore more than he ate. Maybe we wouldn't forget, but celebrations, especially ones that included cake like this, would certainly help.

After we'd finished, Quinn opened the rest of his presents. Then I offered to give the cake-covered birthday boy a bath, after which I ended up reading stories to him and Cara and Lucas until they all fell asleep. They'd stayed up later than usual, after nine by the time the last one fell asleep, and the house was quiet.

I was all sticky from Quinn, so I took a shower and watched some television. But I couldn't stop thinking about the whole evening, how nice it had been to have everyone get along. It made me reevaluate things, realize that I needed to mend whatever rift there was between

Lexie and Eddy. Maybe the way to do that was to let him know I hadn't chosen her over him.

So even though it was almost eleven, I went and knocked on his door, lightly in case he was asleep. He didn't answer, but I really didn't want to wait until morning, so I knocked again. Then I turned the knob and pushed the door open. "Eddy?"

The small light was on by his bed, so the room was dim. His bed was made, perfectly empty. Figuring he was downstairs watching television, I turned to go. But then I noticed the small garbage can by the door, and what lay on top. I picked it up. The Mariners shirt he'd had on the day we went to the ball game. The one like mine.

I dropped it back in the garbage and started to leave, when I heard voices. The yard light shone in the door that opened to the balcony, and the curtain moved with the breeze. I stepped toward the open door. One voice was Eddy's, but I wasn't sure about the other. I tiptoed over to the open door. No one was on the balcony, so I stepped out the door, crouching so I wouldn't be seen.

Through the bars on the balcony, I peered down at the pool area. Eddy's head was just visible above the back of a chaise lounge. And someone sat next to him in another one. I couldn't tell who it was. One of the guards maybe?

Eddy said, "I'm glad they're back, don't get me wrong. Thinking they were all dead . . . that was the worst day ever."

The other person spoke: "This must be hard to get used to."

Tony? Tony was there, in our yard?

I grabbed a hold of one of the metal bars and squeezed. How could Eddy have let him in?

Eddy said, "Some days it all just seems so frickin' weird. I've got my sisters back, only they're different than they used to be. And the little kids. They're cute and all, but, man. I feel like I'm the babysitter that they hate. I'm getting to know them, but it takes awhile. And Eli . . ."

I froze and held my breath. My heart pounded as I waited for him to go on.

"Sometimes he's normal. We get along and do stuff. And then other times, he's, like, my project. Like he's this foreigner that I am forced to teach American ways." He breathed out. "I find myself just feeling sorry for him. And some days, to be honest, all that pity feels like work."

I realized I was clutching the bar so hard I'd lost feeling in my hand. I let go and turned around to head back into Eddy's room. I didn't want to hear anymore. I didn't need, or want, Eddy to feel sorry for me.

But then Tony said, "So you up for it? Should we go?"

Eddy said, "Yeah, let's do it."

I turned back as they headed around the side of the house. I quickly ran out Eddy's door and back to my own room, and over to the windows that looked out on the woods at the edge of the property. As I watched, they walked over to the wooded area, climbed over the fence, and disappeared.

My heart was pounding. Should I tell someone?

I sank down on the edge of my bed.

Eddy had left with someone we knew nothing about. We didn't know Tony's last name or where he lived. Eddy could be in danger.

I picked up the phone on the bedside table, and my finger hovered over the button that went directly to the guardhouse. I would call William, who worked the night shift, and tell him to go after Eddy.

But then I set the phone back down.

The reason I wanted William to go after Eddy wasn't to keep him safe. It was to get him back. To keep him away from Tony.

The truth was I wasn't worried about my brother; I was jealous that he'd rather be with someone other than me.

While I was hard to be with, *work* as he put it, apparently Tony wasn't. And if my own brother would rather be with someone he'd just met, then . . .

. . . that was one more thing in my life that was messed up.

Eddy not only told a stranger who we were, he brought that stranger to our house. And then he snuck out.

My hands clenched into fists.

After all his lecturing to Lexie about not making Mom upset, here he was, doing something that would send Mom over the edge.

My heart pounded. Two could play at that game.

I went over to my desk and picked up my cell phone. I hit #5 on my speed dial.

"EJ?" Verity sounded sleepy.

"Yeah," I said. "Sorry to wake you, but I wanted to ask . . . can you meet me sometime next week?" I swallowed, and then gathered up the nerve to add, "There's something I need to tell you."

CHAPTER EIGHTEEN

Verity and I talked, and made plans to meet the next week. I would've liked to choose somewhere nice, where we could get coffee or dessert, maybe go for a walk; something to make it seem like a real date.

But it would be too hard to get out of the house.

Going back to the Progeria Institute was probably the only place I could talk my mom into letting me go on my own. Even then, I'd probably have to come up with a pretty decent lie.

But when I woke up the morning after we talked, I regretted calling Verity.

I lay there, looking up at the ceiling.

Eddy may have been ready to tell someone who we were, but I wasn't ready to trust anyone like that. No way. And after sleeping on what I'd heard Eddy say about me, I woke up feeling more reasonable about it.

His wanting to hang out with Tony actually made sense.

All I did was worry about things: my sisters, my mom, the little ones. I'd even told Eddy about some of my stranger, more paranoid worries, like the doomsday prepper people following us.

And Phil. Eddy was probably tired of my saying bad things about Phil and our dad.

When it came down to it, I was like an old lady with my constant worrying; being ultra-cautious about everything. Someone like that is no fun to be with.

Not only that, I didn't even have the confidence to choose my own clothes, instead I copied whatever he had.

With a house full of children, Eddy was already reminded every day of how his life had changed. It wasn't fair for me to expect him to sit around waiting for me to catch up to him. Be his equal again. Be normal.

Furthermore, why would he want to?

I got up, changed into running gear, and started on the treadmill.

Maybe Eddy felt like I did, that it was never going to happen.

So, of course, Eddy would see Tony as a better choice than me.

But being reasonable about it didn't make me any less envious. Or curious.

As I ran, I looked out the window at the section of fence they'd climbed over, and the woods where they had disappeared.

Where did they go?

Did they meet up with anyone? Girls maybe?

And how long had they been sneaking out? Maybe Tony had been coming over before then, maybe this hadn't been the first time.

I pushed the button to increase the speed.

The part that made me feel the worst was that Eddy hadn't told me about Tony. He hadn't told me about where they went or what they did.

That part felt like betrayal. Because he was leaving me out.

I finished my run and then went down and poured a bowl of cereal. Sunshine poured in the windows, so I took my breakfast outside. Cocoa ran over to me, wagging her tail.

"Hold on, let me finish."

A FedEx truck pulled up to the front. Joe went out the small door in the gate and came back with a package, which he took into the guardhouse with him.

I finished my cereal and set the bowl on the ground so Cocoa could drink up the leftover milk. Then I walked over to the guardhouse.

Joe was standing there talking to Sam. They both greeted me, and I said, "I can take the package in."

Joe glanced at Sam.

"What?" I asked. I was close enough to see the mailing label with Terese's first name on it, along with Gram's grandmother's maiden name, like we used for all the online shopping. I frowned. Usually Gram's first name was on all the packages, just as an extra precaution.

Sam said, "We kind of have special instructions."

I frowned. "From who?"

Joe pointed at the label. "Your sister. We're supposed to call her when she gets a package from there, and then she comes and gets it."

I glanced at the label again, searching for the return address.

SUGARWORLD, LLC

What the hell?

I picked up the package. "I'll take it to her."

Joe started to protest, but I added, "I promise, I'll tell her you two told me not to." The package wasn't that heavy, a few pounds maybe, and made a shuffling sound when I shook it.

I grabbed my cereal bowl and went into the house.

Even though it was after nine, no one but Gram and Els were in the kitchen, so I set my bowl in the sink and took the box upstairs. I knocked on Reese's door.

She groaned. "I'm sleeping!"

I opened the door and walked in.

She was facedown under the covers, her head covered with a pillow, one dark braid spilling over the side of the bed. Clementine was lying on Reese's back, purring. "Go away." Her voice was muffled.

I set the package on her computer desk. "You've got mail."

Her head shot up, eyes wide. Then they narrowed as she saw the box. Reese shoved the covers aside and the cat went flying with a hiss as my sister leaped out of bed, grabbing for the box just as I snatched it up, holding it over my head.

"Give it to me!" Reese jumped up, flailing with her arms as she tried to grab the box away.

I straightened my arms, keeping the package well out of her reach as she got more and more irritated. Her chin crumpled and she started to cry.

When she saw that getting the box was hopeless, she threw a fist into my stomach.

"Oof." I doubled over and clutched my stomach, dropping the box.

She grabbed it and ran over to her bed, climbing back in.

When I finally got my breath back, I went and sat on the edge of her bed. "That wasn't nice," I said.

"You shouldn't have taken my package."

"What's in it?" I asked, deciding a calm and even voice would be the best way to find out what she was hiding.

She sniffled. "You'll tell Mom."

"I promise I won't. You know it's only a matter of time before she finds out anyway. It's pretty hard to keep a secret around here."

Reese shook her head. "You keep secrets."

"No, I—"

"Yes, you do! You and Lexie and Eddy all have secrets." She wiped her eyes. "I just—"

"You what?" I asked.

"Nothing," she said.

"Reese, just show me what's in the box. I won't tell anyone. Then we can have a secret together."

She didn't look completely sold on the idea, but she

went over to the desk and got a pair of scissors and cut into the tape. When she unfolded the top of the box, I saw a familiar brown label.

"M&M's?"

Reese turned the box upside down, dumping out several one-pound bags of the candy. She tossed the box beside them. "There."

I laughed, but then quickly stopped when I saw the serious look on her face. "Why M&M's?"

Her eyes filled with tears once more, and I put a hand out to her. She came and put her arms around my neck and cried, snuffling into my shoulder.

After a little bit, when she seemed like she was calming down, I asked, "Reese? What is it?"

She shuddered and then stepped back. She picked up a bag of M&M's. "Remember in the Compound?"

I nodded. We'd all had a supply of our own favorite treat. "Those were your treat."

"I ran out."

I smiled. "We all kind of ran out." I remembered my own stash of Snickers, and how, after the years went by, each one I unwrapped looked worse and worse, until I finally stopped unwrapping them and simply kept them under my bed. Maybe it made me feel better to know I still had a small piece of the old world there. An inedible piece, but still.

"No," said Reese. "I ran out two years after we went down there."

"How?"

"I was sad. And they made me feel better. Remember my store?"

I nodded. For a while in the Compound, before the little ones came along, the yellow room had been Reese's playroom. She had a cash register and shelves and play money. I'd only seen it once, when I'd been on one of Dad's early tours of the Compound. I wouldn't know for certain, because I isolated myself very early on, but I could guess she spent a lot of time playing there.

"I put the candy on the shelves. And sometimes Dad would come and give me real money for them. And it made me feel . . . normal. Like we were outside and I was just playing. A normal kid. So then I made Mom and Lexie come to my store, too. But I never . . . I never thought I might run out." She looked at me.

I knew what she was thinking. Why would anything run out when we'd always had everything we wanted?

She swallowed. "So I kept selling them, making Mom and Dad and Lexie play in my store, and I kept eating them, too, and . . . then one day they were gone."

"When was this?" I asked.

She ignored my question. "I looked everywhere. I couldn't believe that I'd used them all up. I knew Dad had to have more, somewhere."

I set a hand on her arm and squeezed. "But he didn't."

She shook her head and a few tears slid down her cheek. "I didn't know what to do. Nothing else was like them and . . ." She shrugged.

"When was this?" I was beginning to put a timeline

together in my head, trying to remember when Reese had become . . . different from who she'd always been.

She didn't answer my question. Instead, she said, "So I went looking for something else. Something that made me feel happy on the outside."

I froze. "*Mary Poppins*." When Reese ran out of her favorite candy, the one thing she had left from the outside world that made her feel normal, she reached for another. And that was when she started watching *Mary Poppins* nonstop. And when she—

"That's when I started talking like I was British. I wanted to be one of those kids, I wanted to live with Mary Poppins. "

I looked over at her. "I always wondered why."

She picked up a bag of M&M's and let them drop on the bed. "See? I'm living proof that candy *is* bad for you." She smiled a little.

I hugged her. "How long have you been stockpiling?"

She sat back and looked down. "Awhile." Then she knelt on the floor beside her bed and lifted up the bed skirt.

I got down beside her.

Boxes packed the entire space beneath her bed. All the same, all obviously from Sugarworld, LLC. "Holy crap," I said. "Do you even eat any?"

She shook her head. "That's the weird part. I don't even want to. I just want to know that they're there." She watched for a minute. "I'm a freak."

"No," I said, and put my arm around her. "Not at all. This is . . . this is about the most normal thing I've seen in a while. But . . ."

"What?"

"I think you have enough now. And if you need more, just tell me. I'll go to Costco or something. Okay?"

She nodded and wiped her eyes, then took a deep breath and smiled. "It's better than talking in an English accent, right?"

I nodded. "Candy is fine by me." Then I picked up a bag and opened it, watching for her reaction. She didn't really seem to care. It was more about having some at her disposal.

So I poured a few into my hand and held them out. She made a face and simply watched as I ate them, then stuffed the bag back into the box along with all the others.

She closed the box and shoved it under her bed. Then she sat back on her heels and tilted her head as she looked at me. "You won't tell anyone, right?"

I rubbed the top of her head, messing up her hair. "Nope. Just between us." I stood up and held out my arms to her, then pulled her to her feet.

"Thanks."

I glanced around. "How have you kept anyone from seeing them? Doesn't Gram come and vacuum?"

Reese said, "I've been cleaning my own room."

Then I realized. "That's why you vacuum! Not to help out, but to keep people out of here."

She shrugged.

"You're too smart for your own good." I smiled and went out into the hallway, shutting the door behind me.

I'd been so worried about Reese. But it seemed like she'd found her own harmless, if slightly obsessive, way to deal with her leftover demons. I only wish the rest of us could be placated with several pounds of chocolate with a colorful candy shell.

CHAPTER NINETEEN

ALL DAY, I AVOIDED EDDY. EVEN THOUGH I WAS TRYING TO be mature about the whole thing, I had no idea how to approach him. If I went in there begging him to hang out with me, then I'd be exactly the person he had been trying to get away from. But if I went in there all cold and calculated, telling him to hang out with who he wanted to . . . that wouldn't work either.

What did I want?

It was easier to think about what I didn't.

And I didn't want to be left out. I didn't want to have to sit there, night after night, knowing my brother was out running around with some guy he barely knew, because that stranger was more fun that I was.

I wanted to be part of it, too. I wanted to be included.

And if that meant throwing aside my paranoia and fear and mistrust of the world, then I would suck it up and do it.

About ten o'clock that night I was watching television and realized I couldn't wait anymore. I turned off the television, not even aware of what had been on the past couple of hours. In stocking feet, I walked down to Eddy's room and knocked.

"Yeah, come in."

I pushed the door open. He was lying on his bed, an arm over his face, with only the bedside lamp for light. "Eddy?"

He didn't move. "I think I'm gonna puke."

"Maybe you caught whatever we all had."

"Yeah. Thanks." Then he jumped up and ran for the bathroom.

I heard him throw up. "Ugh." I walked over to the open door and stood beside it, not looking in. "Can I do anything?"

I heard him spit into the toilet and then flush it. "Get me a pillow. I think I'm sleeping in here tonight."

I grabbed a pillow from his bed and a light blanket off the end of his bed and carried them into the bathroom.

"Thanks." He took the pillow and put it on the floor, then lay down on the tile, knees up, and put his arm over his eyes. "Oh, God."

I set the blanket on the floor beside him. "Want me to stay?"

"No."

"Feel better." I shut the door and turned to go.

His room was getting chilly, and I noticed the glass door to the balcony was open. The sweatshirt he'd worn at dinner was slung over a chair, and I put it on, then turned off his light. I felt like I should stay for a little while, anyway, so I sunk down into the comfy chair by the balcony and stared out at the night sky, which I couldn't see for all the lights. I missed Hawaii, where I could see the stars every night. I hadn't seen the stars since we'd been back in Seattle.

I went to check on Eddy, but his breathing was slow and deep. Maybe he'd actually fallen asleep. I'd done the same thing when I had the stomach virus, slept on the floor of the bathroom all night.

I stepped back into his room, reluctant to leave. Being there reminded me of when we shared a room, whispered secrets in the dark before finally falling asleep.

Something skittered across the balcony. I stepped outside. A little rock hit my face. "Ow."

"Eddy?" A loud whisper came from below.

I leaned over the railing without saying anything.

Tony stepped out into the light and smiled up at me, waving. I knew I was in shadow, at least partial darkness, so he couldn't see my face, my reaction to him. Which was good, because I realized this was an opportunity. A chance to show I could relax about my fears and paranoia.

Better yet, it was a chance to see what Eddy did when he ran off with Tony.

"You coming or what?" he asked.

I hesitated only slightly, then waved back. "Yeah. Be right down."

I put on a pair of Eddy's Nikes, then went out into the

hallway. Everything seemed quiet as I made my way downstairs, but I took every corner slowly in case someone was still up. No one was.

Then I stopped.

Was that how Eddy snuck out? The front door?

I turned back toward his room. There were trellises next to all the balconies. Maybe . . .

I went back into Eddy's room and out to the balcony, pausing before I stepped outside. Could I pull it off? Make Tony think I was Eddy?

I pulled the hood up over my head and went outside.

Tony was standing down below, arms crossed, tapping a foot. "Did you take a dump or what?"

"Sorry." I reached out a hand and grabbed the metal trellis. It was firm and didn't move. I put one leg over the edge of the balcony, pulled myself over, and used it as a ladder, hoping the whole time it wouldn't break and send me falling to the concrete below.

When I was a few feet from the ground, I jumped.

"Cool," said Tony. "You should do that from now on instead of going out the front."

Seriously?

Tony grinned. "Ready?"

I forced myself to grin back. "Yeah."

He turned and jogged away from the front gate, over to the patch of trees at the edge of the property. I followed. When we got to the fence, he climbed up and over, then dropped to the ground on the other side. He turned and looked at me. "Need an invitation?"

I shook my head and reached up for a handhold. I stuck my toe in a gap in the fence and pulled myself up with my arms. Then I lifted one of my legs over and managed to get to the top. I jumped down beside Tony.

I was outside the fence. Unprotected. Or free. Depending on how you looked at it.

I was undecided.

Tony headed through the woods, obviously sure of where he was going. Unless I wanted to climb back over the fence, I had no choice but to follow him, trying not to trip over tree roots in the dark as I pretended I'd been there before. The woods ended fairly abruptly and we stepped out onto a deserted access road where a dark blue muscle car was parked.

My dad had never been into old cars, not even the nice ones. With him, it was always the latest, the newest, the most innovative.

And me? I knew nothing about old cars, but I could appreciate them. And this one was a beauty. I almost whistled, but caught myself. Maybe Eddy had seen this car before. If so, my acting like I'd never seen it before would be a dead giveaway.

"What do you think?" said Tony. He patted the hood as he walked around the front to the driver's side. "1969 Camaro."

Eddy hadn't seen it yet. So I whistled. "She's a beauty." I suspected the answer would be no, but still I asked, "Yours?"

Tony shook his head as he opened the door. "Neighbor's."

I opened the door on my side. The smell of leather rushed out at me as I sat down. "Your neighbor lets you drive it?" I shut the door, and the sound was solid.

Tony turned the key and the engine was loud. He revved it, making it even louder. "I wash it for him. One time he forgot he'd given me a key and gave me another. I kept one."

I turned and looked at him in the glow of the dashboard. "You took the car without asking?"

He shook his head. "He's out of town. He'll never know."

I knew that I should get out of the car. I should get out of the car, climb back over the fence, and go to bed. I knew that I should.

Instead, I buckled my seat belt as Tony pulled out onto the access road, which soon hit the main road. He braked at the stop sign, gunned the engine, and we flew out onto the road, heading for the bridge.

He turned on the stereo, and Iron Maiden soon drowned out the revving engine. I rolled down my window and stuck my head out, letting the wind rush at my face.

I was in a speeding car, possibly stolen, with a kid I hardly knew, no bodyguard in sight. I hadn't even grabbed my cell phone when I left.

I was on my own. Possibly heading into harm's way.

Remember, you're Eddy.

What would Eddy do? Eddy, who didn't have my hang-ups, wasn't afraid of everyone in the world?

I grinned. And then I whooped out the window, as loud as I could, as we flew all the way over the bridge.

Tony slapped the steering wheel and laughed at me.

After a second, I laughed, too.

I realized that if I wasn't so jealous of Tony, I would like to have him as a friend. Eddy certainly did. And, for the moment at least, Eddy was who I was.

I settled back into the seat, ready for the night to begin.

CHAPTER TWENTY

THE TRAFFIC WAS LIGHT AT THAT TIME OF NIGHT. I NOTICED Tony stayed just at the speed limit or barely above, apparently not wanting to attract any unwanted attention. I suppose anyone could drive like that, but it made me wonder how sure he was about his neighbor not noticing the car was gone. For whatever reason, I was glad he wasn't speeding or driving crazy. It was the first time I'd been in a car driven by someone other than my dad or one of our staff.

Maybe it was due to me trying to think like Eddy, but instead of being worried or stressed about it, I felt excited. *Free.*

After about a half hour of driving, I recognized where we were. My heart started to pound as we turned onto the street where our mansion was. Our old house. The high walls of our security fence loomed in the dark, lit up like a 7-Eleven. Had Eddy brought Tony here before?

Obviously.

Tony slowed and pulled over to the side, in front of another walled-in residence. He unbuckled his seat belt and started to get out, then stopped and looked at me. "You coming?"

I nodded. "Yeah."

He said, "I figured it's better to park down here, instead of right in front." He quietly shut his door.

I hesitated before unbuckling my seat belt, then got out and shut my door, letting him lead the way.

My heart was pounding even harder. I didn't know whether there were security guards or not. Even if there weren't, the alarms had to be on and I didn't have a code for them.

When we'd gotten back to Seattle, we hadn't even left the house. And then we'd moved and there'd been no reason for me to learn the security codes.

We headed down the sidewalk. It had started to drizzle, so we stayed under the trees, partially to stay dry but also to stay a bit hidden from anyone who might be looking out.

"The street's so empty," I said, my voice loud in the quiet night.

"It *is* night."

I didn't reply. I'd been talking about the last time I had been there, all the chaos with the news trucks and satellite dishes. But apparently, Eddy had been there since then. I needed to start being way more careful about what I said if I wanted him to think I was my brother.

We reached the front gate.

There was a black box.

Tony looked at me and raised his eyebrows. When I didn't do anything, he said, "Cool, my turn at last." He flipped up the cover, punched in a code, and the gate slowly opened.

My knees threatened to buckle.

Eddy had given him the code? How many times had they been there?

"Hurry up," he said, as the thing seemed to take forever. As soon as the gate opened wide enough, he slipped inside and I followed. The guard building was dark and empty. Why weren't there any guards?

Once we were both inside, Tony went to the black box on the inside of the gate and punched the code to close it.

There we were, in the courtyard.

All was quiet.

I let out a breath I didn't realize I'd been holding.

Despite all the lights being on outside, the house was dark. Lonely. I didn't want to go in. I didn't want to be there without the rest of my family, because it wouldn't be home. At least, I didn't want to walk in there and realize it by myself.

Tony said, "I still can't believe you got away with that."

"With what?"

He pointed at the empty guard building. "Messing up their schedule, so nobody was on tonight. Don't you think they'll catch on eventually?"

I shrugged, but didn't say anything. Again, I wondered just how many times Eddy had been here like this.

With confidence, Tony began striding like he knew exactly where he was headed. Like he'd been here a thousand times before.

I jogged to catch up with him.

We walked across the courtyard and circle drive, then hit the cobblestone walkway that led to the backyard. The lights in the backyard were off, but the pool lights were on, revealing the steam coming off the surface.

But Tony kept going, toward the area I'd only seen from my window, the new addition that seemed made all of concrete.

And I froze when I saw what it was.

A skateboard park. With ramps and tunnels. Everything a skateboarder would want.

My face got hot and my stomach clenched.

When I had been stuck underground—*when my whole family had been stuck underground*—my brother had gotten his own skateboard park in the backyard. When? Before he and Gram went to Hawaii? When they came back to Seattle now and then?

I tried to reason it out, tried to stop being angry.

Eddy had no idea we were still alive. Maybe the skateboard park had been something to make a grieving boy try to get his mind off the loss of his entire family.

I took a deep breath.

Tony said, "This is so sick. I still can't believe you had this in your backyard."

"Yeah," I said, feeling a bit sick myself. I couldn't

skateboard. Well, other than the sad little skills I'd had when I was eight. Which were nowhere close to what Eddy could do on a skateboard. And there was no way I'd be able to convince anyone that I was my twin.

The rain continued to fall as I stood there, motionless.

Tony turned back to me. "Do you really want to do this?"

"Huh?" I asked. Did he know? Was he messing with me?

Tony jerked a thumb over in the direction of the pool. "That thing is heated, right?"

I nodded, unable to breathe, wondering if I was about to dodge one serious bullet.

Tony unzipped his sweatshirt, dropped it on the ground, then peeled his shirt off and tossed that aside, too. He unbuckled his jeans and took them off, standing there in boxers. He grinned. "Last one in's a douche bag." He shoved his boxers to his ankles, stepped out of them, and sprinted to the pool, where he dove into the water, surfacing a moment later. He yelled, "You coming?"

Relieved to not have to showcase my nonexistent skills on a skateboard, I scooped up all his clothes and jogged over to the pool. The drizzle on my face was chilly, and the warm water looked so inviting that I couldn't resist. I tossed Tony's clothes under a table, out of the rain. Then I stripped, threw my clothes under there, too, and dove in, staying under until I couldn't breathe.

I surfaced and gasped. Then I whooped.

Heaven.

With our bodies in the warm water and the cool drizzle hitting our faces, we swam around for a while. Finally, I just floated on my back, looking up at the sky. The rain clouds finally cleared a bit, revealing patches of a few, bright stars. As I lay there, suspended in the warm water, I couldn't hear anything, only see.

How many times had I floated in this pool? Hundreds?

I'm not sure I'd ever felt peace like I felt that moment. Nothing mattered.

It didn't matter what Eddy had done when we were gone or what he was going to do now. We'd made it out. We'd made it back. It was going to be okay. It was. I would figure out whatever I needed to figure out.

Something tugged at my foot and I stood up in the pool. Tony was standing there, a weird look on his face.

"What?"

He pointed toward the front gate, in the direction we'd walked up the street. The glow of flashing red and blue lights was visible. He said, "I think we need to go."

We quickly got out.

Dripping wet, I went to the pool house, relieved to find a stack of towels. I grabbed two for myself, two for him, and we dried ourselves off and got dressed. I draped the towels over one of the lawn chairs, wondering what the security staff would think the next time they checked.

We went to the front gate and Tony punched in the code. We slipped out the gate and he closed it, then we stood in the shadows. A police car was parked next to the Camaro, lights flashing as the officer stood there talking on his radio.

Tony swore under his breath.

"What?" I asked.

"I can't deal with the cops right now."

My mouth dropped open. "You stole the car." I wasn't asking.

Tony looked at me and rolled his eyes. "No, I didn't. It's just . . ."

"What?"

"It's complicated." He sighed. "Trust me. We do not want to walk over there right now. We need to go." He grabbed my sleeve and yanked, pulling me up the street the opposite way. We moved slowly, trying to stay in the shadows of the trees until we reached the first corner. As soon as we turned it, we sprinted, racing down the street.

"Where are we going?" I said, breathing hard as we ran.

"We need a bus." Tony turned and ran down the street to the left and I followed.

We went several more blocks before we hit a street with a bus stop. We stood inside the shelter, doubled over from the sprinting, and just panted for a moment. I asked, "Can I get back home on the bus?"

He nodded. "Yeah. We may have to switch a few times, though." He looked at me. "I'll get you there, don't worry."

A bus showed up a short time later, and Tony paid for both of us. Good thing, because I had no money with me. We were the only ones on that bus. We had just gotten off it to wait for a connecting bus when Tony's phone rang. He glanced at the screen and held up a finger. "Be right back." He stepped away for a minute and I heard him say, "Yeah, boss." He listened for a moment and then said, "Part of the plan. I'll get everything back where it belongs."

His tone was low and I couldn't really hear anything else. Boss? Maybe that car had been stolen and he was supposed to deliver it. Or maybe there were drugs in the trunk. My heart began to pound. Maybe my gut feeling had been right about him. I was glad Eddy wasn't with him . . . But Eddy *was* with him. At least, Tony thought I was Eddy.

Maybe, for Eddy's sake, I should end it. Their friendship. Pick a fight so Tony would never show up at the house again.

Tony hung up and came back over to the bus stop.

"Who was that?" I asked.

"Just this guy I do stuff for. He doesn't always agree with how I get things done." He shrugged.

"Oh," I said. Could I do it? End their friendship right then and there?

But Eddy would wonder why Tony didn't call. And he'd end up calling and then figure it all out. He'd end up being mad at me. Not a chance I wanted to take. Plus, as much as I didn't want to admit it, Tony was fun.

And I could picture the three of us hanging out. So I asked, "Illegal stuff?"

Tony laughed. He laughed so hard he bent over and put his hands on his knees to catch his breath. "Oh, my God."

"What's so funny?" I asked,

He stood back up, still chuckling. "It may be slightly outside the law of certain things, but no. Not illegal."

"I have no idea what that means." I laughed. "I don't think I want to know."

He smiled. "Probably a good idea." A bus pulled onto the street and came toward us. He pointed. "That one will get us back to Mercer."

I said, "You don't have to go with me. I can do it."

He shook his head. "No. I'd probably stay up all night wondering if you made it or not."

I frowned. "No, you wouldn't."

"No, I probably wouldn't." He laughed and smacked me on the arm with the back of his hand. "It sounded sincere, though, didn't it?"

I laughed and shoved him. "Yeah, it did."

The bus squeaked to a stop and Tony handed me some money.

"Thanks. I'll pay you back next time you come over."

He said, "I know you will."

I stepped on the bus and lifted a hand. "See ya."

"Later, Eli."

The door shut behind me.

Eli.

I turned back around. Through the clear doors of the bus, I saw Tony standing there, hands in his pockets, a smirk on his face. He lifted one hand to me as the bus pulled away.

I sunk down into a seat, still looking back at him.

Did Tony know it was me the whole time? I wondered what gave me away. And I wondered what I was going to tell Eddy when he found out.

CHAPTER TWENTY-ONE

I HAD QUITE A JOG FROM WHERE THE BUS LEFT ME OFF, SO by the time I climbed over the fence and snuck back into the house, I was wiped out. I managed to make it into the house and up to my room without anyone knowing I'd left. At least, I thought so.

When I woke in the morning, sun was streaming in my window and my clock read ten after ten. I quickly threw on some sweats and grabbed Eddy's hoodie and shoes I'd worn the night before. He wasn't in his room, luckily, and I threw them in his closet. He tended to be a bit messy, so he probably wouldn't notice. I wondered whether Tony would tell him about our outing.

Maybe he already had.

I heard the little kids yelling and laughing in the playroom, but I passed by and headed for the kitchen. Eddy and Lexie were both there, eating strawberries. I told Eddy, "You look better."

He said, "I feel better."

I poured myself a cup of coffee.

Lexie looked at me. "You slept late."

I shrugged. "Stayed up late reading."

Gram came in with a stack of mail, which she set on the counter. "For no one knowing where we live, we sure get a lot of junk mail."

I pulled the stack toward me and started leafing through one at a time. Every envelope and catalog was addressed to Gram, or at least Gram's real first name and her grandmother's maiden name.

"Junk." I tossed an envelope aside. "Junk." I tossed that one at Eddy's face. "Junk." I threw that one up in the air and it landed on the floor.

Gram narrowed her eyes at me. "Recycle those when you're finished picking them up." She left.

I was just about to toss the next envelope in the air when I saw the name *Yanakakis* on the front. I looked closer. Alexandra Yanakakis. I glanced at the return address. The information about Lexie's birth parents.

Eddy and Lexie had begun to argue about whether the little kids would enjoy going to a mall, so they didn't see me slip that envelope into my lap as I kept sorting the rest.

Eddy stood up and put the empty strawberry bowl by the sink. "Want to shoot some hoops?"

Happy for the invite, I nodded, probably a little too enthusiastically. "Yeah, after I eat something. I'll meet you out there."

"Cool." He went upstairs.

I lifted the envelope out of my lap. "Lex. It came."

"What came?"

I handed it to her. Her eyes widened as she read the return address. "This is it?"

I nodded. "Want me to open it?"

She shook her head. "No. I don't know if I'm ready."

"Okay. I'm here if you need me."

A corner of her mouth turned up. "I know. Thanks." Lexie stood. "I'm gonna go up to my room and open it." She lifted the envelope higher and squinted at it. "Maybe."

I put on some sneakers and went to join Eddy outside. We played one-on-one for a while, until we were both sweating and panting, and needed water. Back in the kitchen, Mom was talking to someone on the phone. She must have just been exercising because her face was red, her temples were sweaty, and her T-shirt was damp. "They're my properties to do with as I want. It's not the company's decision."

Eddy got two glasses out of the cupboard and handed one to me. I filled it with the sprayer in the sink and handed it to him. I'd just started to fill up the other one when Mom finally noticed us. She told the person on the other end, "We'll discuss this later." She hung up and smiled at us. "How was your game?"

"I won," I said.

Eddy smacked me in the chest. "Did not."

"Really?" I aimed the sprayer at him.

He held up a palm at me. "You wouldn't dare."

I sprayed at him, just enough to get his shirt a bit wet.

"You did not just do that." He stepped toward me and I sprayed him more, laughing as he tried to get the sprayer from me.

"Boys!" Mom looked like she was trying not to laugh as she admonished us. "Els will have a fit if you get the kitchen all wet."

"Sorry," I said. Then I spritzed her in the face. "Oops."

She sputtered and blinked, then started to laugh. "Eli!" She widened her eyes at Eddy. "Are you going to let him get away with that?"

Eddy grabbed my arm and tried to twist the sprayer around at my face. I was laughing so hard I couldn't hold on to it, and he turned it on, soaking my shirt. I yelled, "Mom! Help!"

"Eddy!" she said. "Give me the stupid thing."

Eddy handed it to her.

"This is ridiculous." Then, laughing, she took aim and let both of us have it full blast, as we yelled and tried to block the spray with our hands.

"Clea!" Gram stepped in the kitchen.

Mom stopped spraying and let her arm drop to her side.

"The floor is soaked." Gram crossed her arms and glared at all of us.

Mom pointed at us. "They started it."

Eddy and I looked at each other and grinned. "Right, Mom," he said. "Gram? Did you see either of us with the sprayer?"

Gram didn't look like she was going to believe anything that any of us had to say. "All I know is you'd better get this place dried before Els sees it."

Mom laughed as she put the sprayer back in the sink. She told us, "Get some towels. I'll help you clean up."

I said, "That's the least you can do since you started it."

She rolled her eyes at me.

Eddy came back with a stack of towels and the three of us got down on our hands and knees and started wiping up the water. Eddy stopped and looked at me. "That was fun. Like old times."

"Yeah." I grinned, glad that he noticed I could still be fun.

When we'd finished, Eddy took the towels to the laundry room. Mom was making some tea, so I asked her, "Who was on the phone?"

She said, "I want to sell the Colorado house."

Eddy had just returned. "Why?"

She didn't look at either of us. "I don't think we need all our properties. It's too hard for all of us to go anywhere. I think we should sell and think about getting new ones that no one knows about."

I guess I understood that logic. Fresh start and all. But still. "I'd like to see the Colorado house before you sell it. I mean, it's been so long."

Eddy said, "Me too."

Mom said, "It's so hard to travel with all the kids right now. I don't think I could deal with it."

Eddy looked at me. "What if just Eli and I went?"

Mom started to shake her head, but I said, "Yeah, why not? There's staff there, right?" Staff paid nearly as well to be discreet as they were to be efficient caretakers.

Mom nodded.

"And we can take the jet," added Eddy. "It's not like we're unsupervised at any point."

Mom stopped wiping and sat back on her heels, looking at the two of us.

"Please, Mom? Since we're not doing school yet?"

She scratched her head. "I don't know. What if—"

"What if what?" asked Eddy. "No one can get into the place when we're there." He looked at me. "We'll just go for a couple days, right?"

I nodded. "Yeah. Just to see the place again."

Mom sighed. "I suppose."

Eddy grinned.

I went upstairs to get out of my wet clothes and shower. As I headed toward my room, I walked past Lexie's. And I heard her crying.

I knocked. "Lex?"

"Go away." Her voice was muffled.

I twisted the knob and it turned, so I pushed open the door.

"I said go away!" Lexie was on her bed, clutching a pillow, her face and eyes red. "I don't want to talk."

I shut the door and stepped inside. "What's wrong?"

She shook her head and dropped her face into her pillow, sobbing.

I went and sat beside her, then set my hand on her back. She knew it was a long shot, which might not work. Softly, I said, "Hey. We'll find your birth parents some other way."

She croaked out a no, then pointed at her desk.

I went and sat in her swivel chair. Her computer was on, and a balled-up piece of paper lay near the keyboard. I opened it and smoothed it out until I could read the letter from the state adoption offices. I scanned it until I found what I needed. Lexie's birth mother's first name and occupation.

The first name was Laudine. "That's unique," I said. "We should be able to find her. What does she—" My gaze went to the next line. The one where the occupation was listed. The line held one word:

Inmate.

CHAPTER TWENTY-TWO

My intake of breath was so quick it almost sounded like a whistle. I whispered, "Seriously? She's in jail?"

Lexie was still crying into her pillow, so I turned to the computer and jiggled the mouse enough to wake up the screen. The Washington State Department of Corrections website popped up, along with the heading **Find an Offender**. The search results consisted of a listing of prisoners with the last name of Cobb. There were a few men with that last name, but no women. And no one named Laudine.

Had she been released? Is that why Lexie was upset?

I clicked on the next window. It was a death notice. Three years before, Laudine Cobb had developed an infection and died in prison. I leaned back in the chair. But then I noticed several other windows open, so I clicked on one of them. Yahoo search engine, with the search results from the words *Washington+* inmate+ Laudine.

Hundreds of entries came up. One that Lexie had clicked on was from the local NBC affiliate with the head-line CROWD ATTENDS LAUDINE COBB SENTENCING. I scanned the news article from over eighteen years before.

"Convicted murderer Laudine Cobb, 29, was sentenced to life in prison plus 65 years for the murder of her two children."

I gasped and looked over at Lexie. That was why she was upset. Not that Laudine Cobb was dead, but that she'd been . . . a murderer.

I kept reading.

One rainy night, Laudine Cobb called 911, said some-one had broken into their house, shot her in the leg and shot her two children, both of whom died on the way to the hospital. Her tearful pleas from her hospital bed, to find whoever was responsible, made the national news. Prosecutors spent months checking her story and finally found enough evidence to convict her of the crime. She had shot herself in the leg to solidify her story. I checked the dates.

I said to Lexie, "Are you sure this is her? She was in prison when you were born."

Lexie rolled off the bed, and came over to me. Her eyes and face were red, glistening with tears. There were other windows open and she clicked on one of them. The article, dated several months after the first, was short. The first line read: "Under heavy security, convicted murderer Laudine Cobb gave birth at St. John's Hospital in Gig Harbor."

I stopped reading and glanced back at the date. Lexie's birthday.

Lexie said, "She was pregnant with me when she went in. Father unknown."

I grasped her arm. "You don't know this is her. You don't know this is your birth mother."

Lexie asked, "Did you see the photo yet?"

I shook my head.

She reached down and moved the mouse, clicking on another window. There was a posed photograph of a woman and two children. It was small, so I leaned in to look more closely.

The woman had bleached blond hair. She was pretty. Not as pretty as Lexie, but she looked a lot like her. Enough to be her mother?

Most definitely.

Lexie sighed. "Still think it's a coincidence?" She sunk down onto the carpet beside the chair.

"This doesn't mean anything." I said.

She narrowed her eyes at me. "Doesn't mean anything? My birth mother was a murderer! How does that not mean anything?"

"No one has to know," I said. "No one *does* know."

Her face crumpled and she started to cry again. "Did Mom and Dad know? Did they know they had a murderer's baby?"

I slid off the chair and sat next to her on the floor,

putting my arm around her shoulders. She leaned into me. "Did they know?"

I said, "You heard Mom go on and on about that night. About the next year, waiting until the adoption went through. They had a baby. An innocent baby."

Lexie sat up. "What if I'm not innocent?" She pointed to the computer. "I looked it up. She was psychotic. She was narcissistic and histrionic. I looked those up. Psychopathy can be inherited."

"No." I shook my head. "You're not any of those."

With the back of a hand, she wiped tears off her face. "Really? She was egocentric. Antisocial. Manipulative. You don't think I'm any of those?"

I swallowed, realizing I had to tread carefully so I didn't make her more upset. "You can be those without being psychotic! Little kids can be manipulative, for God's sake."

"So you think I am those things."

Oh crap. "No, Lex. I didn't—"

"Like mother, like daughter," she said. "Isn't that how it goes?"

I pointed down. "Your mother, your real mother, the mother that raised you, is sitting downstairs right now, taking care of her children. You should be glad to be like her."

"She's not my biological mom."

"Lex! Your birth mother has had nothing to do with you your entire life. She has had no influence, no impact.

All she did was give birth to you. And she's gone. You are not her and you never will be." I tightened my arm around her.

She breathed in and shuddered, then set her face against my chest. "I can't, Eli."

"Can't what?" I asked.

She sighed, the sound shaky and ragged. "I can't be from a monster. I just can't."

I didn't know what else to say, so I just sat there while she cried.

Someone knocked on the door.

"Go away!" said Lexie.

The closed door muffled Eddy's voice. "I'm looking for Eli."

I told Lexie, "It's fine." Then I said more loudly, "Come in."

Eddy walked in. As soon as he saw us, he frowned. "What happened?"

"Nothing," snapped Lexie. "It's none of your business."

But Eddy didn't retreat as I expected him to. He closed the door, then walked over to us and stood there. "What's going on?"

Lexie looked at me and shook her head. But I wondered if this was the moment that I could stop being their intermediary, stop being the buffer between them. If Eddy was the person I thought he was, then he *was* capable of being a brother to Lexie, just as much as I was.

I would give him this one chance.

The letter from the state was sitting above me, on the desk. I reached up and grabbed it, then, praying I wasn't making a huge mistake, I held it out to Eddy. "Lexie found her biological mother."

CHAPTER TWENTY-THREE

EDDY'S EYES NARROWED, BUT BEFORE HE SAID ANYTHING, he read the letter. His eyes widened. Lexie was staring him down and he met her gaze. "I'm sorry. I mean, I didn't know how you wanted this to work out, but . . ." He shook the paper a little. "I doubt this was it."

He sat down beside us and put a hand on Lexie's arm. "I am sorry."

Lexie asked, "You're not gonna tell Mom?"

He shook his head.

"There's more," I said. I tilted my head toward the computer, but Eddy didn't stand. Instead, he looked at Lexie. "Do you want me to know what it is?"

Lexie studied him for a moment. Maybe she was deciding if she could trust him. "Go ahead. It won't change anything."

Eddy sat in the office chair and started reading all the stuff I'd just read. He didn't say anything, but after a bit, he blew out a breath loud enough that we could hear it. "Wow." He twirled around to face us. "That's crazy."

Lexie shook her head. "No. She's crazy. Was crazy. And now *I'm* crazy."

"Lex." I put an arm around her. "You're wrong." I looked up at Eddy.

Eddy said, "Are you serious? Other than some shared DNA, you have nothing in common with this woman. You are not her."

Lexie sniffled. "How do I know that for sure?"

Eddy scratched his head. "Because you're you. We're your family, not her. The people downstairs are your family." He pointed at the computer. "She had absolutely nothing to do with who you are."

"But it's obvious you hate who I am," said Lexie.

Eddy's mouth dropped open a little, and then closed. He looked as if he'd been caught at something. "No . . . no, that's not it."

"You always pick fights with me. It's like you can't stand to be in the same room with me." Her gaze went from him back to me. "Before we went in the Compound, neither one of you could stand me." She waggled a finger between me and her. "*We* only started getting along when we thought our lives depended on it."

In a low voice I said, "Our lives did depend upon it."

"Seriously?" She tilted her head at me. "So if that hadn't happened, we—"

"No." I held up a hand to get her to stop. "That's not what I'm saying." I sighed. "I'm glad you're my sister, honestly." I looked up at Eddy. "I just need the two of you to figure it out. Because I need to have both of you in my life. But more than that . . . I need you both to *want* to be there." I didn't look at Eddy when I said that, but he shifted uncomfortably in his chair.

None of us said anything for a few minutes, and then Eddy cleared his throat. "I'm sorry. Really. It's been an adjustment having you all back."

Lexie snorted. "Wow, excuse us for not being dead."

Eddy covered his face with his hands and groaned. "God." He dropped his hands. "I didn't mean it like that. I spent so long thinking you were all gone forever. And it took a long time for me to figure out how to go on without all of you. A long time. And when it seemed like it would be okay, that I could go on . . . it all turned out to be a lie. And, except for Dad, you were all back and my life changed again." Before we could say anything, he quickly added, "For the better. I have my family back." He paused. "It's just . . . taking me a little while to figure out my place again. I was the only one of us left. And I got used to that. And now . . . I find myself having to go back to being a younger brother and an older brother"— his eyes met mine—"and a twin."

Lexie shrugged. "You're probably looking in the wrong place for sympathy."

Eddy said, "I don't want your sympathy. I want things the way they were. Before."

I said, "How do you expect that to happen?"

Lexie rolled her eyes. "You don't think we all want that?"

Eddy practically yelled, "Then do it! For God's sake, stop dwelling on the past six years. I'm *sorry* about what happened! I'm *sorry* Dad did that to you! But . . . when are you gonna get over it and live life again? Be like you used to be?" He looked at Lexie. "Maybe I can't stand to be in the same room with you because all you do is walk around looking sad. God, Lex, maybe I pick fights with you because when you fight back I actually get to see who you used to be. It's the only time you seem to forget about being sad and actually act like there's still life in you."

Lexie didn't say anything.

Then Eddy looked at me. "And you. You're like someone who's afraid of life. You don't want to go out because someone might be trying to get pictures of us or ask what it was like." He held his arms out to the sides. "Welcome to the frickin' world of the Internet! Everybody wants to know what everybody else is doing. So what if someone takes our pictures and posts them on the Internet? Maybe they'll say some nasty crap, but they can't really hurt us. They can't change our family. They can't take away everything we have. All we have to do is ignore them, and then someone else will come along and they'll forget about us." He paused. "Eli, it's so hard to be with you because you don't want to do anything if it means leaving the grounds of this house. You're getting to be like Mom. How long do we have to hide out here? How long do we have to wait to be normal again?"

Stunned, all I could do was sit there. Then I said what I was thinking. "Is that why you sneak out with Tony?"

Lexie's brow furrowed. "You've been sneaking out?"

Eddy asked me, "How do you know?"

"I saw you. The night of Quinn's birthday party, I saw you guys go over the fence." I left out the part about listening to him and Tony talk about me. Given that he'd basically just repeated everything he'd said that night, I didn't see the point.

Eddy leaned his head back and looked up at the ceiling for a moment, and then he dropped his head back down. He averted his eyes. "Yeah. I just want to get out and have fun." He shrugged.

Lexie said, "I don't want to sit around and be sad."

I glanced at Eddy. "I don't want to hide here forever." I didn't. It just seemed . . . easier. And safer. But maybe it was time to stop playing things safe. Maybe it was time to *live*. Get back to normal. Whatever normal was.

CHAPTER TWENTY-FOUR

I GOT TO MY FEET.

"Where you going?" Eddy asked.

"Bathroom. I'll be right back." I started to leave, then turned back and told Eddy, "I think we should invite Lexie to go with us."

"Where?" asked Lexie.

Eddy slowly began to nod. "Yeah."

"The Colorado house," I said.

"Why are you going there? Does Mom know?" Lexie asked.

"Yeah." I nodded. "She's good with it. And it's just a visit." I didn't think it would help anything to tell her Mom was thinking about selling it.

Lexie said, "I'll go." She glanced at Eddy. "Wait. Are you sure you want me to go?"

"Yes," he said. "Maybe . . ."

"Maybe what?" I asked.

He offered up a half smile. "Maybe it'll help us get a fresh start. The three of us, I mean."

Lexie's eyes were still red from crying, but she smiled, too.

Eddy said, "Let's go tomorrow."

I frowned. That was when I was meeting up with Verity. But as I looked at my brother and sister, I knew I had to put them first. There was no way I could think about letting in someone else, starting a new relationship, until I had fixed the ones I already had.

I went to my room and picked up my phone.

Verity answered on the first ring. "Hey, EJ."

I wanted so much to tell her that wasn't my name. I wanted to spit out who I truly was, and everything else she needed to know. But I didn't. "Hi."

She said, "I'm really looking forward to tomorrow."

"Yeah, me too, um . . ." I took a deep breath. "Listen, that's why I called. I can't make it and—"

"Why am I not surprised?" She sighed. "Why did you even bother to set it up if you knew you weren't gonna make it?"

"But I planned to! Something just came up and I can't."

"What is it this time? Another paper? Something with your family?"

"You don't understand."

"No, I guess I don't. Care to fill me in?"

Filling her in would mean *letting* her in. And even though I thought I had been ready, I knew I wasn't. Especially after talking with Eddy and Lexie. Even though

Eddy had let Tony in without telling us, I felt like I owed it to my brother and sister to be in on the decision to tell Verity everything. Because it wasn't just me anymore. It wasn't that simple. So I said, "I will. I promise. Just not now." That sounded so lame.

"Oh, okay. Let me clear my schedule and we'll set a date for you to let me know all your deep dark secrets. How about that?" Her voice had a rough edge to it, and had gotten louder as she went on.

I couldn't blame her for being mad. Why would she even waste time on me? "I'm sorry."

"Yeah. Okay. Me too." The click of her disconnecting was loud in my ear. I just sat there, wondering if I should call her back. And I did. The call went straight to voice mail.

I didn't want to face Eddy and Lexie right away, so I turned on the television to something mindless for a while, and ended up dozing off. It was daylight when I woke up.

I went into Eddy's room. He was in the shower, so I stared out the window until he came out with a towel around his waist.

"Hey," he said. "You never came back last night."

"I fell asleep," I said. "I just wanted to check and make sure you were okay with Lexie going. I know I kind of made it so you couldn't exactly say no . . ."

"Yeah, I am."

Was he being honest? "Really?"

Eddy sat down on the edge of his bed. "I know I haven't been the best brother since you guys came back.

Especially not to her. But when you showed me that stuff about her birth mother . . ." He trailed off.

"That was pretty bad."

He nodded.

I said, "Even though she wouldn't admit it in a million years, she needs us."

Eddy said, "I do want to be there for her. I want her to know I'm her brother, too."

"Cool." I smiled. "I had one other idea."

His eyebrows raised.

"You should ask Tony."

"To go with us?"

"Yeah. I think he would be a good distraction for Lexie."

He frowned. "I thought you didn't like him?"

"I was jealous that you seemed to have more fun with him than me."

Eddy started to say something, but I stopped him. "And that's fine. I haven't been very fun. But I'm really gonna try to get back to normal. And I think this trip would be really fun with the four of us."

"Okay," said Eddy. "But what about Mom? She barely went along with Tony going to the baseball game with us."

"She won't be at the jet when we leave. She won't ever have to know."

Eddy grinned. "You are *bad*. Okay, I'll call him."

Eddy picked up his cell phone. "I'll call YK first, make sure the jet is ready."

"I'd better pack." I went back to my room and threw

on some jeans and a black T-shirt, then quickly packed a bag. My phone beeped. A text from Eddy. We'd be leaving at twelve thirty. And Tony would be there.

My phone beeped again. The battery was low, so I opened my drawer to pull out the charger. The cord was tangled with something else that dropped on the floor. I leaned over to pick it up.

Phil's flash drive.

I had time, so I inserted the flash drive into the computer and went down the list of files.

Hadn't I seen it all before? I wasn't looking for anything in particular. I just felt like looking. Then I noticed one of the files was named Barkley.

Dr. Barkley from the Progeria Institute?

The last time I looked at the file, the name would have meant nothing to me, because it was before I visited the Progeria Institute. The thought of which reminded me of Verity.

My heart beat faster. Would she ever speak to me again? Probably not.

I clicked on the file. A bunch of lab reports popped up, all with *PDL Project* at the top of them. I didn't really understand any of them, but I wanted to. I wanted to know what the PDL Project was. I looked up Dr. Barkley's number and called.

A woman answered.

"Hello," I said. "This is EJ Smith for Dr. Barkley. I'm with the YK internship program."

"Is he expecting your call?" she asked, not unkindly.

"No," I admitted. "I just had a couple of questions."

"Of course," she said. "I'm sorry he's not available right at this moment, but he should be able to return your call sometime before noon. Will that work for you?"

That would be cutting it close, with the jet leaving at twelve thirty. "Sure," I said. "Have him call my cell." I gave her the number, thanked her, and hung up.

I went to close my drawer, but saw the printout I'd made the day of Phil's disappearance. I started to read.

Philip A. Whitaker . . .

Philip A. What did the *A* stand for?

There was a knock on my door and Lexie opened it and walked in, wearing jeans and a white blouse with black ballet shoes. Her hair was back in a precise ponytail and she wore makeup. "So we're really going?"

"You look nice," I said.

She started to scowl, thinking I was messing with her, but then she smiled a little as she realized I was serious. "You think?"

I nodded. "And, yep, we're going." I put the paper back in the drawer and shut it.

"Why did you ask me to go?"

I shrugged. "It seemed like it would be fun."

She rolled her eyes. "Since when do you and Eddy think I'm fun?"

"Since . . . you're turning over a new leaf and you're going to start being fun?"

She laughed. "When did you become an optimist?"

I smiled.

She said, "I thought it had something to do with what I found out. About my birth mother. I thought you were doing it because you felt sorry for me."

I shook my head. "I think we can all use a getaway."

"A *getaway*." Lexie seemed amused with the word. "Yeah, maybe a getaway is exactly what I can use."

"Having some fun might get your mind off it."

Lexie slumped against the door. "It doesn't change the fact that I'm the product of a monster."

"Lex, come on." I stood up and went over to her. "You've got to stop saying that. That woman only gave you life. Nothing else."

"I keep telling myself that, but it doesn't sound any better when you say it." She let out a deep breath, just as Eddy showed up. He put a hand on her shoulder. "You packed?"

"Almost," she said. "I'll go finish."

As soon as she left, Eddy closed the door. "Here's the plan. Tony is meeting us outside the airfield. We'll pick him up as we get there. But Lee is out there with the SUV and I don't think he'd keep that a secret from Mom. So you need to stay here and come a little later, with Lexie. I'll go now. I already called another driver from YK."

My phone beeped again, signaling the low battery. "Oh crap." I'd gotten so involved in the flash drive that I still hadn't charged my phone. And I didn't want to miss Dr. Barkley's call. "I have to charge this up anyway."

"Cool. So we'll see you there?" Eddy glanced at his watch.

"Yep." He left. I was glad, because when Barkley called

back, I wanted to take that call in private. I didn't feel like answering a bunch of questions, which I knew would be inevitable when Eddy heard me asking Dr. Barkley about his research.

I was glad Eddy and Lexie were getting along. Despite Eddy blaming it on his own feelings, I knew the rift between them was mainly my fault. Lex and I were a lot closer than we'd ever been before we went in the Compound. Back then, she had been more of an enemy than a sister to the both of us. I could totally see how it was probably hard for Eddy to see such a change and not be part of it. So it was a relief to see him be completely different overnight, making an effort to get along.

I plugged my phone in. While I waited for it to charge all the way, I remembered the hot tub at the Colorado house and added swim shorts to my bag. At eleven thirty, I knew I couldn't wait any longer to leave. I had just unplugged the phone from the charger when it rang.

I answered.

Dr. Barkley sounded very happy to hear from me. "YK has renewed the funding! I don't know how much you had to do with that, but I wanted to thank you." He rattled on a bit more.

Finally, I managed to get a word in.

"Dr. Barkley, I wanted to ask you a few questions."

"Of course, anything."

"I have a question about the fire? The one that destroyed your research?"

He sounded a bit deflated. "Yes?"

I said, "You said you'd figured out what turned on aging."

"We'd isolated the compounds that caused aging, yes."

I wasn't sure what I needed to ask, so I just kept going. "And you said that could lead to a potential cure for progeria?"

"Yes," he said. "Which is why it was so magnificent that Mr. Yanakakis came through so quickly to provide the funds to start over. He was such a great man. It's a shame you'll never have the chance to meet him."

I stifled a groan. I really wanted him to stop talking about my dad and the stupid funding. "Dr. Barkley. Could that discovery, the isolation of those compounds, have had any other . . . ramifications? Besides a cure?" I needed to know what else that discovery could have meant. What interest my dad might have had in it.

Dr. Barkley chuckled a bit. "Well, I suppose that . . ." He trailed off.

"Dr. Barkley? Were there other ramifications?"

"In the right hands."

"What?" I asked. "*In the right hands . . . what?*"

He breathed loudly into the phone. "In the right hands . . . that discovery could have led to the fountain of youth."

My hand tightened on the phone. Holy crap. So that discovery was not just a potential cure for a rare childhood disease. That discovery could have led to . . .

"Dr. Barkley, one more question. What was the date of the fire? Do you remember?"

He sighed. "Of course I remember. One of the worst days of my life." And he uttered the date with more than a trace of contempt. I thanked him and hung up. I worked at the date in my head. That date was . . .

That date was mere weeks before my ninth birthday. Mere weeks before that night when we entered the Compound. I quickly printed out all the pages from the PDL file. Again, it was just a bunch of research, but I checked the date. The date was before we went into the Compound.

My heart started pounding.

Was I looking at Barkley's research?

The research that had been destroyed by fire so many years before?

And if so, how did that research end up on a flash drive belonging to Phil?

CHAPTER TWENTY-FIVE

LEXIE CAME IN. "YOU READY?"

I stuffed my tablet computer into my bag, along with my phone, the flash drive, and the PDL printout. I was still reeling from the phone call and walked downstairs in a daze. I hugged everyone good-bye and was glad to get out in the fresh air. Lexie climbed in the front of the SUV and I got in the back.

I pulled out my tablet. But I didn't even know what to search for. No search engine was going to answer the questions I had.

Had Dad known about the research? When Barkley applied for funding, he could have mentioned his recent discovery. Did Dad have something to do with the fire? Did he steal Barkley's research and then start the fire as a cover-up?

No. Dad never got his hands dirty. I knew that. He

would have had someone else do it. Steal the research. Start the fire.

But why? To find a cure to progeria?

There had to be more to it. Dad could have just funded the research and had Barkley continue.

The discovery must have had more meaning than the cure alone.

I slipped the printed pages of the PDL file out of my bag and scanned them. Barkley had talked about the ramifications of the discovery I held in my hands. A cure for progeria, yes. But also the fountain of youth. What would Dad want with that?

I glanced at the top again.

PDL.

Fountain of youth.

PDL.

I gasped.

Ponce de León?

The fountain of youth. PDL had to stand for Ponce de León. It had to be.

The Ponce de León Project.

What had Dad been up to? Had he considered a vaccine to stop aging? If it was even possible, whoever did that would be the wealthiest person on the planet.

I leaned back against the seat and looked out the window.

Did any of it even matter? Dad was gone. Phil was gone. I couldn't believe anyone else had been involved. I could just give the contents of the PDL file back to Dr.

Barkley. Except, if they were the lost research from the fire, what would I tell him? How would I explain that an exceptional high school student/intern somehow happened to have research that had been destroyed years before?

I couldn't. It would have to be my secret to keep.

We reached the private airstrip and pulled up to the jet. Lexie said, "Will you take my bag on board?" She pointed at the office building. "I want to pee inside before we leave. I hate going on the plane."

I nodded and got out, grabbing both our bags. I climbed the short flight of steps onto the jet. Tony was standing in the back, near the small kitchen area.

Eddy was stretched out on a seat, already napping from the looks of it.

Tony waved at me. "Want some juice?"

I nodded. "Yeah, thanks." I sat down behind Eddy, in the second row of leather reclining seats, and stuffed Lexie's bag under the seat next to mine. I started to shove mine under when my phone and the flash drive fell out. I picked up the flash drive and noticed the tiny P.A.W. on the edge. Did Phil put his initials on everything? I shoved it into my pocket.

Tony handed me a glass and I downed half of it. "Thanks," I said. "I was thirsty."

"Guess so," he said.

"Hey, if you could not mention our . . . outing the other night, I'd appreciate it."

He nodded. "I kinda figured you didn't want Eddy to know you were posing as him."

"Thanks." I took another drink and finished the juice.

Phil's middle name was still bugging me. What was it anyway?

I got out my tablet, went online, and Googled Philip A. Whitaker. The connection was slow, probably because I was on board the jet. Finally it popped up. The *A* stood for Anthony.

As I started to read more, my vision grew blurry. I rubbed my eyes, but it got worse. I stood up, but immediately felt dizzy and collapsed back into the seat.

"Whoa." Was I sick?

Then Tony's face was inches from mine. "Eli?"

"I don't feel well," I said. My words were marbles in my mouth. "Something's wrong."

"You'll be fine." Tony smiled. "Just be a good boy and take a nap like your brother."

"What?" I tried to stand up, but I couldn't. My fingers fumbled and my tablet slid off my lap onto the seat next to me. The screen blurred, but I could still see Phil's name.

"Let me go," I said.

I struggled, tried to stand, tried to push him away. But my limbs wouldn't do anything I wanted them to.

Tony laughed. But then he stopped. "Do you know how painful this has been? To be nice to you all and pretend to be your little family friend? I'm so glad this is almost over."

What? What's almost over?

"I'll tell the pilot." I tried to stand up.

He simply pushed me back down and buckled my seat belt around me, cinching it tightly. "Just sit there and enjoy the ride."

He lowered his head so he could look out the window toward the office building. "And here comes your pretty sister."

I could no longer speak, but in my mind, I screamed at Lexie.

Run!

Get help!

Do not get on this plane!

But then my sister stepped on board and smiled at Tony, who handed her a glass of juice.

Nooo!

She took a drink, and then noticed me.

Her smile faded as she saw me and then Eddy.

She said something to Tony.

And just as Tony reached for her, everything went black.

CHAPTER TWENTY-SIX

I SMILED.

What was that smell?

Lovely. So lovely.

Almost like perfume. But it was some kind of flower.

A tropical flower.

Plumeria?

Yes.

Gram's plumeria trees in her front yard in Hawaii.

Reese made leis for the little kids one day. Pink and yellow plumerias.

I loved the smell.

My eyes fluttered. Blurry.

I could smell, but I couldn't see?

I tried to reach up and rub my eyes, but my arms were heavy. So heavy.

I forced myself to hold up my head, but it lolled, a bowling ball on my neck.

I blinked and blinked, finally clearing my vision.

I was still on the jet.

Hadn't we left yet?

"Eddy? Lexie?"

I heard a groan, but no one said anything.

And then I remembered.

Tony. Tony drugged me.

I had to find my brother and sister.

I tried to stand, but something held me down.

My seat belt. Still fastened.

I shook my head, trying to clear my thoughts, shake off the cobwebs in my brain. "Get a grip, dude." My mouth was dry and tasted awful.

With a loud click, the seat belt opened easily for me, and I held on to the seat in front of me and got to my feet. My legs threatened to give out, but they held as I walked to the front of the jet, grasping seats on my way to steady myself.

Eddy was in the same seat he'd been in when I boarded the plane. He opened his eyes, then squinted and held his head. Lexie was next to him, but she was still out cold.

I found a bottle of water and drank about half of it. Then I took another to Eddy and he downed most of it before stopping to take a breath. "Where are we?"

"I don't know," I said.

I walked to the front of the jet and stepped into the open doorway. I squinted at the bright sunshine and had to hold my hand above my eyes.

A breeze hit me then. A distinctly warm, tropical breeze that held the scent of flowers. I chugged the rest of my water and set the empty bottle on the counter. Then I held on to the rail and, still feeling wobbly, went down the steps and onto the tarmac. A tarmac lined by coconut palms and plumeria trees laden with pink blooms.

Through the trees, I caught a glimpse of water. The ocean. Was it real? Could I smell it?

Yes. There. The scent of salt was faint, almost covered completely by the plumerias.

The jet *had* left Seattle, because I was most definitely on an island.

My legs gave out and I fell to the hot tarmac.

"You okay?" Eddy was behind me, and squatted beside me. He put a hand on my shoulder. "Dude?"

I tried to stretch my arms and legs, then shook them. I also slapped myself on the cheeks a couple times. Finally, when I felt strong enough, I got to my feet, still a bit woozy. "I feel like crap."

Eddy slowly stood up, and staggered into me. "Me too." We held each other up.

I said, "Something was in the juice. Tony drugged us."

Eddy spit on the ground. "I can't believe he'd do that. I trusted him."

"Do you think it's a kidnapping? Did he drug us and let someone fly us here?" Wherever *here* was.

"I don't know." Eddy scrunched his eyes shut and rubbed them. "My vision is so blurry."

We heard a scream from inside the plane.

Lexie.

We got back up the stairs as quickly as we could, and found Lexie still strapped into her seat, eyes wide. She looked relieved when she saw us. "What's going on?"

"I don't know." I got a bottle of water and handed it to her.

She drank almost the whole thing. "Where's Tony?"

Eddy and I looked at each other. He said, "I don't know. We think maybe—"

"Maybe what?" she asked.

Eddy paused before saying, "We think it might be a kidnapping of some sort."

"But it's a YK jet!" Lexie tried to stand up, but fell back into the seat. "Help me up!"

Eddy grasped her arm and pulled, and when she got out into the aisle, I got on her other side for support. We headed for the door and slowly made our way down the stairs and onto the runway.

"Where are we?" asked Lexie.

Straight ahead and straight behind lay nothing but runway, each option ending in what looked like blue water. So I pointed at the trees. "I think we should head that way." They both seemed to agree, because neither said anything. We started walking, and my head cleared more as the blood got flowing. By the time we reached the trees, I felt almost back to normal.

Eddy said, "I feel better."

But the sun was so hot that my shirt was nearly soaked

through with perspiration. Eddy's and Lexie's faces were beet red and sweaty, just like mine felt.

An opening lay between two particularly large coconut palms, and I led the way through, finding myself steps away from a wooden boardwalk. I stepped onto it, and Lex and Eddy followed, our footsteps clunky and loud as we made our way along.

Lush vegetation was abundant alongside the man-made trail, growing so tightly together that I couldn't see anything besides the path and the green. I certainly couldn't see far enough ahead to get an idea of our destination.

"Shh." I held up my hand and we stopped for a second. I wanted to listen, see if I could hear anything.

I froze. Was that—

"Dripping water," said Eddy.

We headed toward the sound.

The boardwalk went on neatly through the tropical foliage, until it ended at a wall. I knew the wall had to be concrete of some kind, but it was laden with a large relief, taller than I was, of a man kneeling by a pond, sipping from his cupped hands. A constant but light flow of water rippled down the wall into a catchment basin below, making the entire thing seem more like a piece of art than a barrier.

At first I couldn't see any way to get by the wall. Lexie said, "Look." There was a slight crack behind the figure of the man. It was a door, almost hidden. I should have noticed the narrow walkway over the water that led right to the door.

Eddy and I stepped over it and ran our hands along the wall, which was cool and wet. Together, we pushed on the outline of the door and it opened.

I hesitated. "Maybe we're being stupid to walk right in."

I shot a glance behind me.

Lexie said, "The only thing back that way is the jet."

I froze. Faint strains of classical music drifted toward me.

Lexie asked, "Is that Vivaldi?"

Eddy said, "Only one way to find out."

I took a deep breath and stepped through the door.

The first thing I saw was a glass house.

We stopped.

The house wasn't entirely glass, but the wood and concrete supports were so sparse that the structure did seem, at first glance, to be made all of glass. Marble steps led up to a large, wide veranda, and Eddy walked up them slowly. Lexie followed, then I brought up the rear.

Once on the veranda, Eddy aimed for a pair of glass doors. We all peered inside, but saw no one.

Eddy pointed around the side of the house. "I don't see another way in."

I took a deep breath and quietly slid open the glass doors. Cool air blew out and felt refreshing on my sweaty skin. I stepped inside, then closed the doors shut as soon as the others were inside with me.

The Vivaldi was much louder inside, but I still couldn't tell where it was coming from. Shiny bamboo flooring lay under our feet, and we tiptoed across the huge foyer. We all stopped before a massive floor-to-ceiling cylindrical aquarium, with a circumference of about twenty feet. I stepped closer to it and gazed at the thousands of tiny creatures inside. Some kind of jellyfish.

"They're all the same," whispered Lexie.

The water in the glass shone with a blue light, which made the jellyfish inside look eerie, alien, as they glowed an artificially bright turquoise. Their tops looked a bit like an oblong globe, with a bright orange spot inside. Their tendrils also appeared blue as they floated like flimsy spiderwebs beneath.

Eddy whispered, "Let's keep going."

We walked across the foyer until we reached a hallway. A tall archway lay to the left. We walked under it and into a massive glass room with bamboo end tables and two fans whirling from the ceiling a good fifteen feet over my head. Vases of orange orchids and plumerias sat on every possible surface, making the room smell heavenly. A large lava stone fireplace took up one entire wall and a white sectional sat in front of it.

"It's beautiful," said Lexie.

"What is this place?" I asked.

Eddy turned around to face me and started to say something else, then his gaze, and Lexie's, wandered behind me to my left. Their eyes widened and their mouths dropped.

"Eddy. Lexie. *Eli.*"

Goose bumps sprouted on my arms.

That voice. There was no way. *No way in—*

I turned around.

Our father stood there, smiling at us. He said, "Welcome to the Yanakakis island. I've been waiting."

CHAPTER TWENTY-SEVEN

MY LEGS ALMOST BUCKLED, BUT I REACHED OUT AND grabbed a table near me, managing to stay upright. Lexie ran into our father's arms; Eddy right behind her. He squeezed both of them in an embrace. They stayed that way for a long moment, then they stepped slightly apart, Dad's arms still around them. My gaze went from my father's face to my sister's to my brother's.

"Dad?" I took a step and found myself in his arms. He smelled of aftershave and pipe tobacco. My face smashed into his shoulder, the silk of his aloha shirt slippery and cool on my cheek.

I stepped back then and looked at him.

My father was alive.

How was he alive?

He looked good. He'd put on weight since the last time I'd seen him . . .

The last time I'd seen him had been that night. The

night he threatened to hurt Lucas. The night we finally escaped him. The night he had died in the Compound . . .

Except he hadn't.

Because he was standing right in front of me.

The spontaneous joy at seeing my dad alive evaporated as all the questions flooded back. But I didn't even know where to start.

Where are we?

Who is Tony?

How the hell are you alive?

Dad squeezed Lexie and Eddy closer to him and said, "I'm sure you have a lot of questions."

I said, "I thought you were dead."

He grinned. "Almost was. I managed to get out at the last second and the helicopter barely made it out."

"With Phil." My voice was low and hard.

"Yes," he said. "With Phil."

"Why?" I asked.

His forehead creased. "Why what?"

Why did you leave?

Why did you let us think you were dead?

Why did you let Phil take over the company when you were alive?

But the one question that made its way out made me sound five years old. "Why didn't you come and see us?" *Why didn't you make things right?*

Dad reached out and ruffled my hair with his hand. "I think that would have been the wrong thing at the wrong time."

"Why?" I asked. "Mom has a new baby. She is trying to do everything by herself. She thinks you're dead."

Dad drew his hand back. "My showing up . . . would have led to a lot of—let's say—*unpleasantness*. It was easier for me to slip away, come here. Phil had been preparing this place for years. My timeline got moved up a bit." He paused. "I just don't think I would have been received well had I gone with you all to Seattle."

Eddy said, "Because the world thinks you did something bad."

"Thinks?" I asked. I was relieved to see my father alive, despite all he had done, but was Eddy delusional? "He kept us down there against our will. Of course it was bad."

Dad said, "See? Better the world thinks I'm dead and buried."

"What about Mom?" I asked. "And Terese? And the little ones?"

"I'll see them soon." Dad let out a loud breath. "Come now. Let's not spoil our reunion. There's plenty of time for talk."

And then I looked at Eddy and Lexie. They were so happy. Why? Why weren't they freaked out that we'd been drugged and taken against our will?

And then it all hit me. Not only Dad being alive, but him orchestrating our arrival on the island. A plan that must have been in motion almost since the day we arrived back in Seattle.

"I've gotta sit down." I went to the nearby glass dining table and dropped onto one of the white damask chairs.

Dad had been behind all of it.

Tony finding Lucas that day couldn't have been a setup, because I'm the one who left Lucas alone. But Tony could have been following us for a long time, simply waiting for the chance to befriend us. Maybe a setup had been coming, and opportunity had simply presented itself early when Lucas went out the emergency door.

Tony. Tony had been the one who'd leaked our outings to Barron. Had to be.

Which meant Dad had been in on it all. Tony was on the payroll.

The trip to Colorado had been just the right moment to get us in the jet, to bring us here.

Eddy asked, "You all right?"

I shook my head.

He said, "I'll get you something to drink."

I nodded.

Dad had come and sat at the head of the table, while Lexie sat on the chair to his right, smiling up at him. He placed a hand on her cheek.

Eddy set a tumbler of ice water down in front of me and I held the cool glass for a moment, and then stuck my hands on my face.

I was so hot.

After a long drink of the water, I set the glass back down. I looked at Dad. "You planned it. All of it."

"Eli, now's not the time for debate," said Dad. "We're here together, can we simply—"

"No!" I slammed my hand on the table. "I need to know."

"All right." Dad sighed. "I needed to get you all here."

Lexie said, "Eli, we're here. Dad's here. That's all that matters."

"Are you kidding me?" My voice got louder as I continued, asking. "You're fine with Tony lying? Drugging us?" I glared at Dad.

"Daddy?" Lexie frowned. "What's going on?"

Dad walked over to the sidebar and picked up a small pair of silver tongs. "Now that you're here, I'll tell you everything." He plucked out an ice cube from the matching silver bucket and dropped it into a glass with a *clink*. "I became aware of Dr. Barkley's research—"

"What?" Goose bumps rose on my arms.

"Who is that?" asked Lexie.

I said, "He's a doctor at the Progeria Institute, where I visited. YK funds his research." I looked at Dad, waiting.

Dad continued. "As I said, I became aware of Dr. Barkley, and his discovery, a few weeks before Eddy and Eli's ninth birthday." He dropped another ice cube. *Clink.*

I sucked in a quick breath and Eddy stiffened beside me.

Lexie frowned at me and Eddy. "What's so special about your ninth birthday?"

"Our ninth birthday was . . . the camping trip. When we entered . . ." I couldn't say it.

"Oh." She frowned and looked back at Dad.

He put a couple more cubes in his glass, poured himself

some water, then took his drink over to the glass wall on the opposite side of the room. My father stared out at the jungle for a moment before speaking again. "His discovery was . . . astounding, to say the least."

Eddy asked, "What discovery?"

When Dad didn't answer, I explained. "He'd isolated the compound that triggers aging."

"Really?" Lexie asked Dad, "What did that have to do with anything?"

He lifted his arms out to his sides. "It had everything to do with everything!" He dropped his arms, still grinning as he walked back over to us and sat back down in his chair. "Dr. Barkley's discovery meant so much more than just a potential cure for progeria." He leaned forward. "It was a possible cure for aging itself."

Eddy cleared his throat. "Is aging something to be cured, though?"

Dad laughed. "Spoken like a true teenager. Wait until you're thirty or forty or eighty. Then you'll understand."

Lexie asked, "What does this have to do with Tony?"

I wanted to know that myself. How Tony got involved in Dad's scheme to get us here. And who the dude really was, because it was apparent he was no skateboarder from the wrong side of the tracks.

"At first I wasn't completely sure what we had," Dad said.

"Wait." I held up my hand. "You skipped a bit, don't you think? How about telling us how you got your hands on the research?" I only had a hunch, but I had to call him out.

Dad shot me a scathing glance and sighed. "Fine, fine." He twirled the fingers of one hand in the air. "I had it taken."

I knew it.

Eddy asked, "Why would you have to do that?"

"Yeah," said Lexie. "Couldn't you have bought it?"

Dad scratched his chin. "I did buy it, really. I wrote Dr. Barkley a very significant check after the fire and—"

"What fire?" Eddy burst out.

"There happened to be a fire at his research facility and I provided the funds to get him back on his feet. Start up his research again."

"Wait." Lexie hadn't acted like the conversation was worth listening to, but now she had a serious expression on her face. "Was the fire before or after you took his research?"

Dad didn't answer.

So I took a chance and said, "The fire was a cover-up. For the robbery. And you ended up with the research and no one was any wiser."

"Very good, Eli." Dad smiled at me. "You always figure out my secrets, don't you?"

Yeah, I guess I did.

Then why did it feel like he was still hiding something?

Eddy fidgeted in his chair. "So what did you do with the research?"

Dad leaned back in his chair. "I took it with me into the Compound. Spent years with it."

"How?" I asked. "You were busy with the cloning."

Eddy asked, "What cloning?"

Dad waved him off. "I'm not God. There was never going to be any cloning."

"But that room, the lab . . . ," I said. "I saw it!"

Dad shook his head. "You saw exactly what I told you to see. Did you open any of the tanks?"

I swallowed. "No, I—"

"Why not, Eli?" asked my father. "Why didn't you check for yourself?"

Why didn't I? "Because I—"

"Because you believed what I told you."

I nodded.

Dad laughed as he rubbed his hands together. "Of course you did."

Lexie said, "What were you doing if you weren't . . . trying to clone things?"

Dad looked at me. "I was decoding the key to aging."

"Why?" asked Eddy.

"I know," said Lexie. "Mom spends a fortune on anti-wrinkle cream." She nodded. "You could make a fortune on antiaging medicine. Everyone would buy it."

Maybe I was right about the vaccine for antiaging. Maybe he had done it after all.

Dad tilted his head slightly to one side. "Not quite what I was thinking . . ."

Confident with my answer, I said, "A cure for aging. The fountain of youth. People wouldn't have to get any older ever again."

Dad smiled at me. "I didn't want to just stop aging." He nodded at Lexie. "Or find a cure for it. I wanted to do more."

Eddy said, "More? How could there be more than that?"

Dad looked at me. "Eli? Don't you have this figured out?"

No one said anything. Suddenly, I felt my heart pound faster and my hands started to tremble. I didn't want to hear him say what he was going to say. Because it would not be anything good.

Dad said, "It wasn't enough to stop aging. I wanted to reverse it."

Reverse it?

"That's impossible!" I said. "No one can reverse aging."

"Really, Eli? You honestly think I can't do anything I put my mind—and money—to?" Dad had this look on his face as he watched me. This smug look.

The same kind of smug look Tony had given me on the plane before I'd passed out.

The same kind of smug look Phil had given me that day in the boardroom.

What was I missing? I couldn't help thinking it had something to do with Phil.

Dad interrupted my thoughts when he asked, "Did you see my jellyfish?"

"The tank in the foyer?" I asked.

Eddy said, "We saw them."

Lexie nodded.

I asked, "What are they?"

Dad said, "*Turritopsis nutricula*. Originally from the Caribbean, but they've spread all over the world."

There had to be a reason for their prominent display in the foyer. "What's so special about them?" I asked.

Dad said, "The *Turritopsis nutricula* is technically a hydrozoan, a cousin of the jellyfish. I heard about it while I was working on Dr. Barkley's discovery. And it's special because once it matures and mates, it is able to revert back to a juvenile form."

Lexie asked, "So it shrinks or something?"

"No." Dad shook his head. "It is the only animal capable of reverting completely to its younger self." Dad set his drink down. "Most members of the jellyfish family die after mating. But this creature has the ability to return to a polyp state, an earlier stage in its life cycle."

"How does it do that?" I asked.

Dad said, "Through trans-differentiation." He must have seen the confused looks on our faces, because he added, "They turn one kind of cell into another. Some animals have the ability to do this in a limited capacity, like how salamanders can regrow limbs. But the *Turritopsis* can regenerate its entire body. It reverses its aging process."

244

An immortal jellyfish. I swallowed.

Had Dad done it? Had he figured out how to reverse aging?

The implications . . .

I couldn't breathe.

CHAPTER TWENTY-EIGHT

I SHOVED MY CHAIR BACK AND DROPPED MY HEAD BETWEEN my knees.

"Eli?" Eddy put a hand on my back.

I tried to breathe.

This can't be true. It can't. I have to be wrong.

Immortal jellyfish? The reversal of aging?

None of it was possible.

Despite the air conditioner, I was sweating, my shirt nearly soaked through. My jeans felt as if they weighed a ton, and something was poking my leg.

I reached into my pocket and pulled out the flash drive I'd shoved in there earlier. I reached up and dropped it on the table.

Eddy asked, "You okay?"

I nodded. "Just a little light-headed."

Somewhere a door opened and shut, and then I heard footsteps.

"Good afternoon, all."

I sat up and barely missed braining myself on the edge of the table.

"Tony." Lexie stood up. "You *are* here."

Tony wore a blue rash guard and flowered swim trunks. He walked right past Lexie, slid out a chair, and sat down. "Family meeting?" he asked. He reached for the platter of sliced mango and papaya at the center of the table, then took a plate from the stack of china next to it and filled it.

Eddy watched him with narrowed eyes. "Did you drug us?"

Tony stuck a forkful in his mouth and slowly chewed, then swallowed. He shrugged. "Figured it would be easier than trying to fly the jet plus keep you all in line."

"You were the pilot?" Lexie frowned. "You work for my dad?" She glared at him. "But you let me think . . ."

Tony looked at her. "Let you think what?" Then he grinned. "Flattering, for sure, but you're not my type, sweetie."

"Watch how you talk to my children," snapped Dad.

"Sorry, Rex." Tony held up both his hands, palms toward Dad. "I'm just used to playing the role."

"What role?" I turned to Dad. *What role?*"

Tony sighed. "Seriously, kid. The role of buddy and protector to all of you. Get in good, make you trust me, then get you on a plane." He looked Dad's way. "I did finish about a month earlier than you expected."

Dad nodded. "Yes, you did. I appreciate that."

"Bonus time, Boss?" Tony smiled.

Eddy shoved a thumb in Tony's direction and asked Dad, "He was part of a plan?"

"From the get-go," I said. "He followed us everywhere we went." I turned to Dad. "Didn't he?"

He nodded.

Tony started talking with his mouth full. "I had a few things go my way. Like you leaving your little brother alone in the bathroom. Tsk-tsk-tsk."

My hands turned into fists. My first instinct, to neither like nor trust Tony, had been right. I reached out and picked up the flash drive, turning it over and over in my hand.

Lexie asked Dad, "How could you send someone like that into our life? We could've had him in our *house*?"

Dad and Tony exchanged a quick glance, then Tony said, "I've been in your house."

Was he talking about the nights at the mansion when Eddy snuck out with him? When *I* snuck out with him? But we hadn't been inside.

Eddy said, "What are you talking about?"

Obviously, Eddy hadn't taken him inside either. So—

I froze and looked at the flash drive in my palm. The initials on it.

P.A.W.

Philip A. Whitaker.

Phil's middle name.

Anthony.

My heart dropped.

I set it on the table and stood up. My heart pounded and my hands trembled as they turned into fists. I strode over to Tony. "Dad had no problem sending him into our lives, because he was already there."

Tony stood up, so we were chest to chest. He said, "Take it easy."

My face mere inches from his, I repeated, *"He was already there*. Had been for years."

Eddy asked, "What are you talking about?"

"This is not some teenager named Tony." I swallowed. "He's a middle-aged douche bag named Phil."

And I punched him in the face as hard as I could.

CHAPTER TWENTY-NINE

Tony went down, hitting a chair on his way, and lay there on the floor, holding his nose and swearing.

Dad was on his feet. "Eli! That wasn't necessary."

"Really?" I yelled. "I've wanted to do that since I was five years old!"

Lexie was standing by Tony, not helping him, just watching him. Eddy stood up and pulled on my shoulder, yanking me around to face him. "What is wrong with you?"

"Absolutely nothing." I looked at Dad. "It took me awhile. I even knew his whole name. Philip *Anthony* Whitaker. Clever to use *Tony*."

Eddy fell back down into his chair. "Somebody seriously needs to tell me what's going on."

"The reverse-aging process works," Dad said matter-of-factly. "I used it on Phil so he could go back and get you all here."

Lexie grabbed on to the table. "What?" She pointed at Tony. "That's Phil?" She made a face of disgust, then covered her mouth. She walked over to the sectional, where she perched on the edge of an arm, eyes wide.

Eddy sat there, shaking his head, as Dad put some ice in a towel and handed it to Tony. "Probably should head over to the infirmary and get that X-rayed." He helped Tony get to his feet. Tony glared at me as he left.

I said, "I want to see the rest of this place. Now."

Dad smiled. "Of course. You each have your own room and—"

"No!" I was so frustrated I couldn't help yelling. But I knew it wouldn't help, so I tried to sound calmer as I added, "I meant the rest of the island."

Dad said, "How about a nice meal first? Then we can—"

"I don't want to eat." I paused, giving myself another moment to chill out. "I couldn't eat right now if I tried. I want to see where we are. What this place is."

Eddy said, "I do, too."

"Not me," Lexie called from across the room. "I'm staying here."

Dad sighed. "Fine. I'll give you the tour. But then we're sitting down to a nice meal."

He led us past the fireplace and out a different door from the one we'd snuck in. Right outside the house was a circular veranda of brick, accented with tropical flowers and plants, and a large fountain in the middle. A bronze sculpture of a man kneeling, resembling the one on the wall, sat next to it, creating the illusion that the man was actually reaching into the fountain.

A few drops from the spray landed on my arm as we passed. I asked, "Is that Ponce de León?"

"Yes," said Dad. "He's sort of our mascot around here."

"The fountain of youth," mused Eddy. "So you really created it?" He sounded impressed rather than disgusted, which was how I was feeling about it.

"Yes, we did," Dad answered.

I asked, "Who's we?"

Dad headed past the fountain and onto a path made of shells that led into an area of thick bamboo. "I always thought money could get people to do anything. But to some, there is something even more valuable than wealth."

Eddy asked, "Happiness?"

Dad kind of laughed. "Actually, no. The people I needed for this project, the *brains* I needed for this project, weren't about to be swayed by money. They were too busy, too focused on research to even entertain a proposal based solely on wealth. Their goals were not based on what they could obtain in their lifetime. Their goals were based on what they could *discover*."

"Time," I said. "You offered them time."

Dad smiled and clapped me on the back. "You got it. They laughed when the offer was for millions. But when I assured them they could get back their youth, get another lifetime—and unlimited funding with which to work on their discoveries—well . . . let's say I didn't have many say no. Can you imagine if Einstein could have

253

been young again, lived fifty more years? What he might have discovered?"

I let that sink in a moment, then asked, "But what about their families?"

"The offer was only extended to scientists who had devoted their lives to their research, never had time for families, or had gotten so old that they had no family left to speak of, only themselves to think about. Most of them were living in homes for the aged, just waiting until their time ran out. My people went all over the world to find them: Prague, Berlin, London . . . I'm still recruiting."

That jogged something in my brain—*old-age homes, London, BBC News.* That day in Reese's room. The missing scientists . . . they had come to Dad's island.

Eddy asked, "What did they have to do in return?"

The shell path ended at a tall fence formed of thick logs covered with dark green vines. Dad stopped there and turned to face us. "In return?" He shrugged. "They would have to leave everything and devote half their time to my aging research."

I said, "I don't see how anybody would do that. Give everything up."

Dad smiled. "You'd be surprised." He reached over and opened a door in the fence. "See for yourself."

I stepped through the door and uttered a shaky "Holy crap."

I stepped onto a vast, seemingly endless cobblestone plaza that webbed out into narrow paths that ended in large, windowless metal buildings. I counted six of them, each the size of a football field. A few palm trees and wooden benches dotted the area, but they didn't make the place look anything other than scientific and industrial. They gave me the feeling that, in order to grow a society, the jungle needed to be razed. Those lonely trees were all that remained.

Several men and women of varying ethnicities, all in white lab coats, walked quickly between the buildings, or were paired off, standing side by side with heads down in what looked like serious discussions.

Eddy joined me and whistled. "Whoa."

Dad came up behind us and set a hand on my shoulder. I turned and saw he had done the same to Eddy. "Boys, this is your legacy, too. I did this for all of us."

"The largest software company in the world wasn't enough?" I asked. Eddy glared at me, but I ignored him.

"Seriously. I think the world's reaction to watching their grandpa turn into a teenager is going to be slightly different from finding out they can get faster Internet." I paused. "Don't you think?"

Dad said, "Exactly why we're working so hard. Can you imagine if man had gone from chisel and stone directly to a wireless tablet? They couldn't have handled it. They wouldn't have believed. They would have thought it was sorcery or something else . . . something inherently evil."

He took a breath. "It's the curse of the discoverers through history, the nonbelief that surrounds them. Look at Galileo. He believed the earth revolved around the sun."

Eddy said, "The earth does revolve around the sun."

Dad held up a hand. "Of course it does. But the Inquisition could not accept an alternative to the pervasive belief that the sun rotated around the earth. They forced Galileo to recant and he spent the rest of his life under house arrest."

"But he was right," I said.

Dad nodded. "*But* his theory wasn't accepted until about a hundred years later. This is exactly why discovery happens in stages. It *must*. Man needs time to adjust and accept. Which is why I intend for the world to get this discovery in stages."

Eddy asked, "What stages?" He pointed across the plaza at one of the men who looked all of about twenty-five. "How old is he?"

Dad said, "Actual age? About seventy-five."

A chill ran up my spine. "That doesn't sound like stages to me."

"Exactly," said Dad. "The public could never adjust if we went directly to the reversal of age. So first we're going to arrest age. Show people we can stop the symptoms of age that debilitate them. Cure the diseases of age. Progeria, for one. Alzheimer's, for another. And then, slowly, we'll introduce them to the concept of curing age. That everyone can be young again. That they never have to grow old. And by then, once they've accepted that, they'll be ready to hear more. In fact, they won't be satisfied until they hear more. They will *expect* to hear more." He smiled. "And I won't be the one to disappoint them."

"Is it about the money?" I asked. "Is that all this is for?"

Dad laughed. "I have more money than I could ever spend." He waved a hand at us. "I have more money than *you* could ever spend." When he spoke, his voice was much quieter. "No, it's not about the money."

"It's proving you can do it. Just like the Compound." Goose bumps covered my arms.

Eddy looked confused. As he should.

He had no idea what Dad had said to me in the Compound, that it had all been a challenge, to see what he could do. His testing us to see how far we would go to survive. And that feeling of powerlessness that overcame me when I found out.

Eddy said, "I don't get what's so bad. I mean, think of all the people who won't have to go through old age." He looked at me. "Maybe we won't have to."

Dad put an arm around Eddy. "Exactly, son. It's a good thing we're doing here."

Was it a good thing? To want to control something as natural as aging?

I understood wanting to cure diseases; those kids with progeria deserved a cure. I even understood, maybe, putting a stop to age-related ailments or discovering how to smooth wrinkles without plastic surgery.

But to actually conquer aging itself?

Wasn't that . . . playing God?

My hands started to tremble and my heart beat faster.

Nothing had changed.

257

My father hadn't changed.

If anything, he was worse. Because, except for the people on this island, no one knew he was alive. No one knew what he had done. What he *was* doing.

And no one knew he had us.

Once again, I was powerless.

And, once again, I had to stop him.

So, once again, I was going to try.

"I want to see the labs," I said. "I want to see how it works." Because finding out how it worked would be the only way to figure out a way to put a stop to it. To put a stop to him.

Dad held his hand out to the left. "This way. Follow me."

CHAPTER THIRTY

UNDER THE HOT SUN, DAD LED US TO A BUILDING DIRECTLY across from where we came through the fence. Double glass doors, so large you could drive a truck through them, opened automatically and we walked in. They closed behind us with a long, quiet *shh,* and I felt a chill on my sweaty skin from the temperature, easily twenty degrees cooler than outside.

Eddy rubbed his arms, which were covered with goose bumps, just like mine. "I wondered how everyone could wear those lab coats and not be dying from the heat."

Dad said, "We keep it a pretty steady sixty-five in here." He walked straight ahead down a long hallway of industrial-tiled floors. We passed several closed doors and my breaths became short and shallow.

We reached a silver door at the end of the hallway and I shivered, less from the cold than from the memory of another silver door. Dad punched a code into a keypad and the door swung open. Dad looked at me and frowned. "You all right?"

I couldn't speak.

He glanced at the door and then back at me. He grasped my arm and his lips turned up in the kindest expression I'd seen on him in years. "It's okay, son. This one is only locked from out here. You can get out any-time you want." He motioned to Eddy, who walked through the doorway. Dad held out his arm and I shook my head. "You first," I said.

He shrugged. "Okay." He walked through.

I followed, ever so slowly.

We walked down another hallway and into a white room. Clear plastic curtains hung down across the entire space and Dad pushed them aside and stepped through. Eddy was next, and I brought up the rear.

The first thing I noticed was something that looked like a large rolling oven with a black half on the left and a white half on the right. The left side bore a large dial in the middle and two small yellow handles beneath it. The right side had a dial on top with a metal tube the size of my arm snaking out of it. The bottom half of the white side contained a glass door, making that side of the contraption resemble a mini-fridge.

"What is that thing?" asked Eddy.

"A particle delivery system." Dad walked over to it and picked something off the top. He turned around and held it up.

The device looked something like a gun. No, not a gun. It looked like a ray gun, like a phaser from the original *Star Trek* series.

"What is *that*?" I asked.

Dad smiled. "A gene gun. It's loaded with genetic information. And this is how we inject the cells and cause the differentiation. How we change from one type of cell to another, reverting the cells to a younger stage in development.

"Like the jellyfish," I said.

He nodded.

"You mean that's how you did it?" I asked. "How you . . . *de-aged* Phil?"

"De-aged?" Dad laughed. "I like that. That's exactly what we did."

I looked at the ovenlike thing. "You invented that?"

Dad shook his head. "Oh, heavens, no. They've been using gene guns for years on plants. But I found that for our purposes, it didn't quite work the way we wanted." He shook the gun a bit. "So I came up with this prototype."

"How does it work?" I asked.

Dad said, "Just like you'd expect." He held the gun to his bicep. "Pow."

Eddy asked, "Does it hurt? I mean, did the scientists . . . did Phil . . ."

"Feel pain?" asked Dad.

Eddy nodded as I cringed.

"Some discomfort at first." Dad shrugged a bit. "But he

was sedated, of course, so when the process was complete, he barely remembered any of it."

I asked, "He just woke up and was younger?"

Dad nodded. "He was the same person, just physically *de-aged*, as you put it so eloquently."

"Wow," said Eddy. "That's cool."

I glared at him. Cool? Seriously? And then I reminded myself that Eddy hadn't been in the Compound. He hadn't experienced what Dad was capable of. To him, all of the stuff in that room probably was . . . cool.

Unable to watch Eddy fawn over our father, I turned around.

At the far end of the room stood a large metal door with a latch that seemed to lock from the other side. I didn't want to know what lay inside. My gaze went to a bank of shelves along the wall. On one of them sat a small black box, almost like a remote. It looked so familiar. Where had I seen something like that before?

"Eli?"

I jumped at Dad's voice and quickly turned around. "What?"

"You look pale," he said. "When did you last eat?"

"Breakfast. Right before I was kidnapped."

Dad rolled his eyes slightly. "Well, let's go eat. There's plenty of time to see more."

I couldn't wait to leave. I'd seen what I needed to see.

I was first out of the plastic curtain, then the silver door, and first to get back outside, happy to be back in the sun and heat, even if I was sweating to death. I quietly followed Dad and Eddy back to the house, as they chattered the entire way. Eddy asked, "Did you consider taking a few years off yourself?"

Dad hesitated a moment. Was he searching for an answer? But then he sounded very sure of himself when he said, "No. I have a family. It wouldn't do to be younger than my kids."

Strange, but that seemed like the most rational thing to come out of his mouth in the past hour. Which made me question whether it was actually the truth.

Back at the house, Lexie was at the dining-room table, eating slices of fresh mango. My stomach growled. I sat in the chair next to her and put several slices of mango on a plate. Then I picked up a fork, stuck it in a slice of mango, and popped it in my mouth. I closed my eyes and groaned. "That is great mango."

Dad sat back down. "We grow our own here."

My eyes snapped open and I finished chewing and swallowed. I realized I needed to know more than just what lay on the island. I needed to know about the island itself. "Where is here, exactly?"

He rattled off a latitude and longitude that lay somewhere south and west of the Hawaiian chain.

He had poured himself a drink and seemed really relaxed, so I decided to keep him talking, spilling information that might help me later.

"Why bring us here?" I asked.

Dad smiled. "That was always my plan. Bring my family here. Start over."

My face grew hot and I couldn't help saying, "We have started over." I pointed my fork at him. "Without you."

"Eli," said Eddy. "Our family has a chance to be together again."

I threw my fork down on the plate and stood up. "Are you serious? You think we can just pretend none of this happened? Pretend that none of the last six years have happened?"

Eddy frowned. "We're family. Family sticks together. Being together should be all that matters."

Dad shook his head at Eddy. "It's okay. He needs time."

"Time for what?" I asked.

"To adjust," he said. "To the island. To me, perhaps." Dad stood up. "The lab I showed you was just part of the island. It's a beautiful place. You don't ever have to see the labs again if you don't want to."

"I don't want to," I said. "I want to go home."

Dad said, "It's nearly evening. That can't happen before tomorrow."

"Fine." I finished eating my mango and pulled my shirt collar away from my neck. I reeked. "Any chance I can get a shower? Change maybe?"

Dad nodded and stood. "Follow me." He called over to Lexie. "Want to see your room?"

The three of us followed him down a wide hallway, lit by wall sconces. Halfway down lay an open stairway, and we climbed up to the second floor and entered a hallway identical to the one on the first floor. Dad stopped at the second door on the right. "Eli, this is your room." He paused. "Unless the two of you want to share a room?"

Eddy shot me a look. Obviously he didn't want to share.

He smiled. "It is good to see you both together again."

My stomach churned. He could have had us together anytime in the past six years. If he had wanted. Instead . . .

He had kept us apart. Let each of us think the other was dead. Let *me* live with the guilt for all those years, the guilt of me thinking I had been responsible for Eddy's death.

I went into the room, locking the door behind me. I closed my eyes and leaned back against the door.

I shut them out.

My father, my brother, my sister.

I needed to be alone.

I took a couple of deep breaths, trying to relax, trying to adjust to the past few hours and all the truths, however horrible, that had come to light.

Dad was alive. Phil was alive. Only he was Tony, because my father had figured out how to reverse aging.

And I was on an island. Somewhere in the middle of nowhere.

But the worst truth of all?

I was back under his control.

And Eddy seemed completely enamored with him, hanging on every word. Stopping my father would be next to impossible on my own. I only hoped I could convince Eddy that our father was not to be trusted.

CHAPTER THIRTY-ONE

I OPENED MY EYES.

Two walls of the room were floor-to-ceiling windows, looking out onto the ocean. Surprised to see the open water after all the jungle, I leaned out the open window. Amid the tops of the trees to the side, three roofs were visible. I stayed there a moment, feeling the breeze and hearing bird sounds.

Rolled up at the top of each window were large white shades, and I reached up to unroll them. I couldn't see any cords, but there was a switch on the wall. I pushed it.

Immediately, the shades began unrolling, slowly covering the windows from the top to the bottom, until the room lay in near darkness.

I went back to the door and flipped the light switch, brightening the room. A king-size canopy bed of bamboo sat along one interior wall, with white matelassé bedding, accented with bright orange and red floral rectangular pillows.

A desk with a large computer sat along the other interior wall, as well as two wooden doors. I opened the first, and a light automatically came on, revealing a huge walk-in closet, full of clothes. I stepped inside and knelt down. Flip-flops, sneakers, even a pair of dress shoes. Shirts hung in a row along one side, while jeans and trousers filled the other. I had no doubt that everything in there would turn out to fit me perfectly.

Just like my old closet in the Compound.

A dresser was near the back, and I opened the drawers. Shorts, T-shirts, swim trunks, underwear.

I pulled out a T-shirt and a pair of shorts, grabbed a pair of black flip-flops, and stepped back into the bedroom. I opened the other door and again, a light popped on.

A bathroom. Nearly the size of the bedroom itself. Double sinks sat under a long mirror. The toilet was off to the side in an alcove, and at the far end of the room was a monstrous open shower made of black lava rock, like the living-room fireplace. The linen closet held large, white, cushy towels, and I hung two of them, along with the clothes from the closet, on hooks next to the shower.

I undressed, left my clothes in a pile on the floor, and turned on the water.

The spray came from all directions: the ceiling, the sides, and when I stepped inside, the soothing jets felt better than any shower I'd ever taken. Clear square containers held thick, pale-colored liquids. I pushed one of the buttons and the contents oozed out into my palm. I held it to my nose. Coconut-scented shampoo.

I stayed in there until the water turned lukewarm.

When I came out, the mirrors were all steamy. I dried off, and in the drawers of the vanity, I found deodorant and toothpaste and floss and everything else I needed.

I felt better, much better. Ready to handle whatever other truths were waiting for me. So I got dressed and went to join my brother and sister for dinner. I hoped it would be the last time we ever had to eat a meal with our father, because I planned on getting us out of there as soon as possible.

Down in the main room, the table was set, but no one was there. I heard water running, and figured maybe the others were showering, too. I wanted to get out to the beach, so I headed back down the hallway and past the staircase, figuring there had to be a door that opened toward the beach.

I reached the end of the hallway and entered a small foyer that set off a large wooden door. I turned the handle and stepped out onto a sidewalk where a breeze hit me. Spread in front of me was the most beautiful white sand beach I'd ever seen. I headed straight for the sparkling, turquoise water.

The sand was like powder under my feet, and not hot at all. I stepped into the water, and it was barely warm. I walked in up to my shins and stood there, letting the waves move between and around my legs. Ahead of me I saw nothing but water, the surface reflecting the sun so brightly that I had to put up a hand to shade my eyes.

Up the beach to my right, I saw several dwellings: the roofs I'd seen from my window earlier. A sidewalk led along the beach. Reluctantly, I left the water and went to see what I could find.

The first house was much like Dad's, only smaller. There was no one in sight. Same with the second. But at the third, the back of someone's head was visible on the small deck in front. As I got closer, I wondered if I should turn around without saying anything. But if my intention was to find out as much as I could . . .

"Hey there!" I called out.

The person stood up. As he turned around, I started to wave. But my hand froze in midair when I saw who it was.

Tony. *Phil.*

And he did not look happy to see me.

CHAPTER THIRTY-TWO

I LOWERED MY ARM AND TURNED TO WALK BACK, MY STEPS fast and light on the sand.

"Wait!" he yelled. "Kid! Hold on! Wait a sec." He jogged onto the beach toward me.

Wondering how good an idea it was, I slowed, then turned around and took a strong stance, ready to fight him off.

He stopped in front of me and held his hands out toward me. "No worries. I won't try to retaliate." He gestured toward the white bandage on his nose. His eyes were both bruised, and would probably get worse before they got better.

"I'm not sorry," I said. "You deserved it."

He shrugged. "Probably. Depends on whose side you're on."

I frowned. "You're admitting there are sides?"

"Aren't there?" He tilted his head slightly.

271

I nodded. "I think so." I held up a hand. "This place . . ." I wasn't sure what I wanted to say. I knew I couldn't trust him. But if he'd had anything to do with the island, which I strongly suspected he had, he would probably drip his own praises from his mouth without much coaxing. "It's beautiful," I finished.

"Yes, it is." He straightened up a bit. "Took me awhile to get it ready. But Rex was pleased when he arrived. Definitely pleased. We'd been up and running for about a year when you all finally got out." He noticed me watching him. "You know I disagreed with that."

"What?" I asked.

He looked out to sea, shading his eyes with a hand. "The whole underground thing. While it was being built, I thought it was brilliant. Think about it." He turned to look at me. "When the world descends into chaos, your family is set to ride it out." He put a hand to the side of his mouth, and lowered his voice. "Honestly, I rather hoped I'd get an invite if there really was an apocalypse." He breathed deep and it came out loud, almost like a sigh. "But when he told me what he meant to do, that you were all going under, with no plans to come out, well . . ." He shook his head. "I'll admit that I'll do just about anything for money, but there's not enough in the world for me to go in there, and live in that situation."

"Smart," I said.

He turned his back to the sun and faced me. "I did try to change his mind, you know."

What? My heart began to pound. "About taking us into the Compound?"

"No." He shook his head. "It was once you were in. Those first couple of days after your brother was left on the outside. I told Rex how devastated that kid was. There was still time, before the world found out. I was the one with the lies to spin into a truth the world would believe. I told Rex that he could fix it, let you all out, tell you all that it was some kind of drill. A test to see how the Compound worked. Everything could go back to how it was."

"He didn't listen," I stated.

"No, he sure didn't." Tony held his arms out to the side. "Instead, it was on to the next thing. Build him this place. That's probably why I felt I should take care of Eddy all those years. Since I'd failed at getting you guys back for him." He dropped his arms. "You know it really threw Rex when you figured it all out."

"How to open the door?"

He nodded. "I never heard him as frantic as he was that night."

I thought of the phone that had sat on Dad's desk in the Compound. "So he did call you from there."

Tony looked almost guilty as he nodded. "Every day. No different from when he called me from his office at YK." He started drawing in the sand with a toe. "I hoped we could go back to that. Once you all were out. I wanted to go back to just being his right-hand man at YK. Meetings. Business trips." He stared out at the sea. "You might not believe it, but kidnapping kids and trapping people underground are not what I signed up for."

"You had no problem with the age reversal."

He whipped his face around toward mine. "You think I wanted to be a guinea pig? I had no choice in that! Rex *owns* me. Everything, every single dirty thing I've done for him, is documented." His shoulders slumped. "I knew it from the start. I knew what I was getting into." He put his hands on his face. "I never expected to be an experiment, though."

He didn't say anything else, and the breeze and waves were the only sound.

I shrugged. "You make a pretty good teenager. You fooled me. Fooled Eddy and Lexie."

He smirked. "It has been kinda fun. Being a kid, yet being able to afford all the toys."

I rolled my eyes. "That Camaro was totally yours, wasn't it?"

He laughed. "Well, it belonged to Philip A. Whitaker. Tony the teenager would have had a hard time explaining that."

I smiled. "I gotta say, it's much harder to hate you as Tony. Phil was such a prick."

Tony laughed. "I deserve that. I mean *Phil* deserves that."

I pointed at the house. "It's yours?"

"Of course." He smiled. "There are perks to being

a henchman. Mine include room and board with ocean-front property."

"What's next?" I asked.

Tony quickly turned and looked out at the water again. He shrugged but didn't say anything.

I needed to know, and I felt like he was going to open up to me. So I kept at him. "Tony?" I couldn't get myself to call him Phil, even though I knew that's who he really was. "What's next? What's the plan?"

Finally he turned back around and met my eyes. "Eli, you know what's next. You know what has to happen."

"I don't," I said.

He let out a breath. "Think about it. Think about what Rex wants." He held up his hands, palms up. "What would make this paradise complete for him?"

I started to say something, then I stopped. I knew my dad, how he thought. There was only one thing that would make the island complete.

"My family," I said.

Tony nodded. "They're next."

My father wanted us all on the island. To keep. To control. Just like he told me when we were still in the Compound. Only once we were back in Seattle, I had thought we were safe.

I was so wrong.

"But Dad said we were all flying home tomorrow."

Tony frowned. "He did? In those words?"

"Yeah, he . . ." I trailed off and looked down at the sand as I tried to remember. What had he said? "I told him I wanted to go home and he said that wouldn't happen before tomorrow." My heart sunk as I realized it meant nothing of the sort. "He's not letting us go."

Tony shook his head slightly. "He has no intention of letting you go now that you're here. At least, not all of you."

I blurted out, "But my mom will never come here. She'll never let him bring the others here. She won't let him."

Tony said, "Really? There's nothing on earth that would get her to change her mind?"

"No, she—" I stopped. Dad would use us. Me, Eddy, Lexie. "He'll use us. He'll use us to get her here."

Tony nodded. "He's going to send you. Alone. I'll be flying you out tomorrow. And he knows if you ever want to see Eddy and Lexie again, you'll bring the rest of your family back."

I studied his face. There wasn't a trace of smugness in his face or the tone of his voice. So what was left? Could it be remorse? Guilt?

I said, "I can't let him do this to us again. Make us prisoners in his private world."

And then I did something I never thought possible. I dropped to my knees in front of Philip A. Whitaker and begged, "Please help me stop him before it's too late."

CHAPTER THIRTY-THREE

"OH, GOD, KID, DON'T DO THIS." TONY REACHED OUT AND grabbed my elbow, pulling me back up to my feet. "Get up. You know I can't help."

"Why not?" I grabbed him by the arms so I was right in his face.

"You know why not." He tried to push me away, not unkindly. "You know my loyalty lies with him."

I dropped my arms and stepped back. My hands turned to fists at my side. "Why?" I asked. "Why do you have to be loyal to him? The rest of the world thinks my father is dead. Eddy and I are set to inherit everything." As much as it disgusted me to say it, I did. "We could give you a permanent place at YK, just like you wanted. You could have your job like it was. I would see to it."

Tony stepped back, shaking his head. "That's not what you want and you know it."

I clasped my hands at the back of my head and looked up at the sky. "What I want is to be back in Seattle with my family. My whole family."

"And Rex? You want your dad, too?" he asked.

That was the worst part. I wanted what any son wanted: a father to be there for me, pick me up after my failures, feel pride at my successes.

I dropped my arms and faced him again. "That man . . . is not my father. Not the father I knew. That man . . . that man . . . is a *monster*."

And in that moment, I knew how Lexie felt, knowing the truth about her birth mother and the atrocities she'd committed. Powerless. I knew my dad's genes were coursing through my own body, my own brain, and I could do nothing about it. Rex Yanakakis, and everything he was, was what I came from.

The difference was that Lexie had the comfort of knowing she had not been raised by her biological monster, that our mother had been nothing like that.

But everything I was—everything I knew—had been affected, cultivated, *bred* by my monster. Nature *and* nurture. There was no escaping that fact. Which meant the only chance for me was to escape *him*.

I asked, "What time do we leave tomorrow?"

"Long flight. Would rather get an early start." Tony glanced at his watch. "About eight?" His eyes were wary. "Listen, whatever you're planning, I can't help you—"

"I know."

He watched me for a moment. "So you'll be ready to leave at eight?"

"Yes." And then I added, "You'd better have the jet ready to go."

So I would be flying out the next day. Without Lexie and Eddy. I would be the one sent to bring back the whole family. But I would never do it. I would never allow Mom and the others to get on a plane and come and be prisoners again. But the only way to prevent that would be to get Eddy and Lexie on the plane with me.

Back at the house, Eddy, Lexie, and our father were seated at the table. They had all showered and changed as well. Eddy wore board shorts and a T-shirt, while Lexie wore a flowered dress.

"Sorry," I said. "I wanted a walk on the beach before dinner."

Dad smiled. "It's lovely, isn't it?"

I answered honestly. "Most beautiful beach I've ever seen in my life." I slid into a chair next to Eddy and he handed me a plate with rib eye steaks on it. I stabbed one with my fork and set it on my plate, then passed them on to my father.

He took one and set the plate down. "I thought we could all walk the beach after dinner."

I dished up some salad and asparagus, then started eating. I was starving and had eaten half my plate before I set my fork down. "So are we leaving tomorrow?"

Dad paused, his fork in midair. "I'll make sure the jet is ready."

Eddy said, "But we just got here."

"Yeah," added Lexie. "I wanted some time on the beach."

Dad smiled. "You two are staying. Eli will go back and get the rest of the family."

Eddy sat up. "They're all coming?"

"Everyone will be together?" Lexie asked. She glanced at me. "Mom is on board for a vacation?"

"It's not a vacation." I turned to my father. "Isn't that right, Dad?"

He looked slightly uncomfortable before catching himself and putting a smile on his face. "We all belong together, and this is the most beautiful place I could find."

How was I going to convince Eddy that he and Lexie needed to be on the plane with me? He was so happy; he'd just gotten his father back, and the island was paradise.

The rest of dinner was small talk, and then Dad stood up. "Should we take that walk now?"

We all went out on the beach, Lexie in front, then me, then Eddy and Dad, all of us walking on the wet, hard-packed sand, leaving footprints that washed away as soon as each wave came in. Behind me, Eddy told Dad, with a slight wobble in his voice, "It is so wonderful to be back with you."

Dad put his arm around Eddy's shoulder. "I missed you, son. Leaving you out of the Compound was the hardest part of the whole thing."

Did he say *leaving him out?* I forced myself to keep walking, pretend I wasn't listening.

Dad continued, "But one of us had to stay in the real world, keep the name going. Otherwise YK might have been broken up, gone downhill."

I whipped around, standing in their path and forcing them to stop. "You're a liar."

Dad's lips trembled for a moment before he forced them into a smile. "It's been a long time, Eli. It's probably hard for you to remember."

I shook my head. "No, I remember it like it was yesterday. And it was not part of your plan to leave him out!"

Eddy said, "Dude, just chill. You were a little kid and—"

"No!" I shouted. "I remember it like it was yesterday because I thought about it every frickin' day for six years! Dad didn't plan it! He was shocked when he closed the door and you weren't there. I remember!"

Dad said, "Son, you may not have known it at the time, but leaving Eddy out was definitely prearranged."

"No, it wasn't!" I screamed at him.

Dad looked as if I'd hit him.

Eddy turned from Dad to me, and then asked, "How are you so sure?"

I stood there, trying to catch my breath. My heart pounded and my face burned. "I know, because . . ."

Lexie came up beside me and put a hand on my arm.

She knew my secret. I'd told her and Mom in the Compound when we thought Dad was dying. She said, "Tell them."

I looked at Eddy. "It was my fault. I did it. I was the reason you were left out."

CHAPTER THIRTY-FOUR

VISIONS OF THAT NIGHT, THE NIGHT OF OUR NINTH birthday, all came back to me.

Our ninth birthday. We were excited to be almost in double digits. The annual big party was held the day before, so we could head to the cabin on the actual day. Dad's acreage in eastern Washington was huge, with a ten-room log house we called the cabin. We had an RV, too, which we used to drive farther into the wilderness to go camping. Not that an RV was roughing it, but that's what we called camping anyway.

Gram came with us, sort of. She followed the RV with the Range Rover. She said she always liked to be prepared for emergencies. Although to her, an emergency might constitute running out of marshmallows for the s'mores we made over the campfire. A trip in the RV wasn't a trip without Gram driving back to the cabin at least once.

As we drove along, Dad told us he had a big surprise for us. And he did. He'd just bought a new two-seater airplane. It went along with the new landing strip in the middle of the property, which is where we went with the RV. It was already dusk when we reached the site, so Dad promised we'd go flying first thing in the morning. We'd flip a coin to see which birthday boy would go first. Of course, I wanted it to be me.

We were getting ready for bed when Eddy started wheezing. Dad discovered a kitten in the RV. Terese admitted to finding it at the cabin, then smuggling it onto the RV. She started to cry and apologized to Eddy. She said she just wanted to make sure the kitten had a home.

The RV medicine cabinet always had some antihistamine for Eddy, but Mom came back empty-handed. "We better go get some at the cabin."

Gram volunteered.

Eddy said he felt better. Gram insisted. "Just let me tuck Terese in. I'll take the kitten back to the cabin and get it set up in the garage."

Eddy and I crawled into bed. The airplane ride was still on my mind. "Hey, Eddy. I heard Dad and Gram talking. They said they have another surprise back at the cabin for us. What do you think it is?"

Eddy's eyes widened. He loved surprises.

"Guess we'll have to wait for tomorrow." I rolled over and shut my eyes. I counted on the fact that Eddy also loved a mission.

"Eli? I've got an idea."

"What?" I tried to stop them, but the corners of my mouth wanted to go up.

"I could hop in the back of the Range Rover and go with Gram. I could find out what it is."

I sat up. "That's a great idea. But you have to go now, while she's with Terese."

Eddy opened the window and dropped to the ground. I lay back, grinning. I knew once Eddy was in the Range Rover with the kitten, he would start wheezing. And Gram would keep driving to the cabin; insist on staying there overnight. I would be the only birthday boy around in the morning when it was time to ride in Dad's new plane.

The rest I didn't plan on: waking up to shouts, the RV moving wildly from side to side, falling out of bed. Then the darkness, running blind outside, Dad's shouts telling us which way to turn . . .

And then we were in the Compound. The silver door had shut and locked, not to be reopened for twenty years. And I had called for Eddy, even though I knew he wasn't there.

My lie had caused him to be left outside. And at that moment, and for six years after, I'd believed he was dead. Just as I believed my lie had killed him.

Eddy stood there, mouth slack, thick creases in his forehead. "How could you do that?"

"I was nine years old." He was missing the point. "I felt guilty all those years." I pointed at Dad. "Because he let me believe all those years that you were dead!"

Eddy's gaze moved slowly to our father, who was staring out at the water, and the sun that was slowly sinking. His face was entirely relaxed.

"Dad," I said. "Is this it? You don't want to explain any of it to him?" My hope was that Eddy would realize how messed up Dad was. That he wouldn't want anything to do with him, and he would fight to get us off the island.

But Eddy turned to me. "Why are you doing this?"

I froze. "Doing what?"

Eddy shook his head. "You're grasping. Somehow you've built this all up in your head, that Dad is evil." He looked at Dad, who had turned to listen to him. Eddy continued, "But it was just a plan. Dad had a plan and now you're all back and everyone's fine."

Lexie scowled. "Eddy, seriously. You think we made it all up?"

And I realized that we had left out all the bad parts about the Compound. We'd made it sound like we were fine there. Because it wouldn't have done him or Gram any good to know the whole truth. So there was a lot that Eddy didn't know. And maybe it was time he did.

I turned to Dad. "Are you going to tell him about the yellow room or should I?"

"No." Lexie pulled on my sleeve. "Eli, don't."

Dad ignored me and started walking again.

"Stop!" I yelled. "Tell him! Tell him the frickin' truth!"

Eddy grabbed the collar of my T-shirt and bunched it up in his hand, pulling me toward him. "That's enough. I get it. You felt guilty about what you did. But don't start blaming it all on Dad."

And suddenly I had Eddy's neck in my grasp and I pushed him backward into the sand. We rolled a few times, then I pinned him to the beach. Lexie had her arm around my neck and was trying to pull me back, while Dad had turned around to watch, an amused expression on his face.

"You need to listen!" I yelled at Eddy. "You need to understand! Don't you get it? He messed up the food supply! He tried to push us to the edge. He wanted to see what we would do to survive." I looked up at Dad. "Tell him about the yellow room. Tell him."

Dad didn't say anything, just crossed his arms.

Eddy tried to shove me off him, and I slipped, so suddenly he had the upper hand and had rolled me over, so he was sitting on me. I was pinned, but it didn't matter. I felt hot tears well up in my eyes as I yelled, "Tell him about the yellow room!"

Eddy leaned down, almost to my face. "What! What was in the yellow room?"

His knee was in my chest and it was hard to get a full breath.

Lexie said, "Don't, Eli! Don't!"

I squeezed my eyes shut but tears still managed to leak out. "The Supplements."

Lexie turned away.

Eddy frowned. "I don't know what that means."

My breathing was even more constricted, and I fought to get free, but he shoved me back. So I gave up and lay there. "Do you really want to know?"

Eddy nodded.

"The Supplements. Lucas. Quinn. Cara. What Finn would have been."

Eddy looked confused, and started to say something, then he stopped. Realization spread across his face and his mouth fell open. He looked over at our father. "What is he saying?"

Dad said nothing. So I did. "They were going to supplement our food supply when it ran out."

"Oh, my God." Eddy got off me and fell face forward into the sand as he tried to get up. When he finally got to his feet, he started walking backward, his horrified gaze going between me and Dad. Finally, he turned and ran up the beach.

I got to my feet and went after him.

Eddy was fast, but I was the runner, and I soon caught up to him. I ran behind him until his legs gave out, then he dropped to his knees and covered his face with his hands. I dodged to the side, then stopped, and turned to face him. "I'm sorry. I never wanted you to find out."

Eddy lowered his hands. His cheeks were tear streaked and he blinked back more. "I should have been there. I should have been there."

I sank to my knees in front of him. "No."

"Maybe I could have done something." He slapped a hand into the sand. "I feel so guilty that you all went through it and I didn't do anything!"

"You did," I said.

He just looked at me.

I nodded. "I missed you so much. And I felt so guilty for what I'd done. And it was that, the guilt and your absence, which sent me into your room. That's how I found the laptop, and eventually found the wireless signal."

Eddy said, "But I feel terrible I wasn't there! I feel so guilty that I didn't suffer like you all did!"

I grabbed both of his arms. "Don't you get it? If you had been there, *we would still be there.* I wouldn't have found the wireless, wouldn't have discovered Dad was lying to us, and we would still be there, thinking the rest of the world had perished."

Eddy looked off into the distance for a moment, maybe digesting it all. "But we would have all been together."

I didn't say anything. He needed to figure it out for himself.

His voice was almost a whisper. "But it wouldn't have been enough. To be together. Would it?"

I slowly shook my head. "We would still have been Dad's prisoners. Living a lie. Which isn't living. Trust me."

Eddy looked back down the beach, where Dad and Lexie stood about fifty yards apart. "He's doing it again. He's going to get us all here and do it again."

I nodded. "He told me about this place when we were still down there. That is what he planned to do as soon as we got out, bring us here. But I thought he was dead. So I never even considered . . ."

"I'm sorry," he said. "I'm sorry for not . . . listening to you."

I shrugged. "Not the first time."

"So what do we do? How do we get out of here?"

I said, "I think I have a plan."

CHAPTER THIRTY-FIVE

AFTER I TOLD EDDY MY PLAN, WE WALKED BACK TO LEXIE and Dad. Eddy smiled. "Sorry. We just had to get all that out. We're good."

Lexie scowled at us, but I tried to give her a look to say I'd explain it to her later.

I asked, "So, is there dessert?"

Back at Dad's house, all the dinner dishes had been cleared and the table was reset with dessert plates and forks, and a cake with white frosting and coconut sat in the middle of the table. I dished up slices and passed them around, trying to look much more cheerful than I felt.

We started to eat. Eddy said, "I could get used to this."

Dad said, "You'll all have plenty of time for that."

Lexie finished chewing. "Dad? We're going home to Seattle, aren't we?" Her gaze darted to me and then back to Dad. "I don't want to stay here forever."

Dad shut his eyes. He put a hand on each temple and rubbed. "When will you three get it through your heads that"—suddenly, his eyes snapped open and he pounded both fists on the table, hurtling his plate through the air and onto the floor, where it smashed, cake skidding everywhere—"I am your FATHER AND I KNOW BEST!"

Lexie shrunk back from the table as Eddy grabbed my arm.

My throat tightened. "Dad. She didn't mean anything."

Dad slowly tilted his head to one side, then the other, with a slight *crack*. "Really, Eli? She didn't mean anything? She was questioning me, wasn't she?"

Lexie slid out of her chair and came around to stand behind our chairs, putting Eddy and me between her and Dad. I felt her hand on my shoulder and I reached up to grasp it. I said, "She's just saying that she doesn't want to stay here forever. None of us do."

"IT'S NOT YOUR CHOICE!"

The three of us jumped.

I swallowed. We had to get him calmed down. If we didn't, he might not let even one of us leave. And for my plan to work—my loose, probably lousy plan—I needed that plane fueled and ready, with Tony in the cockpit ready to fly.

"Dad," I said. "Remember you talked about adjusting to things slowly?"

He glared at me, but didn't say anything.

I continued, "You need to give us time. Just to . . . get

used to the idea. This place is beautiful and I know we'll all be happy here." Eddy's hand tightened on my arm as Lexie's hand squeezed mine. *Let me work here*, I wanted to tell them. I kept going. "You are already used to the idea, you've been living here. You need to know we'll all need some time. It's another new home for us, and the moving is hard."

Dad let out a sigh and his eyes softened. "I just want things to happen now. I've been without you for so long. I want us to be a family again."

I had to make him believe we were on board. So I nodded. "We all want that. Right?" I widened my eyes at Eddy and, since Lexie was still standing behind me, I squeezed her hand.

"Yeah," said Eddy, probably too forcefully, but Dad didn't seem to notice.

Lexie's voice wobbled as she added, "I want us all to-gether, too."

Dad smiled as he looked at each one of us. He rubbed his hands together. "Well, then that's settled. Tomorrow we'll send Eli to get the rest of the family."

The steak I'd eaten threatened to come back up as I stood and walked over to my father. "I can't wait for our family to be whole again." Then I leaned forward and wrapped my arms around him.

When I stood back up, a man with a dark crew cut, wearing an aloha shirt and khakis, was holding a pitcher of ice water. He filled our glasses and left.

Lexie asked, "Who was that?"

"Gerard." Dad cut into his replacement cake. "One of the staff." He took a bite of cake. "He'd retired from one of my favorite restaurants in Seattle a few years ago." He swallowed and bit off another piece. "He was very happy to get out of the rain. And the retirement home."

Lexie looked at me and I glanced at Eddy. The look on his face proved that he was definitely as ready to get out of here as I was.

CHAPTER THIRTY-SIX

WHEN DINNER FINALLY ENDED, AND WE'D PLAYED SEVERAL hands of cards, Dad yawned and headed up to bed. Eddy, Lexie, and I all went to our separate bedrooms. After an hour, when I was sure Dad would be asleep, I knocked on their doors and they followed me back to my room. The three of us sat on my bed.

Lexie asked me, "What's going on?"

Eddy said, "He's got a plan."

"Will it work?" asked Lexie.

"No clue. But it's all we've got." I sighed. "Tony . . . *Phil,* I mean, is planning on flying me out of here in the morning. But plan on him flying all of us out of here."

"I can't believe he is Phil," Lexie said. "I feel so stupid."

Eddy said, "I'm the one who should feel stupid. I brought him into our lives."

"It was planned," I said. "He would have found a way in."

Eddy said, "Yeah, maybe. I just felt so comfortable the first time I met Tony, like I already knew him."

"Because you did already know him," I said.

Eddy made a face.

Lexie perked up. "How are you going to get him to help us?"

"Even though he's a teenager now, I don't think Phil has changed that much, when it comes right down to it. And that's what I'm counting on." I didn't want to explain further. My plan hinged on nothing more than a couple of hunches, and if my gut instincts failed me . . . "I need you guys to go down to breakfast tomorrow like everything is normal."

Lexie sighed. "Right."

I set a hand on hers. "You have to do this."

She nodded.

Eddy asked, "What else?"

I rubbed my chin for a moment. "I wish we had cell phones or some way to communicate." I sighed. "We just have to time it right. I will leave during breakfast, say I want to go for a run before the flight. You guys need to keep Dad busy. Keep him here. And keep him happy."

Eddy asked, "Shouldn't we be at the jet?"

I shook my head.

Lexie broke in, "But I thought we were all—"

I held up my hand. "I won't leave without you. But you need to keep him here as long as you can. I'll come back for you. I promise. Okay?"

They looked at each other and nodded.

Eddy yawned. "I'm going to bed." He stuck his hand out. I put mine on top, and Lexie set hers on mine. No one said anything, just let them stay like that for a moment, before Eddy pulled his back and Lexie and I did the same.

Eddy left, but Lexie lingered by the door. She turned back to me. "I asked Dad. About my birth mother."

"And?"

She lifted and lowered a shoulder. "He said they took babies from everywhere, that all the babies got a fresh start no matter where they were from."

"Was that it?"

She shook her head. "He said he never wanted to know about any baby's background, and he never asked the people that ran the home. He also said he had never planned to adopt anyone. But Mom fell in love with me and wouldn't stop pestering him until he gave in." She smiled. "He said they both fell in love with me and couldn't imagine life without me."

I said, "There you go. You have *your* answer."

She frowned. "What do you mean by that?"

I looked down at the floor. "You have your answer. That's what I meant."

She came over and sat beside me. "What's wrong?"

"You know that you don't . . . that you aren't . . ." I sighed. "You know that you aren't your birth mother's child. I mean, she didn't raise you, she didn't affect your upbringing in any way."

Lexie nodded. "Yeah. That's a good thing. To know I'm not a monster."

I met her eyes. "But I was raised by mine."

"By your what?"

"Dad is . . ." I swallowed. "He's not right. And I'm his son. Eddy only had nine years, but I had my entire life to be affected . . . molded by his thinking." I shrugged. "What if I'm like him?"

Lexie put an arm around my shoulders. "You're not."

"But what if I am?"

She shook her head. "If you were like him, you would leave tomorrow. You would leave us here." That sentence hung in the air for a moment. "But I know you won't."

I hoped she was right.

She asked, "Eli, if we do leave here tomorrow . . . will we ever see Dad again?"

If we left, would I ever *want* to see him again?

The answer to both questions was the same. "I don't know."

That night, with all the thoughts racing through my head, I was barely able to get any sleep. When the bedside clock said seven, I got up. I threw on some running shorts and a T-shirt and dug in the closet for socks and shoes. I opened the drawer of the desk and took out a pen, which I put in my pocket. Then I went down to breakfast.

As planned, Eddy and Lexie were there, plates of eggs and sausage in front of them, pitchers of juice and milk on the table. Dad was nowhere in sight. "Where is he?" I asked.

Eddy looked behind him, then leaned forward and said in a low voice, "Haven't seen him yet."

Lexie said, "Maybe he's still sleeping?"

"I don't know," I said. "When he comes, tell him I went for a run on the beach." I started to go, then turned back. I took the time to look at them both, hoping I would see them again in just a little while, when I came to get them, so we could leave there.

Lexie stood and came to my side. "Be careful." Then she hugged me. Eddy came over and put his arms around both of us.

Then we each stepped back for one last nod, and I left.

Trying to hurry, I jogged as much as I could on my way to the lab Dad had shown us the day before. The doors opened and I stepped into the cool interior. I paused there for a moment, letting myself cool off before heading down the hallway to the silver door with the keypad.

I stood in front of the silver door. My plan was to try a couple of codes, hope something worked. A very lame plan, but it was all I had. Dad had punched in only six numbers yesterday, I was sure of it. My first thought was a date.

But which one?

It could have been when we went into the Compound or when we got out of the Compound. Or his wedding to my mom. Or the birth of any of us.

The real problem was how many wrong tries would I get before it locked me out?

I took a deep breath and punched in my parents'

wedding anniversary. Two short beeps sounded, and nothing else happened.

Sweat dripped off my forehead. I rubbed my fingers together. "Please, please, please . . ." I tried again, punching in my, and Eddy's, birth date.

Two short beeps sounded, like before, only the door slowly opened.

I whispered, "Oh, thank you—"

A pretty blond woman in a lab coat stepped out through it. She frowned at me.

"Oh, hi!" I forced a big grin on my face and wiped my forehead with a trembling hand. "Wow, Dad didn't warn me how hot it would be here."

Instantly, the lines on her forehead disappeared as she smiled. "Are you one of the twins?" Her accent sounded Scandinavian, Norwegian or Swedish, I couldn't tell for sure. "I heard you arrived yesterday."

I stuck out my hand, willing it not to shake. "Eli. And you are?"

She held out her hand and grasped mine for a moment, then let it go. "Dr. Sylvia Jorgenson."

"Oh, perfect!" I said. "Dad actually sent me here for you. Since I was going on a run anyway. He needs you . . ." I snapped my fingers and scrunched my eyes shut. "Shoot, I forgot the name, but it's that building next door."

"Building B?" she asked.

Wow, would she buy that I had forgotten a frickin' *letter*? I needed to sound dumber, if possible. "Oh, duh." I rolled my eyes. "Yeah, that was totally it."

She looked confused. "Are you sure?"

I shrugged. "He was talking all fast and loud, yelling actually, but I think that's what he said." I made a point of frowning. "I hope I didn't get the message wrong. Is there a phone where I could call him and check?"

"No, no." She waved her hand frantically, apparently not willing to show a lack of confidence in the boss, no matter how small. "I will go there and meet him." She brushed by me, then turned back to the open door. "I need to close that."

"Oh, I've got it, ma'am." I put my hand on it and started pushing it closed. "No problem."

She nodded at me. "Thank you." Then she marched off down the hallway, heels clicking on the floor.

I slipped inside the door, then took the pen out of my pocket and stuck it in the opening so the door wouldn't close all the way. I fell back against the wall for a moment, and placed my hand over my pounding heart. "That was too frickin' close."

CHAPTER THIRTY-SEVEN

WHEN I HAD CALMED SLIGHTLY, I RAN FOR THE ROOM with the gene gun, pushing through the plastic curtain. I went over to the shelves and picked up the black box I had seen the day before.

My heart started to pound. I was right.

The black remote was exactly like the one in the Compound: the one Dad had used to set off the explosion.

My plan was nothing more than a gamble, but I was betting on the whole island being rigged to go off, just like the Compound had been.

My plan counted on it.

I would go back to the house, Dad would be there with Eddy and Lexie, and I would wield the remote, threaten to blow up the island if he didn't let us go. And if I was right, if Tony still held all his Phil-like qualities, he would want to save his own skin. So he would happily fly us off in the jet.

I heard a sound from the back of the room. I looked that way and saw the closed door I'd seen the other day. I needed to leave, and I headed for the plastic curtain and the way out. But I heard the sound again, almost like a mewling.

Were there research animals back there?

The least I could do would be to release them. Give them a chance to survive on the island. I didn't give a damn what it did to Dad's heinous research.

The latch was locked from the outside, so I easily unlocked it and pulled the door open, releasing a smell of floral-scented disinfectant that didn't entirely mask a much less pleasant odor.

From inside came a mechanical and steady *whoosh whoosh whoosh* that grew louder as I walked farther into the room. But that wasn't the sound I'd heard.

Then I heard the mewling again.

The room held several structures that resembled cribs, except they had solid sides instead of slats, and they were much bigger than those that held babies. Each had a machine hooked up to it, the source of the whooshing sound.

Were they respirators of some kind?

I slowly stepped nearer to the closest one and peered over the side.

I gasped and jumped back, my free hand clasped over my mouth.

What in the—?

My heart began to pound.

That crib held something unnatural. Something impossible.

I took one step only, then leaned forward to look again.

Something lay there on the white mattress. Something human, but not human. The being was the shape of a human, with normal-size limbs for an adult, only they looked deflated, like a balloon with no air. Suddenly, one of the saggy arms reached up and the creature rolled toward me. Under an oxygen mask, the flesh on the face looked like it had fallen off the bones. "Help me," it mewled. And the mewling turned louder, until the sound turned to an inhuman shriek. "Help me!"

My throat tightened, and I backed away until I couldn't go any farther. I had backed into another of the cribs, and I twirled around to see another creature that resembled the first, holding out its alien arms to me.

I cried out and stepped back, my hand on my chest, where my heart threatened to pound its way out.

More mewling came from the back of the room, where a curtain was drawn. I trudged forward and reached up to grasp the edge. The metal rings at the top clinked as I yanked it open a few feet.

The room was larger than it first appeared, and went on for another hundred yards at least. Enough space to hold dozens more of the cribs, all with respirators making the same *whoosh whoosh whoosh*. And, spurred on by the two shrieking creatures in the front of the room, a chorus of mewling arose from every crib, growing louder as I stood there.

Did every single crib contain one of those creatures?

"Oh, my God." I started to back up toward the door.

"Pity, but it's not an exact science yet."

I whipped around.

My father stood there, between me and the door, blocking my way out.

CHAPTER THIRTY-EIGHT

My throat was so tight, I could barely swallow, but I managed to squeak out, "What are those things?"

Dad shrugged. "We're still working on being able to dictate the precise age. Some of the people didn't *de-age* as expected, especially when we went beyond forty years or so. But all their memories and knowledge seem to remain."

My knees started to buckle and I grabbed hold of the nearest crib to stay upright. "Oh, my God! They still know everything? They're still aware?" I looked down at the creature in the crib, huddled in the fetal position, making the mewling sound I'd heard from outside. "How can you let them suffer like this?"

Dad shook his head slightly. "They did all sign waivers." He noticed the remote in my hand. "Going to blow us all up?" He started toward me. "All that will do is set off a warning that will only be a drill." He held out his hand. "Eli, save us all a wasted day of resetting the alarms and hand it over."

"You're lying!" I backed toward the wall, trying to edge my way toward the door.

Dad kept coming toward me as he still blocked my way to the door.

I raised the black box up. "Stop! Or I'll push the button."

"Eli," Dad repeated. "It will only set off a drill." But his eyes weren't as calm as his voice. Was he afraid?

I took a chance and held up the remote, my finger poised above the button. "Back off or I'll push it."

"Fine, fine." Dad held up his hands and moved to the side so I could get to the door. I backed through it in order to keep an eye on him the whole way, and kept going until something stopped my progress. I glanced behind me.

The machine with the gene gun.

I grabbed the gun and held it out in my other hand.

Dad laughed.

I glanced down at the machine. The dial made no sense, but I saw what looked like a power button and pushed it. With a whir, the entire thing started vibrating. I held the gun out and said, "Stay back."

Dad shook his head. "Or what? You'll de-age me?" He laughed again.

I said, "That's why you didn't use it on yourself. Because the process isn't perfected yet."

The machine beeped. I wondered if that meant it was

ready. Dad kept advancing toward me, and I took a firmer hold on the gun in one hand, the black remote in the other. "I won't let you have my family."

Dad frowned. "They're my family, too. You're all my family."

I shook my head. "Not anymore. Not after what you did. And I won't let you do it again."

"We can talk about this later," said Dad. "There's been a slight change of plans. I've decided your brother and sister should go back to Seattle. You can stay here until the rest of them come."

"They won't leave without me," I said.

Dad laughed. "Really? You think they love you that much that they'd stay here and wait for you to come get them? You really believe that?" He shook his head.

The gun trembled in my hand and I felt my chin wobble.

Would I stay for them?

And I realized that I already *was* staying for them. I was standing here in this room in order to take them with me, get us home. I swallowed, and said with the most conviction I could muster, "I do believe it."

Suddenly, Tony was there. He told Dad, "The jet is ready to go." He looked at me. "You ready?"

Dad had lied to me. He hadn't changed his mind. At least, not the way he told me he had.

"No!" Dad shouted. "None of them are leaving! My wife can bring the rest of my family here if she ever wants to see them again." He lunged for me.

I stumbled, trying hard to hold on to the gene gun, that as I fell, I accidentally squeezed the button on the black remote.

Immediately, a deafening high-pitched electronic beeping began.

Dad was on top of me, grabbing for the gene gun. I shoved it out toward him, my finger pulling the trigger with the hope it would shock him or something. As it connected with his stomach, my finger got stuck, keeping the trigger on for several seconds. I heard several mechanical punching sounds.

Dad rolled off me to the floor. His eyes widened and he tried to get up, but fell back. His limbs began to shake and he started convulsing.

I jumped to my feet and backed away.

As Tony and I watched, my father's hair turned darker and thicker and curlier, growing longer before our eyes. Immediately his limbs began to shrivel and shrink; then his fingers folded in on his hands and his feet curled up.

"What's happening?" I yelled.

Tony yelled back, "He's de-aging!"

My father's limbs continued to shrivel, but they stopped getting smaller. They were deflating, like a balloon that had lost its air. And then he was suddenly still. His flesh hung there, saggy, just like the creatures in the cribs.

Tony said, "My, God, it didn't work on him."

CHAPTER THIRTY-NINE

MY FATHER, THE CREATURE THAT HAD BEEN REX Yanakakis, reached up for me and mewled, "Son."

I stood there, looking down at him, unable to move.

"Kid!" Tony grabbed me. "This place is gonna blow."

I yelled, "He told me it was a drill!"

The expression on Tony's face was serious when he shook his head. He didn't need to say a word.

I said, "But we have to help him!"

Tony pointed at the open door to the room with the cribs. "Like he helps them? Leaving them in there like that?" He shook his head. "They need to be put out of their misery." He pointed at my father. "So does he." Tony grabbed me. "Do you want to live?"

I nodded.

"This place will be a chain reaction. As soon as I hear the first explosion, I'm going," he said. "With or without you.

You've got about nine minutes, kid." And he disappeared through the plastic curtain.

I turned back to my dad, who still lay on the floor, curled up and mewling. I knelt beside him, wanting to throw up, wanting to run away. I set my hand on his arm. It was soft and mushy, and I yanked my hand back.

Dad tried to say something, but I couldn't understand what it was. I didn't want to understand. I stood up. "I'm sorry."

Only thirty seconds behind Tony, I ran through the plastic curtain and down the hallway. Outside, the sun hit me. And I realized Eddy and Lexie weren't going to be at the jet.

Maybe, when Dad hadn't shown up at the house, they decided to go to the jet, ignoring my orders?

But if I went to the jet and they weren't there . . . I'd have no time to get them. I couldn't risk it.

If I wanted to save them, there was only one option.

The electronic beeping was everywhere, increasing in speed and volume. As fast as I could, I ran through the plaza toward the house, dodging people who seemed to be unconcerned about the alarm. Apparently, they'd been told, and believed, that it was just a drill.

I hurried through the fence and onto the path and into the house, screaming, "Eddy! Lexie! Where are you?" I ran into the living room and saw no one. I screamed their names a few more times, then made a decision. They had to be at the jet. They hadn't listened to me.

I ran down the hallway and out the back. I leaped

down the steps of the marble veranda, hit the path, and went through the door in the wall.

I heard a roar. The jet.

"No!" I yelled. I tried to run on the boardwalk through the jungle, but it was slow going and I was forced to shorten my steps, pounding my way toward the runway. Finally, I reached the trees and caught a glimpse of the runway. I sprinted the rest of the way, triumphantly emerging out of breath where the jet had been the day before.

But the jet was gone.

CHAPTER FORTY

ABOUT A QUARTER MILE AWAY TO MY RIGHT, THE TAXIING jet was just about to reach the end of the runway, where it would turn around and accelerate down the length of the runway and take off.

"No! Wait!" I screamed. "I'm coming!"

And I pushed for the aircraft, my legs and lungs already burning. My heart was nearly pounding out of my chest, and I pumped my arms like my life depended on it, which I was pretty sure it did.

The jet reached the end and circled around until the left side faced me, but it was still far from me. It paused there, not moving.

Was Tony waiting for me? Were Eddy and Lexie on board?

I slowed to a fast jog, relieved.

I would get there, make sure my brother and sister

were on it, and then we could go. Tony said he'd wait for the first explosion. And that hadn't—

BOOM!

The ground shuddered beneath my feet and I stumbled and tripped, falling onto the hot tarmac. I got to my feet, my knees skinned and bloody.

The jet had started to roll.

As fast as I could run, I headed straight for it, wincing at the pain in my knees. I aimed for the front of it, trying to cut off some distance. The smell of jet fuel made me want to gag, and the roar of the jet deafened me.

Just as I got closer, the jet passed me.

Tony was leaving without me.

I slowed to a jog, not wanting to give up. But there was nothing left to do.

It was over. Done.

Then, suddenly, the door opened and Eddy's head popped out. "Run!" He screamed something else, along with Tony's name, and the jet slowed slightly. The speed was not yet so fast that I didn't have a chance to catch it, so I mustered up every ounce of energy I had and gave chase.

My lungs threatened to burst as I pumped my arms, running faster than I ever thought possible. Eddy was lying on his belly and reached out to me with both his arms. "Grab hold!"

I had to sprint even faster to get ahead of the wing, and then I lunged, reaching with my right hand. Eddy grabbed my hand, then clutched my arm with his other hand, so he had me with both. My left hand still held the gene gun, which I heaved over Eddy's head before grabbing onto the side of the door.

"Hold on!" Eddy yelled as the jet increased in speed.

"Don't let go!" I screamed. My legs could no longer keep up so I curled them up using my abs, pulling myself off the runway, but putting more strain on my grip on the door.

And Eddy's hold on me.

His face inches from mine. I was all sweaty, and my hand and arm began slipping from his grip. "Don't let me go!" I screamed. "Eddy!"

And then we were speeding down the runway, heading to take off as I still hung halfway out.

Over the roar of the jet, I heard another explosion and felt the jet tremble, then another.

From the cockpit, Tony yelled, "We're not gonna make it!"

Eddy grimaced, his face red with exertion as he struggled to hold on to me. But I felt my own grip on the door failing, my legs were too heavy to keep holding up like that, and Eddy's hands began to slip.

I grunted, trying to hold on. But I couldn't any longer and I started falling—

Then Lexie was there, kneeling, half on top of Eddy, yanking on my other arm with a strength I never knew she had. I was almost in, on top of her and Eddy, part of my legs still dangling outside the door.

But none of us had leverage inside the jet, and with Lexie's added weight, I felt us start to edge our way out the door. My upper half was barely inside the door, and the metal legs of the front seat were just out of my reach. I strained for them with my fingertips, as my brother and sister did everything they could to hang on to me and keep us all from sliding out the door.

My fingers reached out. *Come on!*

Just as Lexie screamed, "I can't hold on!" the front of the jet began to lift, sliding us back far enough so I could grab the metal leg. I pulled with everything I had left, dragging myself all the way in, where I fell on my side on the floor. Lexie and Eddy scrambled backward to safety, then Eddy reached out and shoved the lever for the door, which closed as the jet left the ground.

Eddy and Lexie collapsed beside me, and the three of us lay there, chests heaving. We heard a series of booms, all rocking the jet, causing enough turbulence that we had to grab on to the legs of the seats.

Tony yelled, "You all in?"

"Yeah," yelled Eddy.

The jet shuddered.

"Better buckle up!" Tony yelled.

I crawled up into the seat by the window, Lexie beside me, and Eddy across the aisle. I doubled over, trying to catch my breath as I strapped myself in. Tony slowly circled back around to head east. I looked out the window.

The entire island was ablaze, explosions still bursting. Even if the scientists had tried to leave, it was obvious that none had made it.

Lexie put her hand on my leg and I turned to face her.

Tears streaked down her red face. "When Dad didn't come home, it was my idea to meet you at the jet. I thought we were leaving you. Why weren't you with Tony?"

I managed a bit of a smile. "I wanted to make sure you and Eddy weren't at the house."

"You were worried about leaving us?"

I nodded.

She leaned her head on my shoulder and sighed. "Neither one of us are."

"Are what?" I asked.

"Monsters," she said. "Neither one of us are monsters."

Eddy reached across the aisle with his hand. I grabbed it and held on. He was crying, too.

Lexie sandwiched our hands between both of hers. She said, "It's over."

Yeah. Finally, it was.

Leaving my hand where it was, holding on to my twin's, both snug in our older sister's embrace, I turned once more to the window. My knees stung, my legs and arms felt like I'd run a marathon, and I was still panting. My own eyes filled with tears as I watched the island, in flames, recede from my view, until there was nothing below but blue, blue water. Lexie's head was still on my shoulder, so I leaned my head on hers, closed my eyes, and let Tony fly us home.

EPILOGUE

Now that we're back home, I am trying to come to terms with it all. What my father did to those people. Maybe they all knew what they were getting into. Maybe not.

I told my mom only what she needed to know: Dad's plans to bring us all there and keep us prisoner, again. I told her enough about the research to make Dad appear insane, as he was.

But that room with the cribs? I keep *that* to myself. I didn't even tell Eddy or Lexie. No good will ever come from anyone knowing that.

I told Mom that Dad died in the explosion. Not a lie.

Eddy, Lexie, and I don't agree about Tony. We left that part out when we told Mom everything. We fudged the truth a bit, making up a story about a rogue pilot who saved us in the end.

Obviously, Phil's days at YK are done. Even if we were

to somehow explain how Phil Whitaker, CEO, was now a teenager, Mom would throw him out.

So, for now, we keep Tony as a family friend. Sort of like that saying: Keep your friends close, your enemies closer. He knows we control him. But then, he was always controlled by my dad, so it's not that much of a change for him. He has enough money to see him through this second life he has acquired.

And honestly, Tony is the only person besides me who knows about that crib room. . . . Maybe I need someone around that I can talk to about it. Plus, we would still be on that island if he hadn't flown us home.

Somehow, deep down, I feel like that redeems him, at least a little bit. But I know very little about redemption, so who am I to judge?

Today, I finish it.

Lee is driving me in the SUV to the Progeria Institute. My backpack sits in my lap, my hands resting on the outline of the object inside. We drive through the gate and Lee parks next to the first red building.

I walk inside and head right to Dr. Barkley's office. He's expecting me, and greets me at the door. I take a seat across the desk from him, still holding my backpack in my lap.

I tell him, "There's something you need to know that I've been keeping from you. My name is Eli Yanakakis. I am Rex's son." Saying it aloud wasn't as bad as I had anticipated.

He started to say something, but I kept going. "I have

something that may help your research. But you cannot ask where I got it."

He nods. "No questions. I understand."

I open the backpack and pull out the gene gun. I set it on his desk.

His eyes widen as he carefully picks it up.

I say, "I think . . . I hope there may be genetic material in there that can help your research." I don't tell him that I had his original research on the flash drive for weeks, and that it was recently destroyed in an explosion. I hope the contents of the gene gun will make up for that.

He looks at me. "But where—"

I set a finger on my lips and shake my head.

He smiles. "No questions."

We shake hands and he walks me outside.

On my way back to the SUV, I notice the large building with the pool. I go inside and hear the sounds of laughter and splashing water. I watch the kids in the pool and sit on the bench Verity shared with me that first day.

Will I ever stop being conflicted, wondering whether blowing up the island has hurt any chances there ever were of curing progeria? My only hope is that Dr. Barkley can do something with the gene gun.

I sit here, hoping no one will ask what I'm doing. Because I'm sitting here, waiting, for only one reason: I am hoping Verity might show up.

After forty-five minutes pass, I realize she's not going to be here. I glance at my watch, wondering whether I should stay a few more moments. Or give up.

"EJ?"

My breath catches in my throat as I look up.

Verity is standing in front of me, wearing a flowered miniskirt and bright orange hoodie. She looks so wonderful to me.

All I can do is smile at her. Now that she's here, I'm not sure what to say.

She asks, "Why are you here?"

I say, "I had an appointment with Dr. Barkley."

She rolls her eyes slightly. "Another paper to write?"

I start to say something to appease her, then stop. My plan is to be honest with her, and that means being true to myself, who I am. I am done trying to run from it. "No. There was never any paper."

She frowns.

I say, "And my name isn't EJ. It's Eli. Eli Yanakakis."

She sinks down onto the bench beside me, like her legs have given out.

Go ahead. Make your judgments. Decide I'm some spoiled, rich-kid freak.

"Why?" she asks.

I am confused. "Why what?"

She asks, "Why have you been lying to me?"

The question throws me off for a moment. "Because . . . of who I am."

Verity raises her eyebrows. "So you lie whenever you meet someone?"

I shake my head. "No. I mean . . . I never meet anyone. You're the first girl I've met since—"

"Since you came back from . . . down there."

So she knew. The moment I said my name aloud, she'd probably had news reports flash through her head.

I nod. "And you must think I'm a freak."

Her tone softens. "God, no. I mean, I don't know what happened down there. But I think you're nice, and—" A look passes across her face. "Is this what you were going to tell me the other day? When we were going to meet?"

I nod.

"What happened?"

I blow out a breath and don't say anything for a moment. "It's kind of a long story."

"I have time." She smiles.

I smile back. "Next time." I look down at my hands. "Listen, it's . . . it's hard for me to trust people. And I'm sorry I lied." Then I reach out with both hands and lightly grasp her elbows, pulling her toward me. "If you give me another chance, I—"

She doesn't pull away, but her eyes narrow. "You'll what?"

I don't know.

Part of me wants to let her go, back away, give up on it all, and never see her again. That would be the simple way.

But I *am* Eli Yanakakis. And it seems to be a genetic flaw that I never do anything the simple way.

I take a deep breath, then move my hands up to cradle her face.

I lean in, close my eyes, and kiss her. When I pull my

face back, she smiles up at me. "That's what I wanted to do when I saw you."

My face gets hot and my grin widens.

"So can we reschedule our date?"

"It was a date?" she asks, smiling.

I take a chance. "Yes. It was. It was absolutely a date."

She laughs. "Then I would be honored, Mr. Yanakakis."

"Call me Eli."

"Eli."

Then Verity grabs hold of my hand and squeezes, like she never wants to let go. And that happens to be fine with me.

ACKNOWLEDGMENTS

Kudos to Scott Mendel and Liz Szabla, who always do and say the right things to spur me on. I am grateful to Jean Feiwel and the entire team at Macmillan. Without them, my words on a page would remain simply words on a page.

As always, love to Tim, Bailey, and Tanzie for dealing with a messy house/hungry pets/lack of meals at times. All my extended family is amazing: extra mahalo to Wendy and Rudy, who provide me with an ever-ready Big Island retreat.

There are people who make my life better just by being in it. And they make me laugh. In case you don't know who you are: Jessi Eaton, Karen Dinsmore, Jalyn Thompson, Linda Beck, Maranda Robbins, Lori Dresen, and Kristi Hanson.

Thanks to Mark Roughsedge for early feedback, and the rest of my fellow blogging Spuds on One Potato . . .

Ten: Your support as we all traverse this crazy business together means the world to me. But when it comes down to it, this book would not have happened without the readers of *The Compound*. All the letters, e-mails, and the students I met in schools and through Skype all wanting to know: What happens next? You finally persuaded me that I needed to know, too. I hope you like what I found.

Author S. A. BODEEN talks about

THE FALLOUT

THE SPACE BETWEEN

The Fallout was released five and a quarter years after *The Compound*, quite a long gap for a sequel, I know. And the main reason is that there was never going to be a sequel. For one thing, I didn't want to be *that person*. You know, the one who wrote a crappy sequel. And for another, to me, the story was done. A *tad* open-ended, maybe, but still finished in my mind. And then I started doing a lot of school visits. And Skypes. And at every single one, at least one reader asked, "What happens next?" I quickly assured them, "Nothing. Nothing happens. The story is done." Funny, but no one ever liked that answer. And after being asked so often "What happens next?" I began to wonder myself. In 2011, a full three years after *The Compound* came out, I was watching the news, as I usually do, and a science story came on, one of those revealing a remarkable discovery that always gets my mind reeling with possibilities. And I came up with a potential twist for a sequel to *The Compound*. I couldn't stop thinking about it. A few weeks later, I happened to be on a panel with my editor and had a chance for some one-on-one time. I said to her, "You might think I'm crazy. . . ." I told her my idea and she loved it. So in the fall of 2011, nearly six years to the day that I started writing *The Compound*, I began *The Fallout*. And now here we are. I realize that those five years were necessary. I wasn't ready to write a sequel before that, and if I had, it most certainly would have been bad. I needed those years to get to know my readers, hear the things they had to say about *The Compound*, and figure out the best way to continue the story. Not to mention, I've written a couple novels in the meantime and gotten a bit better at the writing thing in general. And hopefully, for the readers, the wait will turn out to have been worth it.

First appeared on the blog I Read Banned Books (www.jenbigheart.com).

BUILDING A WORLD

Now that *The Fallout* is published, I find myself wondering what readers will think about the setting, because it is quite different from that in the first book. Readers ask me all the time about the room with the yellow door in *The Compound*. The compound itself was quite static. By that, I mean the reader was privy to basically the whole layout: the rooms, what was in them, where they were located. And that wouldn't do. Not at all. I needed a secret. I just knew that there had to something that made Eli uncomfortable, and maybe something he didn't know about, which then gave the reader something they didn't know about and perhaps made them uncomfortable. (Because a comfortable reader is a *bored* reader. And I didn't want that.) So I came up with the room with the yellow door. At first I had no idea what was behind that door. And then I figured it out, and I love how uncomfortable the contents of that room make the readers. While *The Fallout* doesn't have a room with a yellow door, there is a room that, I suspect, will create a lot of discomfort among readers. . . .

First appeared on the blog Live to Read (livetoread-krystal.blogspot.com).

FOOD FOR THE END

Whenever I have a new novel come out, I try to send a little gift to my editor, usually involving some of the items from the book. For *The Compound*, I think the gift involved Snickers, Tic Tacs, and of course, a roll or two of Tums. My husband always asks why my books have so many snacks in them and I'll tell you what I told him. *I like snacks.* And because my books typically have a lot of unpleasant things in them, why shouldn't they also contain things that I think are nice, like foods that I myself enjoy? In *The Gardener*, I put my characters through a lot, but I did let them have a quiet moment with some cold Yoo-hoo. And in *The Raft*, a bag of Skittles has a starring role, and I'm often asked about the recipe for my Better than Anything cake, which is described in detail by the main character of that book. (In real life, I make that cake a lot. I've actually heard my kids and their friends *discuss* that cake.) So, you may ask, what about *The Fallout*? Come on, how could I *not* have food in *The Fallout*? As you've read, not only is there food, there is a trip to the Costco food court, the Mecca for snack-lovers like myself. (I cannot leave a Costco without vanilla FroYo. Cheapest brain freeze ever.) And, I suspect, now that *The Fallout* has hit the shelves, there may be a rush of e-mails in my inbox asking for my Kalua pork recipe.

First appeared on the blog Word Spelunking (workspelunking.blogspot.com).

GOFISH

QUESTIONS FOR THE AUTHOR

S. A. BODEEN

by V Imagery and Design

What did you want to be when you grew up?
An author, of course.

When did you realize you wanted to be a writer?
Grade five. Someone else won the creative writing award and it made me insanely jealous. (I did get the spelling prize, though.)

What's your first childhood memory?
When I was four, getting charged by Eleanor, one of our Holsteins. She had a calf and I got too close and I remember screaming and running for the porch. (I made it, obviously.)

What's your favorite childhood memory?
I grew up on a farm in a small town in Wisconsin. Every summer, my Aunt Connie and Uncle Bud and four cousins would come from Los Angeles. I thought they were like the Brady Bunch and they added color to my black-and-white life.

As a young person, who did you look up to most?
Captain Kirk. He always triumphed over the bad guy, was loyal to his friends, and protective of his crew. I watched *Star Trek* reruns every day after school. You let someone into your living room five days a week and they tend to be fairly influential (as Oprah fans can attest).

What was your worst subject in school?
Art. I got a D+. No chance of me ever illustrating my own work.

What was your best subject in school?
Social studies. Although I couldn't take typing because world history was at the same time. Probably why I have a very unorthodox way of typing . . .

What was your first job?
I always had to help around our farm, but my first paying job was picking strawberries the summer after sixth grade. Ten cents a quart. My take at the end of the summer was $34. I blew it all on a camera.

How did you celebrate publishing your first book?
It was ten years ago and my kids were little. I think we took them out to a McDonald's Playland or something.

What do you consider being a success in the field of publishing?
When your book is an answer on *Jeopardy!*

Where do you write your books?
Usually at the kitchen table.

Where do you find inspiration for your writing?
In things I read, see, watch. I'm also an eavesdropper out in public. Nosiness is good for inspiration, too.

Which of your characters is most like you?
I'm not sure I've written that one yet. But some days, I feel very akin to Eva in *Elizabeti's Doll*.

When you finish a book, who reads it first?
My critique group. I used to hand it off to family members, but that doesn't always work so well.

Are you a morning person or a night owl?
Definitely morning. I rarely stay up after 10 PM.

What's your idea of the best meal ever?
A pregame grill-marked bratwurst with sauerkraut at Lambeau Field.

Which do you like better: cats or dogs?
Cats, but dogs are a close second.

What do you value most in your friends?
Loyalty. Them liking me for who I am. And laughing at my jokes.

Where do you go for peace and quiet?
A hot shower that wastes much water. Or a movie by myself.

What makes you laugh out loud?
The Office. And Stephen Colbert.

What's your favorite song?
Toss-up between "Pride" by U2 and the "Moonlight" Sonata.

Who is your favorite fictional character?
Owen Meany. Harry Potter a close second.

What are you most afraid of?
Deep water. And tornadoes. Basically, Mother Nature in general.

What time of year do you like best?
Spring.

If you were stranded on a desert island, who would you want for company?
The Professor, so he could make me a laptop from a coconut.

If you could travel in time, where would you go?
To 1977, to see my seventh-grade self. I would tell her she will survive those years, and to soak up the drama and angst, because it will make for terrific story material one day.

What's the best advice you have ever received about writing?
It's easier to revise lousy writing than to revise a blank sheet of paper.

What do you want readers to remember about your books?
That they got them thinking.

What would you do if you ever stopped writing?
I'd be a spokesperson for Carmex, can't live without that stuff.

What do you like best about yourself?
I make a really good grilled-cheese.

What is your worst habit?
Putting things off that I need to do.

What is your best habit?
I am a religious flosser.

What do you consider to be your greatest accomplishment?
Actually finishing a novel. And maybe my master's degree.

Sixteen-year-old Robie's cargo plane hits nasty weather and crashes in the middle of the ocean. She is stranded. No water. No food. No hope of survival. Because no one knew Robie was on the plane when it crashed— and no one knows to come find her.

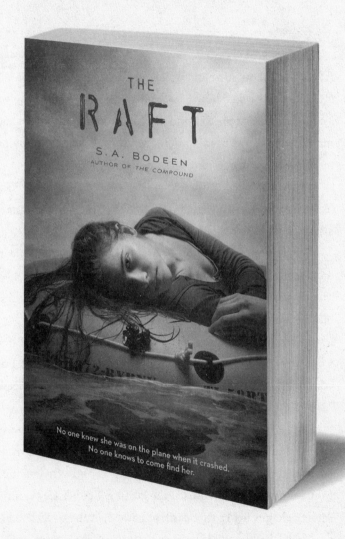

Read on for a taste of S. A. Bodeen's hair-raising survival story.

AJ called at about nine and woke me up.

When she asked how I was, I lied, told her everything was fine and Bobbi had stopped in the day before. I felt bad, but what did it matter when I was heading home anyway? Then I tried my parents, but the phones still weren't working.

When I stepped in the elevator to head down to Starbucks, my heart pounded until I reached the lobby. The security guard who always smiled and called out "Aloha!" wasn't at his post.

Back upstairs, I packed, then went to the pool for a while, made a ham sandwich for lunch, and took a nap. About four, I got dressed. The drive to the airport, and waiting around there, would be hot, but the plane would be chilly, so I had my standard outfit for flying: khaki Bermuda shorts, a white camisole, and my green hoodie. I wore white flip-flops, but shoved a pair of socks in my bag. I debated adding my new Converse, but put them in my suitcase instead. Then I called a taxi.

As usual, the loading of the G-1 at Oahu Air Services was pure chaos, people hauling boxes and cartons and barrels out to the plane. I left my bags by the door to the waiting lounge and went looking for the woman who usually organized the loading. I didn't see her anywhere. A tall, bald guy held a clipboard, so I asked, "Where's Suzanne?"

"Sick." He shook his head. "Of all days. The Costco order didn't get delivered and there's a new copilot." He waved at a couple guys loading the plane. "Hey!" He headed off, leaving me standing there.

The pilot, Larry, came around the plane, wearing black pants and a short-sleeved white button-down shirt with gold pilot epaulets on the shoulders. Tall with dark hair that never had a strand out of place, he swaggered a bit.

I waved.

His forehead wrinkled for a moment, and I called out, "Hi, Larry."

"Robie?" A slow smile spread across his face. "I didn't even recognize you. Nice hair."

"Thanks. I'm trying to catch a flight home."

He nodded. "We'll be stuffed, but there's always room for you."

"I didn't see Suzanne."

He scratched his head. "Yeah, she's gone today. It's a mess, especially with communications down at Midway. My new copilot is around here somewhere, trying to make sense of it all. Max. He'll get you on the manifest. Why don't you wait inside where it's cool? I'll come get you."

The waiting lounge inside Oahu Air Services was air-conditioned and I dropped my bags, then plopped down on the couch. There was a little fridge near the seating area, and I pulled out a Coke, and then grabbed a handful of chocolate-covered macadamia nuts from the koa wood bowl on the table. A golf match blared from the television mounted high on the wall, but there wasn't a remote to change the channel, so I flipped through a *Glamour* magazine for a while.

The flight was supposed to be wheels up around five, putting us on the ground at Midway about eleven or so. During nesting season for the albatross, the Midway runway had hundreds of thousands of bird crossings a day, potential disaster if a jet engine sucked one in, or even if the G-1 collided with a bird. Albatross weigh about fifteen pounds; they're like a flying cannonball with feathers. So flights could only land and take off there at night, when the birds were less active.

I never really got used to flying all that way over water at night. I wasn't scared, because I'd been flying since I was little, but I still tried my best not to think about it. Knowing Larry, and trusting him, helped a lot. I'd taken the G-1 back and forth to Midway probably twenty or so times, most of those at night. Larry could probably fly the route blindfolded.

I waited for them to come and tell me to get weighed. The G-1 could only hold 3,800 pounds of cargo and people, because that's how much it could still fly with if one engine went out. Since we got a supply flight only once a month, and that was all our mail, groceries, parts they needed for the generator and other equipment, it meant we did without a lot that was simply too heavy. Like milk. A gallon of milk weighed eight pounds, and milk for fifty people added up too fast. Thinking about it, I fell asleep on the couch.

Larry shook me awake. "We're ready to go." Then he asked me something about Max and weighing in and paperwork or something.

Still groggy, I just nodded. My watch said nine, which meant we were getting a late start.

He carried my big bag; I took my small one and my backpack. I climbed up the short flight of steps and ducked my head as I stepped aboard. All nine rows of the red upholstered seats were chockful of boxes and cargo, except for two seats halfway back, right next to the starboard exit. The new copilot was already up in the cockpit. Max looked about twenty-five or so; I couldn't tell. Younger than AJ anyway. His dark hair was very short, like in the military, and he wore the same black pants and white shirt as Larry, only he also sported a black tie. Max glanced my way and didn't say anything.

I smiled. "Hi."

For about a millisecond, he nodded and smiled, but his eyes didn't. They seemed sad.

My dad was tall and always had to stoop to avoid the ceiling, but I could walk normally, albeit sideways, through the narrow cabin back to the fifth row of seats. The bin above my seat was filled with a blue mesh bag of satsuma oranges, my favorite. I noticed the Sharpied *Mitchell* on the label and grinned. Part of Mom's grocery order. I undid the top of the bag, pulled out two oranges, and then folded the bag and slammed the bin shut. The bin across the way was also stuffed, so I just put my bag in the seat next to mine. Then I sat down and buckled up.

Although Larry had said it numerous times, he gave me the emergency safety spiel, pointing out the exits, the compartment that held the emergency raft, the flotation device under my seat. He came across a little cocky, but I'd rather have a self-assured, ultra-confident pilot than an insecure one. As always, I listened, but hardly.

I'd heard it all before.

Larry went back to the cockpit and put on his headphones.

Not long after that, the propellers started to turn and air rushed out of the vent above my head. Sweat trickled down the side of my face, so I twisted the knob open all the way and held my face upward, smiling into the cool blast of air. Soon, the propellers buzzed and the plane moved forward, lining up for takeoff.

I looked out the window. A United Airlines jet rumbled as it lifted, probably heading toward the mainland.

A few minutes later, Larry's voice came over the intercom: "Here we go."

My knuckles weren't white as I grasped the seat, but my grip would definitely pass as tight. I wasn't usually this nervous, but I'd just watched the plane crash on *Lost* and was trying hard to put it out of my mind.

The engines motored up to full throttle as we stayed there, so it felt as if we were a dog on a leash, raring to go as someone held us back. My eyes went to the spinning propeller, already going so fast it was invisible, then to the words *Rolls-Royce* on the engine. Larry once told me that Rolls-Royce propellers went counterclockwise. Good *Jeopardy* question.

I leaned my head back on the seat as the G-1 surged forward, rocketing down the tarmac until we gained enough speed. The front wheels lifted and we were airborne, lights below us, the steady drone of the engines loud. Out the window I saw lights from ships in Pearl Harbor, then ships farther out, until they slipped away from my view, leaving only darkness beneath.

The G-1 flew steadily up until it leveled out and I relaxed to the familiar drone of the engines. Home was only a few hours away. Releasing my grip on the seat, I took off my flip-flops, put on my socks, and got comfortable. Still wiped out, I fell asleep.

When I woke up, my watch said one a.m. Lights glowed in the cockpit, but except for the small lighted track along the floor and the galley light, the cabin was dark. The ride was a little turbulent, but I'd been through a lot worse on other flights. An especially rough one had led my mom to say to Larry, upon landing, "Earned your money today, huh?" He had shrugged, then said he didn't think it was a rough flight at all. Since then, I'd read that turbulence didn't ever cause a plane to crash, so bumps didn't really bother me.

Five rows up, Larry sat in the cockpit and Max stood in the galley, sipping from a Styrofoam cup of coffee. Not as tall as Larry, Max was thinner, rather wiry, and athletic looking.

Max went back to the cockpit and Larry stood up. He got a cup of coffee, noticed I was awake, and came my way. "There's a storm front that moved in a little quicker than we expected. I'm going to skirt to the north a bit, but it shouldn't slow us down too much."

"Okay."

"Help yourself." He lifted his cup and went back up front.

Despite the late hour my stomach grumbled, so I unbuckled and went to the galley. A drawer held ice and drinks, and I grabbed a pink can of guava juice before rummaging through a big blue plastic cooler full of sandwiches. I chose a thick turkey one, and then went back to my seat. Unlatching the tray in front of me, I dissected my sandwich, taking off the tomato, lettuce, and white cheese before replacing the top of the onion roll.

At my first bite, the plane shuddered and bumped below me, and an especially large lurch shoved my stomach up into my throat.

Larry's steady voice came over the intercom. "Robie, make sure you're buckled in tight, it might get rough for a little bit here. We should be out of it soon."

I wrapped up the sandwich, saving it for when the turbulence calmed down. Maybe bumps didn't bother me, but I didn't really like eating during them.

As far as I could tell, we were only about an hour and a half from home. The ride got rougher and rougher, so that my knuckles were white as I held on and wished for Midway. Out the window were occasional flashes of lightning, but they didn't illuminate anything except for the rain pelting my window.

Constantly lurching in the dark, it was as if we were in a car sliding on ice. Leaning out in the aisle, I tried to watch the pilots in the cockpit, see if they looked especially concerned, but their backs were to me and their hands just looked busy. Larry hadn't announced anything for a while. I seriously wanted to call up to him, ask when we'd be landing, but it seemed stupid.

We'll get there when we get there. Grow up.

Then the sound of the engines got louder. I tried not to think about the dark and the water underneath us. Nothing but dark and all that frickin' water.

Ten minutes later, although I wouldn't have believed it possible, the turbulence got worse. Now it felt as if we were in a snow globe that someone just shook and shook and shook. The lurching turned into deep plunges that made me feel like we were nose-diving, before we finally came back up, all the while bumping. One huge thump sent all the oxygen masks tumbling down, where they swayed from side to side. Mine swung right in front of my face.

Oh my God! Was I supposed to put it on?

A glance up front showed neither Larry nor Max had donned a mask. I couldn't very well ignore mine, so I tied a big loop in it, just to get the thing out of my face.

Another huge thump popped open a few of the overhead bins.

All of a sudden, a quick barrage of soft but forceful punches pummeled my head and shoulders, but the assault was over before I could even shriek or fend them off.

Oranges from the bin above my head.

One landed in my lap, and others lay all around me, rolling up and down the aisle with every shift of the plane.

I wanted to scream, but held it in.

Panicking wouldn't help anyone, especially not the pilots. Again, I tried to see what they were doing, their demeanor, their attitude.

Were they worried?

Struggling with the controls?

It was impossible to tell from my vantage point.

I felt an overwhelming need for reassurance, for someone to tell me everything would be okay.

That *I* would be okay.

But no one did.

As we bounced around, tears started sliding down my face. I stopped myself and wiped my eyes with the back of my hand.

You baby.

There was no need to cry over a little turbulence.

Tons of things are worse than this.

And then there was a hush.

Not totally quiet, but there was just less of a drone than there had been. I leaned over and peered out the window at the starboard engine. At the end of the wing, a blue light winked. Usually, the propellers were nearly invisible in flight, because they were turning so rapidly. But as lightning flashed, I could very clearly see the propeller, circling slowly, turning only with the movement of the plane.

That engine had stopped.